A Gryphon's Journey

Kathryn Brown

The Quill and Claw Series

Book One: A Gryphon's Journey

Book Two: A Gryphon's Trial

Book Three: A Gryphon's Mercy

Copyright © 2020 by Kathryn Brown

Published by Kob Publishing

Illustrated by Jen Elliott

ISBN: 978-1-7363046-1-7

ACKNOWLEDGEMENTS

I dedicate this to my family, who believed in me first, and to all others who continue to fill my life with joy. They are the breeze that keeps me aloft.

A special thanks to my friend Danielle Lincoln Hanna, who showed me what is possible when you put action to your words; Yadira Perez, who always made time for me despite her busy life; my dear friend Amber Mielke for her encouragement and laughter; and to Travis Trazor for being a steadfast set of eyes on my work. Here's to many more years together!

CONTENTS

Prologue	I
Chapter One	1
Chapter Two	14
Chapter Three	29
Chapter Four	36
Chapter Five	47
Chapter Six	89
Chapter Seven	113
Chapter Eight	162
Chapter Nine	174
Chapter Ten	210
Chapter Eleven	252
Chapter Twelve	279
Chapter Thirteen	299
Chapter Fourteen	325

APPENDIX OF CREATURES

Gryphon: Diurnal, carnivorous predators that boast eagle-like heads and lion-like bodies. Possess wings and can live solitarily, in small units, or in large flocks.

Strigigryph: Nocturnal, carnivorous predators. May or not possess a crest. Have owl-like heads and lion-like bodies. Possess wings and are capable of nearly silent flight. Typically live in small groups, with larger flocks being extraordinary.

Ardeigryph: Crepuscular, piscivorous predators. Opportunistic feeders. Possess crested, heron-like heads, long legs, and lion-like bodies. Typically live in large flocks.

Alicorn: Diurnal herbivore possessing the body of an equine, with pale coats, wings, and a single horn. Have the innate ability to manipulate magick, and are long-lived and peaceable, with the tendency to live in herds.

Hydra: Crepuscular, serpentine carnivores possessing wings and five heads. Have the ability to spout acid from four heads and flame from one. Venomous. Territorial, long lived, and solitary.

Basilisk: Crepuscular, serpentine carnivores that are largely opportunistic in their feeding habits. Capable of paralyzing prey with their piercing gaze. Solitary and territorial, with most living according to a basic hierarchy.

Aquila: Diurnal, predatory raptors possessing the ability to form storm clouds and harness the electricity therein. Typically live solitarily or in pairs.

Tweeter: Diurnal, feathered insectivores.

Fae: Diurnal, nocturnal, or crepuscular depending on their type. Possess wings and a basic ability to manipulate magick. Reserved and aloof, they are typically peaceful and live in colonies.

Satyr: Diurnal herbivore possessing cloven hooves and goat-like horns. Known for walking on two legs, they tend to be peaceful and live in groups in the forest.

Ursos: Diurnal, omnivorous predators possessing a heavy coat of fur, long claws, and muscular builds. Solitary, and dangerous if provoked.

Tusker: Diurnal, mid-sized omnivores possessing two tusks that curve upward on either size of their snouts. Distinct for the grunting sounds with which they communicate. Typically live in small herds.

Peryton: Crepuscular, deer-like herbivores possessing wings and cloven hooves. Males grow antlers during their breeding season. Typically live in small to large herds.

Longear: Crepuscular, small herbivores that possess large ears and soft fur. Common in many environments, and typically live in small colonies.

PROLOGUE

Sheba flew with a swiftness she hadn't used in years, taking painstaking care not to pierce the tiny cub she cradled in her talons. This would be her first time journeying to her destination, but she knew the way well. It was inscribed into the minds of every leader, and described in the tales a Gryphon heard from cubhood. The way the trees gave way to rolling hills, then a sprawling plain, and finally a mountainside that climbed craggily up to the heavens. As she flew, everything looked exactly as she'd imagined it. The closer she got, the more fear shook her body to its core, but she pressed on.

It was true that many creatures never saw the place she was journeying to, whether out of fright or from actual loss of life. The great Hydra that guarded the region would be flying out to hunt soon, and far be it from her to disturb him from any task… she gulped and skimmed over the towering mass of earth, her eyes scanning for any sign of the giant beast. It wasn't long before her anxiety manifested in an acidic mist that had begun to pour out from a cavern blasted into the mountain side. The hulking figure within, half hidden in the darkness, fixed the yellow gazes of five heads on her.

Against instinct and common sense, Sheba swooped off to the side and perched at the lip of the cavern, her heart slamming like a wild beast against her rib cage. A fearsome roaring tore through the air before she could even think to catch her breath, and she flinched away from the opening. Without meaning to, she crouched preemptively, eyes wide and wings prepared to carry her away with haste.

"I'd know the scent of a Skyhaven Gryphon anywhere."

Naugi's many voices were so deep that the sound was like the mountain itself speaking. His fangs glinted against the glowing acid in his throats as he peered at Sheba and said, "You may be Matriarch of your flock, Sheba, but only a fool disturbs a Hydra before a hunt."

Sheba fumbled for words, suddenly made dumb. "Wait! Please hear what I have to ask of you!"

Naugi roared again, the green cloud rising from his nostrils increasing with his impatience. He stepped out into the sunlight, and his red scales blazed like the sun itself. "Enough, Gryphon. I will not speak again."

"Please…!"

"I said enough!" He opened all of his maws at once, and the acidic glow in the throat of one of his heads changed, brightening with the threat of white-hot flame. Sheba cowered, pushing the cub she'd been carrying before her in desperation. She sensed, more than saw, Naugi pause.

The cub's eyes were barely open, but the irises that could be glimpsed within were a curious pink in color. His coat was just as mysterious, being patternless and as white as snow. The cub tottered forward, unaware of the danger the mighty Hydra before it posed, flapping its tiny wings with animated interest. Naugi brought a head closer to peer at the minuscule cub, a single one of his serpentine eyes dwarfing it.

"In all my years of living…" the Hydra said, "I rarely see ones such as these. But why did you bring it here, Matriarch?"

Sheba ducked her head out of respect. "This one belongs to me. He is the last offspring between Meshin and me, conceived just before his death three moons ago. But his color is bad luck according to the lore of our kind, and I fear my own flock will slay him to protect themselves. I'm ashamed to say that I cannot make a decision as to whether to end his life, as is custom, or to let him live in secret. I've come for your counsel, Naugi."

The Hydra sat back, heads weaving as he considered. "It's unfortunate that any predator be born such a color. He will find neither good hunting nor an understanding mate later in his life. Consider that you're doing him a kindness, Sheba."

Sheba cast a sorrowful look at the cub, at the naive lump of fur and feathers that was crafted of her own bone and blood. She gave a small nod, but she couldn't still herself as she watched the Hydra open one of his mouths, reaching over to poise a huge fang over the small creature. She felt the beginnings of a retort spring to her throat, but before any sound could issue, a high-pitched whinny cut through the silence.

"What's going on here? Passing judgment on those too young to walk or talk now, Naugi?"

A white Alicorn landed neatly on a nearby ledge, wings still held open should he have to dodge a bad-natured spout of acid or flame. The stallion's body was distinctly equine, save for the magnificent horn that spiraled up from his forehead.

"Mind your own business, Xio," Naugi growled, but the Alicorn was already stepping lightly over to have a better look at the cub, his horn glowing a faint blue as he picked the nestling up with his magick.

"Surely you weren't going to kill this defenseless little cub, were you Naugi?"

"I'm still going to," The Hydra spat matter-of-factly.

Xio placed the cub gently on his back and shot a look at Naugi. "You seek to kill what you simply do not understand, friend. Sometimes ones like these survive just fine. Sometimes they don't. We should leave such things up to fate, and not be so hasty to decide life and death."

Naugi flicked his forked tongues, acrid smoke pouring from his nostrils. "This is my forest. I'll see to what does and doesn't happen here. Take your pandering elsewhere."

Xio was silent for a moment, and then he calmly said, "You share this forest with my herd, Naugi, and with many other sentient beings like the Gryphons. I respect your rule, as I always have. You know I don't mean to test you. I ask of you as my better to reconsider killing this little one." He bowed deeply, and the smoke stopped pouring from Naugi's nostrils as he narrowed his eyes instead.

"And what do you plan to do with the cub, Xio? Sheba's flock will not take it."

"We'll raise him in the herd."

Naugi laughed deep in his throat, a hollow, hissing sound. "And how will you feed it? You're forbidden to kill another, are you not?"

Xio tossed his mane, his muzzle wrinkling in distaste. "Not my first time scavenging to keep another alive."

Naugi seemed more amused than annoyed now. He cast his piercing gaze over to Sheba, who was still poised near the edge of the cavern. "And this is all right by your standards, Gryphoness?"

Sheba nodded mutely, in disbelief at the unexpected turn of events.

Naugi turned back to the Alicorn. "Then you may take the cub, Xio. But know this. A Gryphon is not a simple beast. It is unlike the ursos, or the longear, or the peryton, or any of the other creatures that prowl this land. You may have experience in rearing such, but you must not raise this one the same. We are creatures of mind, you and I, and while perhaps not to the same extent, so too will he be. Take care. I'll be loath to regret letting you leave with him this day."

Xio chuffed in understanding, and bowed once again. "Thank you, old friend. Your kindness does not go unnoticed! And go in peace Sheba, Matriarch of Skyhaven. This little one will be in good company. Please know that I'm truly sorry for the death of your mate. He was certainly a good Sire, but you've done well leading without him."

Sheba dipped her head gratefully, and both Alicorn and gryphoness flew off, each in their own direction. Naugi settled to watch the sun slip behind the distant hills, his body as still as the mountain itself. The moment the last ray vanished into twilight, he spread his tattered wings, sucked in air, and roared so loud, the firmament itself seemed to shake.

The master of the land was out to hunt. Every creature not protected by a pact with him hid at the sound. Nothing survived if so unlucky as to cross paths with him under the moonlight.

VII

CHAPTER ONE

A delicate nose quivered in the stagnant air, and liquid eyes trembled. The long ears after which its kind were named waved to and fro, alert for anything amiss. After a few tense murms, the longear went back to eating yellowed grass in the shade of the cliff, unaware of the danger that lurked just above it. It was a good thing for Arias and Brynne.

Brynne's fiery orange coat and feathers blended in perfectly with the burnt, earthen color of the smooth rock beneath her claws, but Arias stood out brighter than the moon in the midnight sky. His white coat and pink skin were the first thing prey noticed, but he still made a point of going along on these hunting outings. His companion signaled him with the slightest tilt of her beak, the fluff of her last victim still clinging to her lower jaw. *Your turn, Arias,* her eyes said eagerly.

Arias tried to resist sighing. Gryphons were

made for hunting, but that fact of nature seemed to firmly exclude him. He hoped Brynne was prepared to see another perfectly good meal run merrily away to its escape, because he was sure that was what was about to happen… again. The strange thing was, he really didn't mind. The chase was fun, but killing wasn't really his thing.

Slowly, Arias lowered himself against the baking rock as he'd seen Brynne do a million times, his eyes locked onto the small, fuzzy creature in the canyon just below. He could taste the dust on his tongue as he forced himself to concentrate, scarcely breathing. The longear casually looked up from the greens it was nibbling. It froze, poor eyesight failing it, but two twitches of its dainty nose told it everything it needed to know. It blurred into motion as it bolted a hasty retreat.

Arias sprang into pursuit, eyes trained on the white tail that was disappearing into the canyon. Somehow, Brynne was faster. She was always faster. In a flash, she scaled across the smooth stone to cut the beast off, and in an even swifter move, she snapped it up and shook away its life. Arias dropped his head in legitimate disbelief at how fluid her movements were, and then added in a huff of angst so his disappointment would seem doubly believable.

Brynne already had caught three longears today. Arias's tally remained at a firm zero. But he liked it that way, secretly. If he was lucky, the Alicorn herd back home may have found him some half-edible carcass left behind by an ursos or another predator. He salivated just thinking of the potential leftovers that potentially awaited him back in Glendale. On an unlucky day, he'd have to scavenge marrow from dried bones left to crack and splinter in the sun. Or worse, have nothing at all.

Arias's stomach growled, and he was angry at it for reminding him of just how empty it was. He didn't like killing, but that didn't mean he didn't enjoy having a full belly. The Alicorns tried their best, but finding meat for a growing Gryphon wasn't their strongest suit. However… now that the longear was dead and hanging lifelessly from Brynne's jaws, it suddenly looked far tastier than it had when it was alive and well.

"Well what are you doing, showing off?" he snapped as Brynne stared at him, longear still in mouth. Then, more dejectedly, he said, "Just eat it already."

Brynne stared at him, long tail waving. She dropped the preymeat on the ground. "You can have this one."

Arias peered at her suspiciously. "Don't you want it?"

"I have to teach you how to be a Gryphon, because for whatever reason you're horrible at it. Does an adult ask a cub why it hasn't flown yet? Take it, before I change my mind." Brynne's eyes glinted with a mischievous sparkle that betrayed her voice, and while Arias was vaguely aware that perhaps there was an insult somewhere in her words, hunger was no easy force to contend with. He lunged to take the meat, and she wrestled him over it for a few seconds before relenting. The two were both scrawny and ragged for their age, though Brynne's coat was additionally patchy from all the fights she picked back at her eyrie. Arias never asked if she won or not. She'd never admit to losing. He downed the prey in a couple of appreciative gulps.

Brynne scanned the area, combing every rocky crevice for their next target. Arias found himself trying his best to copy her confident movements. He had no interest in being the great warrior and hunter she aspired to be, but the only time he was able to see her was when she was going on a hunt. The Alicorns had raised him and, whether intentionally or not, he saw the world as they did. All life was precious. Rarely, instinct managed to override his thinking… but the older he got, the less rare the instances were becoming.

"Come on, let's try that ravine next!" Brynne said, cutting into his thoughts. She cuffed him between the eyes before dashing out of reach, and the two were off, nipping and tussling along the way.

***

Arias always enjoyed his outings with Brynne. He had never expected to come across another Gryphon of his age while off on one of his sneaky adventures. The Alicorns knew about their little outings and approved, but only after making Brynne promise she'd never take him into her eyrie. Arias understood, having been warned since early cubhood to be wary of other Gryphons. His albino coloration would not be welcome among their superstitious ranks, and the threat of being slaughtered for his odd appearance was very real.

However, Brynne was different. The time the two cubs spent together zoomed by in mere murms, and while the Alicorns likely wouldn't be happy to know just how far from the safety of Glendale they roamed, Arias didn't care. He was too happy to have someone more like himself to spend time with for once. The Alicorns and the lesser beasts didn't like to run and play the same way he did.

After they'd been hunting fruitlessly for a few murms, Arias chanced to ask, "Hey, what's it like? At Skyhaven eyrie, I mean."

"The same as it was the last time you asked me," Brynne said, adding a roll of her eyes. "It's definitely not like it is out here with you, though. Everyone is always fighting for everything. This drought has made it way worse than it usually is, though. No one has ever bested our leader, Sheba. She killed a fully grown ursos sow when she was barely fledged, and no one has wrested leadership from her ever since she ascended to Matriarch. Anyone who tries ends up in the dust. Can you believe that? I want to be like her someday. Then maybe everyone will see me differently…" Her voice trailed off, and she seemed to think better. "It's impossible to find good preymeat today. I hope this drought ends soon. Let's check over there."

Arias didn't ask any more questions. It felt

strange to be a Gryphon, yet know next to nothing about what that meant. Learning from Brynne had awakened a desire in him to know more about this side of himself. The Alicorns well understood his nature as a predator, perhaps even more than he understood it himself, but it wasn't enough. He sometimes felt filthy beside them, beings that seemed so pure of thought and action. No creature ever fought in the herd lands of Glendale, and the Alicorn's powerful magick enforced it. Any who wandered into their borders were lulled into passivity.

The older Arias grew, the more he heard rumblings from within the Alicorn herd about him. He'd been raised by kind and gentle souls, and yet at the same time he felt another more primal side of himself awakening with each passing day. As much as he wished he could deny it, the forbidden nature of Brynne's eyrie dragged him to it.

***

Arias followed Brynne's tail, wrapped up in his thoughts, until he nearly bumped into her backside. He shook his head and looked up, but before he could speak, he saw why she'd stopped. Three big keythongs—adult male Gryphons— had emerged from beneath the shadow of a rock formation where they'd been lazing away from the sun. The scrawny, well-picked remains of a doe they'd shared lay in the midst of them. All had pelts that were zigzagged with white gouges from battles long fought. Arias had never seen an adult Gryphon up close before. Just as he was processing their miraculous size, one of them picked his head up and fixed his gaze on them.

He chuckled deep in his throat, and it wasn't a happy sound.

"Here I thought that Sheba's runts knew to stay close to home," he said, alerting the other two to their presence. The ruff of feathers at his neck barely covered the white scars that ran deeply across his chest and side. "But then these ones show up to prove me wrong. You— lowborn. Why are you hunting together with a Spirit Walker?"

Arias turned to Brynne, confused, but she didn't look at him. Her tail twitched.

"The Matriarch of Skyhaven allows you to live and hunt on our land, but only if you don't spill the blood of those in her flock," she said in a voice that cracked despite her best effort.

The male bristled, but his voice stayed level. "That's not what I asked you, lowborn. You so fancy from pampered flock life that you don't know how to answer questions from us Primals?"

The other two keythongs flattened their ears. "Let's just kill them both and get on with it," one said. "I've been starving for a bite of anything after that boney doe. They'll tide us over until we can get into some real meat."

"I agree," the other said. "There won't be much left after. We can toss the rest in the river. A Spirit Walker and a lowborn? Sheba herself might even let us into the flock if we send the pale one back to the void. He's probably the one that's been scaring off all the good preymeat of late. And that little hen has a mouth on her that I don't like."

Brynne didn't waste an instant. She turned tail and ran in a flash, and Arias followed after her with such speed that he nearly tripped over his own legs. There was a chorus of rustling wings as the keythongs all took flight, shrieking as they followed them down the narrow trail. A pair of claws snatched at the dust to Arias's right, and he cried out at the proximity. A guffaw of laughter was immediately followed by the screeching reprimand of the group's scarred leader.

"Stop playing with the food!" he yelled. "Kill them! Kill them, before Sheba hears all this commotion and sends guards to skin us alive!"

Another male swooped low, snagging Brynne by the scruff of her neck. The keythong didn't anticipate her twisting in her own skin, spitting and clawing, to eventually take a chomp out of one of his toes. He yelped in pain, dropping her back to the ground, and she took off again, just behind Arias.

Arias felt his speed flagging. They couldn't keep up a quick enough pace to stay out of the clutches of the adults forever. He wracked his brain for an escape. They were too small to fight. There had to be something! His eyes settled on a couple of huge boulders lining the path up ahead, and the dark spaces between them beckoned to him. That was it! He hissed for Brynne's attention before pushing hard and stuffing himself into the crevice, wedging himself in so tightly that his limbs immediately began to ache. It was an unspoken agreement that they both had to fit. Brynne wasn't far behind him, and they were immediately neck and neck with how zealously they'd squished together.

The exasperated sounds of the keythongs from above filled the air, and the thud of subsequent attempts to gain entry to the hiding spot followed. Neither cub dared move. A hooked bill was forced into the small space, and promptly began to pinch and pull bits of feathers and fluff off the two. They squirmed and screamed until it was finally withdrawn, then were subjected to the vicious tries of the other two keythongs. It was long murms before silence finally fell along with the night.

Arias shifted, and, pricking his ears, heard nothing. He chanced to begin backing his way out of the space, eager to return circulation to his limbs. No sooner had Brynne grabbed him and held him back than he felt the hot sting of multiple talons scrambling to drag him out by his tail. His heart leapt into his throat as he curled what was left of his tail as tight as he could against his body.

"Don't try that again," Brynne snapped. "They'll wait us out."

She was right. Dawn came, and it came with a blistering heat. The sun was quick to dry the morning dew with its insatiable rays. Arias and Brynne had shifted gradually over the night, each breathing shallowly in the stale air. None-too-small insects ran into the small opening to shelter from the heat and, realizing it was occupied, scuttled back out. Thirst pricked at the tongues of each fledgling, but at least they were in the shade. It wasn't long before they heard the heavy panting of their pursuers outside.

"How 'bout one of us stay to guard the hole, and two can go hunt and slake their thirst?" one of the grizzled males growled to the others.

"Then it'll be ye! We wouldn't be in this mess had you not played around instead of catching and killing the cubs proper," came the answer.

"You're the dumb gizzard who brought up eating them in the first place!" called out the first voice, much angrier this time.

"Listen, you two dumb giblets. One of Sheba's could be along any moment, and you better believe these youngins' are gonna start screaming the moment they even so much as think help is around." The voice dropped into a whisper. "If we really lean into it, we can fly out of this territory before they can squawk on us. They won't know which direction we head in. Follow my lead."

Arias and Brynne heard frantic rustling, and then nothing. Arias lifted an ear and rotated it all around, and while he heard nothing, his stinging tail encouraged him to be cautious about believing he was safe.

The cubs stayed put for another few long murms purely out of fear. Finally, and with much deliberation, Arias decided to check. He was shaking so hard he felt like a leaf in the wind, but it was a relief to be out in the open air again.

"Anything?" Brynne asked so quietly that he barely heard her.

Arias cast his eyes around thrice more, afraid he'd missed the three predators hiding someplace inconspicuous. He tried to keep his voice from shaking. "No. They're gone."

Brynne came out from under the boulders and stretched, wincing as muscles that hadn't been used for long murms were finally utilized. Arias was still trying to shake the pins and needles from his paws.

"Had we been a little bit older, we wouldn't have fit there. Good thinking, Arias," Brynne said.

"I've never seen Gryphons like that before."

"They're called Primals. They have no flock, and roam around like nomads. The ones around here typically obey our Matriarch when it comes to hunting in our territory. I'd been told some Gryphons are cannibals, but I never believed it to be honest… I'd better tell my mom about this when I get back."

Arias nodded. All he could think of was getting back home to Glendale. In his anxiety, any hunger and thirst were forgotten. He wished he could tell the Alicorns about the Primals, but he knew that if he did, they'd probably never allow him to go adventuring with Brynne ever again.

Brynne drew in a horrified breath. "Oh, no! Your tail!"

Arias hadn't thought about the stinging in his tail. It seemed to match the way the rest of his body felt after having been in that tiny space for so long. He glanced back, and his eye rested first on the bloody stump where his tail used to be, and then at the discarded white tuft on the ground that the Primals had removed in their efforts to eat him. His defeated whimper did nothing to reattach the stricken tail, but he realized he could've been far worse off. The wound had long ago stopped bleeding, and he'd seen the Alicorns work enough to know that it couldn't be saved. At least he was alive.

Arias and Brynne hung around their hiding spot, working up the courage to venture home. It wasn't long until the sun began its decline. They both fixed their eyes into the distance, where there would be greenery and plenty of shelter to hide in, and with a mutual glance, they took off at a sprint.

Arias hardly felt his feet touching the ground. When Brynne broke away to head to her eyrie, there wasn't even a goodbye uttered. Arias expected claws to descend on him at any moment, his worry intensified now that it was only his set of eyes and ears to detect danger. But the attack never came.

CHAPTER TWO

Arias hadn't been so happy to reach Glendale in ages. The home territory of the Alicorns was a beautiful place, a fact that was easy to appreciate when it also brought with it the promise of safety. Moss hung from the trees in long, trailing tendrils, the paths below the branches lit by bright insects and luminescent mushrooms. Arias felt the peace of the Alicorn's magick wash over him as he finally halted his manic running, his senses stifled by the arcane calm. A wandering longear stopped to nibble at some foliage off to its side, unconcerned by his presence. Even it knew that there was no bloodshed to be had in Glendale.

"Out late again, young Arias."

Even without properly seeing her, Arias automatically dipped his head in greeting to Hlaena, the mate of the stallion who led the herd, Xio. She melted out from the greenery and extended her nose curiously toward him, waiting for an answer.

The truth flashed through Arias's mind in an instant. It nearly came tumbling out of his open beak until he snapped it shut. Of course he couldn't say what had happened, especially not to Hlaena! She'd never let him out of her sight again. But what if the keythongs came back at some point to finish him and Brynne off? He scoffed at the thought. They wouldn't. Besides, he'd just stay here for a while, long enough for them to give up for sure. No creature could hunt him here, and Brynne was smart, smarter than him, even. She would definitely be safe with a Gryphon like the Matriarch of Skyhaven around.

"You're hurt." Hlaena furled her muzzle worriedly. Arias whirled around to dodge her before she could examine his tail, but then he felt the warm trickle of her magick flowing over him, immobilizing him.

"You'll lose your entire tail if we don't see to that. What happened?"

"I'm fine," Arias mumbled, although he had no idea whether that was true or not. The aching in his backside was probably a good enough indicator that it was serious enough.

"That's certainly not what I asked." Hlaena picked him up entirely with her maroon magick and placed him on her back, then scrutinized him in the failing light. Arias didn't like it when she stared at him like that.

"Brynne and I were just playing a little too hard," he said, avoiding her gaze. "I didn't know she'd nipped so hard. She didn't mean to." He was practically muttering into his chest feathers.

"Hmm." Hlaena walked slowly through the tangled paths, her horn glowing faintly as she picked little bits and pieces of greenery with her magick as she went. The plants all hovered above her head as she counted and examined them, a symphony of activity taking place at her command. With the prodding of her magick, berries stripped from their bramble, leaves trembled and pulled free, and the fluff from long reeds joined her processional.

Arias noted all the plants as he always did, well versed in the uses of all from long murms spent watching his Alicorn family. Sometimes they even let him help with their concoctions, although they didn't think he knew his way around the herbs as well as he did. He wished he had the same magick the Alicorns did. They could grab things they needed, even from up very high. And they could heal nearly any injury. It was oddly satisfying to watch how they could take a sick or wounded creature and patch it back together. Even simple beasts knew there was safety to be found in Glendale.

Arias focused on perching on Hlaena's back as she walked to one of the many streams that cut through forest. She stopped to add half of an empty terrapin shell to her floating menagerie, which she filled with water before tossing all her herbs in.

"You're going to drink all of that tonight." Her eyes were still chastising from over her shoulder. She searched the canopy and pulled down a long string of ringed moss. "And you're going to sleep with this on your tail."

Arias looked at the moss in disgust. "Fairywort? But that stuff stings."

Hlaena allowed herself a wry smile. "Just tell yourself that means it's working."

***

Arias slept fitfully. For the first time ever, the openness of his grass nest in the meadow seemed too exposed. He rationalized that the three keythongs couldn't get to him here, but found himself awake and searching the dark sky anyway. And, just as he knew it would, the puree of fairywort dribbled over what was left of his tail was causing him as much misery as he'd imagined. It felt like millions of angry insect jaws chewing voraciously at his hide, and he wanted to do nothing more than to rinse it off. After he'd drunk Hlaena's potion, she'd left him some water and used a bit of her magick to help him sleep— but just a bit, because as he'd feared, she'd sensed he'd been lying to her earlier.

The Alicorns all peered at Arias as he rested, striding past him softly on their long legs. They moved to the center of the meadow, their coats pearlescent under the moonlight, and started to talk. Arias cracked an eye open, but concentrated on keeping his breathing slow and regular. Every now and then, one of the Alicorns glanced in his direction, and he made sure they always found him just as he had been when Hlaena had put him to sleep.

"We knew this day would come from the moment you brought him here," one of the herd mares said to the group. "He isn't a grass eater, he isn't a lesser creature, and we can't expect to keep him locked up in this portion of the forest forever. The life of a Gryphon is short compared to ours; he must be allowed to live it as he naturally would've."

"There's nothing natural about what's happening with that little keythong," another, this one a stallion, added. "He's been kept from death twice—once when he hatched out looking like that in Skyhaven, and again when Xio saved him from Naugi. He's obviously been venturing out. There's no way that little fledgling hen he plays with could've done that to him."

Heads swayed in agreement.

"He's growing curious, as is to be expected," the first mare who had spoken said. "Only next time, what will it be? Perhaps it won't be just his tail that he's in danger of losing on the next occasion. He needs to learn how to be what he is; he can't fight against himself forever. Respectfully… maybe we were wrong to take him, Xio."

"They have a point," Hlaena's tired voice said. "He doesn't know what is expected from him as a Gryphon. The local flocks believe his coat color is bad luck, and there are even stray individuals who prey upon their own kind. It's dangerous for him out there, and he doesn't know how to defend himself. He doesn't even know what *is* a threat to him. He'll keep going out, and he'll keep coming back like this—or worse—soon enough. What are we to do?"

The Alicorns began to debate amongst themselves, but before their voices could rise, the leader of the herd stamped his hoof and whinnied silence from the others. "I'm well aware of all of these things," Xio said. "I've been aware from the moment I took him from Naugi's jaws. He will stay with us for the time being. When he recovers and is well, we'll decide what to do then."

The soft hoof beats of the retreating herd melded into the sound of the wind blowing through the meadow. Arias pressed himself deeper into the fragrant grass and closed his eyes. Brynne was right. He would be a yearling soon, but he really didn't know anything more than a daft cub. However... he knew where he might find the answers.

***

Arias was to stay strictly within the boundaries of Glendale, and Xio himself stuck around to enforce it. His days were outlined. It was to the stream... and back. Or out to scavenge so he could eat his fill... and back. Or into the herd to mingle if he wanted to... And then he was ushered directly back to the meadow. Xio spoke little during this time, and it made Arias uncomfortable. He looked up to the herd stallion, and this punishment hurt more than he thought it would. But after what he'd heard, he knew the leader of the Alicorns had more weighing matters on his mind than seeing him guilty for lying.

Arias wished he could promise that he'd stay here, surrounded by the greenery of the Alicorn's beautiful forest. But he wasn't sure that he could. There was a world out there, ripe for exploring. With every outing he took alongside Brynne, he hungered more for the meat of fresh prey, not the jerky-like seconds other predators left behind. The thrill of pouncing leaves caught in the wind was nowhere near the excitement of the actual chase he engaged in with prey, though he never wanted to kill. His mind strayed to wondering where Brynne was. Even knowing the risk involved, he knew that she could take him to Skyhaven to meet her flock. He just needed to convince her.

Arias found a pale rock and stretched over it, letting the heat warm his belly. Xio stood nearby with droopy eyes, only shifting to groom his shoulder and to flick his tail a couple of times, enough to keep a roving swarm of small insects at bay. Then his ear swung sideways, and he snapped to attention.

"Xio!" a voice sailed out, "Come quick!" It was Hlaena, her alarm apparent as she tore through the undergrowth. "This one is bad, he's on the edge of death. Merwyn keeps trying to heal him, she won't listen to anyone. She'll kill herself!"

Xio didn't wait for further explanation. He

darted off after the mare, and Arias wasted no time in shooting off his rock like a spring doe, curious to know what was happening. Never had he heard such urgency in Hlaena's voice. His short strides only just allowed him to keep sight of the two Alicorns as they ripped across the land. When they finally skidded to a halt among their herd members, he stayed well enough back, peering through the fronds of an oversized fern.

In the midst of the Alicorns lay a Gryphon, nearly hidden beneath the shadow of dense vegetation. His breath came in ragged gasps, foam spilling from his bill as he struggled to breathe. It was hard to make out his features, and Arias tried to tip toe forward to get a closer look. Merwyn, a younger filly, was blocking his view. She had her horn aimed at the Gryphon, her eyes closed as her magick enveloped its limp body. The hairs in her mane were slowly darkening, like grass being consumed by wildfire. With each breath the Gryphon took, another section seemed to be affected, until finally it started to work its way into the rest of her coat. She sank to her knees, her eyes fluttering open, unable to break the magickal connection she'd created. The rest of the herd moved away, their voices rising in terror, but Xio reared up and barreled toward her, shoving her away from the Gryphon with a high-pitched squeal. Something between them exchanged, like the bright flash of a lightning bolt, and he cried out in pain, but immediately turned on her in anger.

"Fool!" he yelled, stamping. "You'll kill yourself! You gained control of your magick only a moon ago, and you think you understand the laws that govern it? His wounds are mortal, can you not see that? You cannot give what you do not have to offer!"

The filly's mother hurried to stand protectively in front of her, but she also lowered her head apologetically and didn't look the herd leader in the eye. "I should have watched her more closely, Xio. This is my fault. I'm ashamed that you were the one to save her, and not I. Will you be alright?"

The anger dragged away from Xio's eyes. "I'll be just fine, don't worry. You've never broken a connection before, and you were smart not to try. Done incorrectly, we'd have three bodies lying here instead of just the one. What is more concerning here is that this is the second creature we've found in this condition this season. I shall have to speak with Naugi about it. Either someone has invaded his territory, or one of his scale-kin has gone rogue. Nothing else could create wounds like that..."

The Alicorns spoke on, but Arias was concentrating on the Gryphon now. The instant Xio had broken the connection created by the filly's magick and it, the Gryphon had heaved its last sigh and promptly died. It was definitely a keythong, and not a small one, either. How such a specimen had succumbed to anything in this forest was a mystery. An adult as scarred as he was would've been skilled in combat. Arias's eyes widened. Amid all the injuries crisscrossing the keythong's pelt, a white scar that crossed his chest stood out to him. Under different circumstances, he would've probably been almost giddy with the dosage of indirect revenge that had been dealt. *How does it feel?* He would've thought. Instead, all he could think of was that there was something out there that had been powerful enough to tear down such a formidable foe as the Primal he'd encountered with Brynne.

"It's amazing that he was able to drag himself this far with wounds like that," Hlaena said. "We should reinforce our boundaries until we know what did this. Just in case..."

Hlaena was still talking, but Arias's thoughts were elsewhere. The Alicorns were all preoccupied. Not a single eye or thought was cast his way. He needed to make sure Brynne was okay, that her flock knew of this new danger. He'd be careful. If he was going to Skyhaven, the time was now.

Arias dropped to the ground and scurried away. As soon as he was out of hearing range, he ran west, the wind at his claws, headed in the direction Brynne always went whenever she headed home for the day. He was finally making his way to Skyhaven eyrie.

***

Naugi twitched in his sleep, brought to wakefulness by an odd sensation against one of his boney heads. A tapping. He opened his eyes, and the source of the irritation was made apparent in the form of a red Tweeter. It shrieked when he glanced at it, flying in loops and ruffling its feathers, crying out in its shrill, primitive voice.

"North! North!" it said, pumping its small wings vigorously. "Help!"

Acrid smoke drifted from Naugi's nostrils. Tweeters were the worst of the lesser sentient beasts when it came to getting worked up. This one probably had its nest knocked down by a strong breeze, or had been startled by a predator. Things not worthy of his time. He closed his eyes to begin the hard work of ignoring the annoying creature. It wasn't worth the effort to silence it. They were surprisingly swift. The tapping began again, and this time, more words accompanied it.

"The gale! It kills!"

Naugi's eyes shot open with understanding. He growled, murder springing into his heart. *Barsum.* Trespassing into his territory again. It had hardly been a full turn of the seasons since the beast had tried its luck with him. Naugi touched skyward, his huge wings lifting his heft into the air, and tilted his trajectory northward.

Already, Naugi could see an ominous storm cloud hovering on the horizon of the otherwise clear day. A feathered figure darted from the cover of the thunderhead and swooped over the ground, snapping up screaming figures as it went. When the Aquila noticed Naugi's approach, he returned to the safety of the clouds. Naugi was used to Barsum's tricks by now. He shrieked and dove headfirst into the mass of rumbling vapor. If he could get his claws on the creature, he'd kill him.

The eye of the storm was a welcome respite from the torrent that pelted against Naugi's hide in a maelstrom of stinging droplets, but it did nothing to stave off the lightning bolts that struck wantonly throughout the gloom. He tasted a metallic taste on his tongues, and maneuvered to the right to avoid a lightning bolt that lanced above his head. *That one had been particularly close.* Its brightness had flashed through the thunderheads like an angry grimace, dazzling Naugi's eyes. But not before he'd seen the outline of its creator silhouetted against the grey backdrop. Before he could start toward Barsum, the wind changed direction, and he was blown sideways. The metallic taste returned again, promising more lightning, and he roared in frustration. Barsum was a coward to trespass and then hide from retribution. Typical.

Naugi snorted and swept his gaze over the grey mass, his anger growing. He didn't have time for games. It was impossible to pick Barsum's form out from the surrounding haze, but that didn't mean he couldn't flush him out. He flew up through the muggy air, took a deep breath, and spewed flame and acid in a wide spiral. The dark clouds glowed orange as their rain transformed into boiling steam, and almost immediately, the storm abruptly broke. Each of Naugi's heads scrupulously scanned for the Aquila, but confusion ensued. The sky was empty. Had he escaped so swiftly?

A small sound reached Naugi's ears. There was a commotion on the ground. He dove back toward the earth, to the sight of both Tweeter and Satyr fleeing the forest with haste. He watched closely. The Satyrs were all pointing toward the tree line, fear etched into their tiny faces. Naugi flew over the forest and started laying down lines of flame and acid, and it only took until his second pass for Barsum to rise from his hiding place, the feathers on his back alight with fire.

Without a head start, Naugi was faster than the Aquila, and he pushed to catch Barsum before he could slip away as he had in the past. Barsum was flying as fast as he could—which wasn't very fast with all his now-missing feathers—but just as Naugi reached out to grab him, the taste of metal danced on his tongues again. Barsum was looking over his shoulder at him, and there was a smugness on his feathery face that didn't belong there. It was too late to dodge. Naugi spat acid just as the storm clouds reappeared enough to generate electricity, and Barsum redirected them to cross over to him. The Aquila's cry of pain as the acid contacted his flesh was music to Naugi's ears, but then a bright flash and a loud bang filled the air.

Nothing could ever prepare Naugi for the excruciating heat that filled his body. He staggered and fell a few feet before regaining himself enough to land in the remains of the forest below. Barsum was already just a speck in the sky, although even from the distance his flying was awkward. Naugi wondered what injury he'd managed to afflict on the nuisance. If any acid had contacted a wing, there was a chance he'd be rid of him once and for all. The thought brought him a small measure of joy.

The torn forest began to crackle with activity, and Naugi watched as a grizzled old Satyr buck approached him on two unsteady hooved legs. He used a smooth cane equally as much for balance as to feel his way around; his vision had been failing for years, and he had to be just about blind by now.

"Thank you for saving your people, my lord," he praised in a feeble voice. Naugi silently wondered how the old leader had survived the attack. He was so frail that it looked like falling over would be enough to kill him.

"I've saved very little," Naugi said. "Your homes were destroyed in the gale. Your food stores were demolished by Barsum. And he's eaten countless numbers of your people over the years."

"We will rebuild—"

"No!" Naugi growled. "You will relocate. Your homes are at the far reaches of my territory, and the Aquila is persistent because his own land is right next to it."

"But, my lord! This is our ancestral home, we cannot simply leave it."

"Then stay." Naugi curled his lips, revealing rows of teeth that hooked backwards. "But know that should Barsum return, I will not protect you any longer. Let the Aquila have this forest; he has

fairly earned it, because I no longer wish to
continue dueling with him over it. Either learn to
fight, or leave."

Murmurs of dissent immediately sprang up
among the herd. The elder looked shocked.
Naugi didn't wait to see what they decided. He
leaped skyward and turned back toward his roost,
annoyed. Three of his heads remained light-
headed after the lightning strike, and they closed
their eyes and dropped their necks across his back
to rest. Fighting Barsum wasn't worth it. There
were other, more lucrative parts of his territory
that were far more deserving of defending. It was
true that the Satyrs were great hunters and thus
presented him with some of the best offerings,
but he received plenty of preymeat from his other
indebted creatures. The Gryphons were
particularly good to him at offering time. Naugi
licked his lips. That would be soon enough, now.

CHAPTER THREE

The calming magick that surrounded Glendale dispersed as Arias crept beyond the Alicorns' territory, and he stuck to the shadows and crevices of the forest, his eyes glued skyward for danger. Dangers that wouldn't present themselves directly, but that could be sensed all around. The plaintive cries of an exasperated party of hunting Primals sounded far above the treetops, and down in a ravine he passed, the horrifying sight of an ursos eating a fresh kill awaited. The muscular creature looked like just a dark smudge in the shade, menacing even with the distance between them. And there were the frequent calls of scavengers that stayed with Arias throughout his journey, no doubt keeping an eye on him should he slip up and make himself into an easy meal.

The going wasn't difficult, as all the paths were well worn and covered in a soft padding of detritus from fallen leaves in years past. Arias was just figuring that he must be making good time—

he wasn't really aware of how much distance existed between Glendale and Skyhaven—when his ears shot up. The sound of something approaching came from directly ahead, and he darted up the trunk of the nearest tree, his mind already flashing to thoughts of massive keythongs. But instead it was a hen and her cub that were travelling together, and he immediately identified Brynne's orange coat. He chirped a happy greeting down, to which the gray hen spread her wings and hissed, her crest raised in alarm.

"Come no closer, Spirit Walker," she mused. "Please, don't curse us! My daughter and I only seek passage to Glendale."

Arias recollected what Hlaena had said about other Gryphons in regard to his color, and adopted a more passive stance.

"Don't worry. I'm a friend," he said brightly, hoping to alleviate her concerns. He deduced that she must be Brynne's mother, and noted how unusually subdued Brynne herself seemed. "Is everything okay?" he asked.

"If you mean to curse us or kill us, please get it over with."

"I promise I won't do anything to you. I can't. I'm no different than any other Gryphon. I just look different."

The hen seemed ill at ease, but she nodded and nibbled reassuringly at the feathers on

Brynne's head. The orange cub didn't react. Indeed, she remained passively resting her head against her mother's leg, her eyes barely open.

"She was off where she shouldn't have been, being much too grown for her own good as usual," the mother said in a tone that would have been chiding had it not been so tinged with worry. "She's lucky she wasn't killed. She told me she was attacked by Primals, but I didn't realize how badly she'd been hurt. I hoped she'd get better, but today she's burning up. If the Alicorns don't help us, I fear I may lose her. I'd be there by now if I flew, but she won't let me carry her. And there are Primals everywhere… it's safer down here."

Arias frowned at the mention of Primals again. "I was there when the Primals attacked," he said, showing the hen what was left of his tail.

"So, she hasn't been alone in her exploring. Halada, help us," the hen said. "Yes, white one, Primals are flockless Gryphons. They're lawless these days. Something has been severely injuring, even killing them, and they're fearful on top of starving. This drought won't let up. Some have begged to join Skyhaven, but Sheba won't let them. They've been retaliating by attacking our hunters. They only want to join for protection and food, and this is what happens when they're denied. Even one such as yourself, Spirit Walker, should take care out here."

Arias tilted his head sideways, creeping closer to Brynne. The feathering around her neck where she'd been grabbed by the Primal was matted and dark. He'd seen wounds like that before, many times. If they were treated before infection could truly set in, the victims were usually fine. He realized that just because he wasn't in Glendale didn't mean he wouldn't be able to find the herbs he'd need to help his friend.

"I can help Brynne," he said confidently, beginning to search the tree he'd been hiding in for any sign of fairywort. He deflated slightly when he found none, but then he saw the tell-tale purple flowers of another helpful plant creeping around the base of the trunk. He paused. Blackroot. The potent medicine was a poison in excess, and for a creature as small as a cub, it was hard to determine exactly how much was too much. He clamped the fibrous stem in his beak and pulled, fanning his small wings for extra leverage, and the plant gave way in a shower of powdery earth. The roots all ended in plump bulbs, and he carried the yield back to the hen.

"Have her eat these, but only one of the smallest of them each night," he said. "It tastes horrible, but it'll make her feel better much sooner than you'd think, trust me! And…" he bounded off again, and this time searched among the treetops, ears pricked as he rummaged. He thought he'd heard a particular humming somewhere close by, and his searching wasn't in vain. The buzzing of pollinating insects filled his ears as he crested the precarious upper limbs of a stout tree. For the umpteenth time, he wished he had the Alicorn's helpful magick. He took a deep breath, closed his eyes, and he braved a multitude of hot stings from the hive's denizens to break free a sizable piece of honeycomb. He nearly fell in his haste to descend, shaking himself vigorously before extending the comb to the hen. Her expression didn't hide her surprise and suspicion.

"Put this on her wounds to keep them from turning bad, but be careful! Ursos really like the scent, and it draws them in like nothing I've ever seen before. You'll probably be safe in your flock though… right?"

"What are you?" The hen took a step back. "And why are you helping me? Spirit Walkers are bad luck, you're said to curse those you cross paths with. Are you tricking me? Are these actually poisons? If so, I beg of you to simply end both of us now."

Arias felt a surprising sting at the accusations. "My name's Arias," he said. "Brynne had helped me before, she's my friend. I'd never hurt her. You won't believe me, but I'm from Glendale, that's how I know all of this. If you make it, the Alicorns will give you the same remedies, but you can save time if you just take them now. Brynne can use all the time she can get to heal. If she were well, she'd tell you that I'm not lying."

The hen stared at him for another few tense murms. But then, slowly, without taking her eyes off him, she bowed so low that her beak brushed the ground. "My name is Iba, and I thank you and choose to trust you, Spirit Walker. I won't forget the kindness you've shown me. It's rare among us lowborn."

Arias's mind caught onto the word. "Lowborn? Aren't all Gryphons born the same way?"

The hen shook her head. "No, dear cub. Not in our world. I wish it were so. I have neither strength nor cunning to offer, and that isn't worth much in a flock." She blinked and cut herself off, seemingly a little embarrassed. "I-I wish I had something to give you. If you were to come back to the eyrie, you might have a bit of meat, but hiding you…"

"It's okay, I understand," Arias said. "I'd better get back home anyways." He didn't want to cause trouble. Maybe it was better that he stayed away from Skyhaven eyrie after all. If a single hen, Brynne's own mother, reacted so extremely to him, he could only imagine what a guard or a hunter may do to him. He decided that he'd tell Xio and the herd the truth about him and Brynne being caught by the Primals. He'd vow to stay in the forest and focus on being more obedient from now on. Maybe Xio would still allow him to spend time with Brynne, after she recovered and things calmed down a bit.

"Perhaps what I was told about your kind was untrue, Spirit Walker. Thank you for your help," Iba said.

Arias puffed his feathers, feeling proud at the appreciation. Then he turned to go. Before he got too far, he looked over his shoulder and called out, "Bye Brynne… When it's safe, I hope to see you again sometime… if it's okay with Iba!"

Iba nodded gratefully before nudging Brynne ahead of her, and Arias watched them slowly wind their way back in the direction from which they'd come. The shadows would be growing tall before long, and Arias crept back into the darkness to look for the safest passage back from where he'd come.

CHAPTER FOUR

Arias's mind remained on Brynne, but he was confident that she'd recover soon. They'd be back to their adventures in no time! He was glad that he'd been able to help her, but he was already reconsidering the wisdom in trying to leave Glendale to head to Skyhaven in the first place. Now he was hyper alert, hugging the tree line and jumping anytime the wind rustled through the leaves. He found himself unable to shake free from the knowledge that Iba had confirmed there was something slaughtering Primals. Something in these very woods.

Arias tried to dismiss his behavior as just being nerves, but in reality his instinct had detected danger long before his mind had processed it. He stiffened as he realized that he was being watched, and it was too late to hide. A pewter hen, young and unkempt, not much older than himself, melted out from a nearby berry bush. She didn't look particularly threatening, but Arias was already drawing several conclusions, the most important of which being that he could fight her if he had to. Maybe. Just treat her like preymeat, he told himself. Go for the throat like Brynne showed you…

"I can't believe my luck!" the youngster exclaimed the moment she spotted him. She leaped on all fours in jubilation. "A Spirit Walker! We'll be safe at last! No one will dare attack us now!"

Arias didn't speak nor move. Was she a Primal? Dangerous? Either way, she was acting really weird.

"You're going to escort us to Skyhaven, and Sheba is going to let us join her flock," she said.

Well, that answered that. Definitely a Primal.

"Why aren't you avoiding or trying to kill me like every other Gryphon?" Arias asked.

"Let's go," she commanded, gesturing in the direction of Skyhaven with a hiss. Arias narrowed his eyes and sized her up again, intending to fight her. But before he could dip into pounce, a blur cut around his periphery, and an adult keythong appeared between him and the hen. He was gaunt and older, and his fur and feathers sported a healthy coating of dust from a lack of grooming. His ribs showed through his dull coat. But his eyes were still and dangerous.

"You heard her," he said solemnly. "Let's go."

***

The moment Skyhaven loomed in the distance, Arias felt unease drop into his gut. The eyrie had been formed on a majestic caldera, and its sheer size seemed to engulf everything around it. Any sound Arias made to his unwelcome company was only met with being clouted briskly by the keythong, so he learned to stop speaking. The otherwise silent journey was generously dappled with meaningful threats.

"If Sheba doesn't accept us, it's your throat," the young hen reminded him.

"Don't make any quick movements when we get there, or we'll make sure you regret it," the keythong echoed behind him.

As they began to ascend the side of the caldera, Arias heard the cries of sentries all around them, and he faltered. Would the sentries simply kill them on sight? Torture them first? Hand them over to whatever had been killing Primals in the forest? Another rough shove from the keythong forced him to continue moving, however, and he walked the trodden path to what he was sure would be his doom. He felt terribly stupid to have even begun on this journey.

Arias couldn't see around the lip of the caldera, and the two Primals were just as jittery as he, their heads whipping around at every noise. The young hen was glaring at him incessantly, as though with every movement he were trying to send veiled signals to the flock. The instant they crested the caldera, a group of guards surrounded them. When they rested their eyes on Arias, however, they fell away, warbling uncertainly as they took in his appearance. They gave him a wide berth despite feigning bravado, their eyes flashing in their sockets. And then a hen that could only be the Matriarch herself descended.

Arias quickly realized that Brynne's reverence for Sheba was well-placed. Even alongside her formidable guards, Sheba was absolutely massive. Her silver pelt coursed over her muscular form as she moved, the fur broken in countless places where the scars of numerous battles peeked through. She wasted no time in sorting out affairs, a roar already on her sharp tongue.

"You two again! I ordered you once already to get out. I won't tell you so quietly this time."

Arias jumped as the keythong draped a filthy talon over his back and drew him closer to him.

"Let us into your flock, or this one will curse you."

Sheba's guards practically wheeled in terror before remembering their jobs and stopping themselves, their hocks trembling. Sheba didn't reply. She gave no indication of preparing to move, but in the time it took for Arias to blink, she'd thrown herself onto the keythong. Arias struggled free from between the two as they tussled against one another, the sound of claws meeting flesh ringing in his ears. The keythong yowled as Sheba ducked with breakneck speed to bite him deep in the thigh, and he retreated in a flash.

"You can't just leave us out there with those things hunting us!" the younger female interjected, her tail standing straight up in fear. "We're all Gryphons, it shouldn't matter where we come from!"

Sheba's eyes were hard. They scanned the ragged pair before her, but her expression was unmovable. Arias balked as her gaze lingered on him longer than he felt comfortable with.

"Make your own flock with the other Primals if you're so desperate to be flocked," Sheba told them. "We are at our limit here in size for our territory. I have enough on my claws with protecting my own, and I've no idea who or what your enemy is, but it hasn't concerned us yet. Defend yourselves against it, or die a worthy death; I've no other words for you, save that the next Primal to try to sneak in here with threats will see their entrails emptied out on this caldera."

The Primals cast baleful glances over the eyrie, but at the snapping of the beaks of Sheba's guards, they edged away slowly back to the forest. Arias hovered between the two hostile groups. The Primals evidently didn't share the Skyhaven Gryphons' fear of him, but the hateful looks they gave him assured him that there wasn't anything good in store for him once they were away from here. Sheba was eyeing him again, and he couldn't place the expression she wore. He took a deep breath. He didn't even know what he was saying, but the words tumbled out liberally.

"As Spirit Walker, I'm sure I can do something to ward your flock against this unseen enemy," he said. If there really was something killing Primals in the woods at night, there was no way he was making it safely back to Glendale by nightfall. No way he would try, at least. Especially not without flight. The fear he'd seen in the eyes of the two Primals as they'd pleaded to enter the flock had been real.

To Arias's relief, Sheba seemed intrigued by his proposition.

"Come closer," she said.

He did so.

Sheba's sentinels made strangled sounds and backed away, and Sheba immediately shushed them with an acidic screech. "Stop your mewling. Go on, make sure those two Primals get out of here, and head back to your posts after. And not a word to any of the others about him."

The sentinels rocketed off gratefully the moment she gave the order.

"You should never have left Glendale," Sheba said quietly. "But since you are here, I'll give you a choice. Do as I say and be very quiet, and I'll find you someplace safe to spend the night. Or you can return to Glendale alone, and embrace whatever fate awaits you in the woods this night."

"How do you know I'm from Glendale?" Arias asked. The Matriarch didn't answer him.

She waited for his reply to her proposition, and he realized that he felt very small and very foolish to be all the way over here. Alone. The Primals, he was sure, wouldn't let him escape a third time. Sheba started to move away, and he nearly tripped in his haste to fall in after her. She was leading him toward the center of the caldera, where her flock had decidedly made its home. With the sight of it, Arias's mind was on fire with the knowledge that, despite circumstances, he was finally about to truly set foot in Skyhaven eyrie.

***

Skyhaven teemed with life. Vegetation clung to every stony precipice, and a pool of crystal-clear spring water bubbled up at its center. Huge dens had been dug into the ground and shielded with branches and dried grass. Guards were stationed at regular intervals along the lip of the caldera, some peering down into the forest below for trouble, others scanning the sky. The place was so well guarded that it must have been impossible for anyone to approach the eyrie without being seen.

Curious heads poked out at Sheba's approach, and Arias squeezed his eyes shut even though he knew that they couldn't see him. He was pressed close against the Matriarch's back, and her wings were folded over him like a protective canopy, obscuring him from view. He could only catch glimpses of the eyrie through the wispy spaces between her feathers, but his bright eyes took in as much as he could. He could hear her flock mates calling out respectfully to her, and he felt the vibration that rippled through her body as she replied back. He tried not to dig his claws into her flesh as her solid shoulders rose and fell, causing him to shift from side to side. It felt like he had been lying silently for a small lifetime, wondering where she was taking him and what would happen next. He couldn't believe he was finally in Skyhaven. His heart beat with a mixture of fear and excitement.

"Here we are, Spirit Walker," Sheba presently said, raising her huge wings to send the fading light of sunset spilling over him. "You'll stay with the low born tonight… out of sight, mind you."

Arias leaped unsteadily down from her back, and found himself in the shelter of one of the dens. He exhaled in surprise when he was greeted by the sight of Brynne and Iba. His orange friend nuzzled him weakly and even managed to chirp a greeting to him before lying back down to rest.

"Those herbs you gave me work quickly, Spirit Walker," Brynne's mother said happily. "I must say, it's good to see you again so soon, unharmed."

Sheba's eyes flashed with surprise. "I see you already somehow know the lowborn, Spirit Walker?"

Arias bristled at the word. "You shouldn't call them lowborn. They're the same as you and I."

Iba's eyes widened at the response, and she started to stammer an apology, but Sheba was already pinning her ears at the retort. It was a ferocious sight to see, and Arias tensed for his oncoming punishment, fearing that he'd spoken too freely. But after a pause, Sheba instead crowed with laughter.

"You've no respect, Spirit Walker!" she said, "And you speak before you think. But then again, you are not like the rest of us. I never thought I'd hear such sass from one as young as you. How interesting. Iba! I ask that you explain how you know this young one. I'm sure it makes for a very interesting tale."

***

Sheba's expression changed many times during the recounting Iba told her, but she seemed most perplexed toward the end, when Iba spoke of how Arias had managed to find all the herbs needed to heal Brynne.

"The Alicorns taught you their healing magicks?" Sheba asked.

Arias shook his head. "I don't have their ability to use magick, but I've learned which herbs are helpful as remedies. I remembered things from watching them, like the way certain plants look and what their effects are."

Sheba blinked, astounded. "Very interesting," she said, and after a few quiet murms of thinking, added, "Well, I'm sure you all must be tired after such journeys. Spirit Walker—Arias—please feel free to stay as long as you need to, provided you stay out of sight. As I said earlier, it isn't safe in the forests anymore, especially alone. The Primals are searching for any means of defense possible, and I fear you will come to harm now that you are no longer under Xio's protection. Skyhaven flock has always adhered to certain traditions, ones that began long before I hatched, so know that you will not be greeted happily if you are seen by any aside from us three. If I could escort you back to Glendale myself I would, but I am too needed at the moment. You must remain hidden, and Iba will ensure you get enough to eat and a chance to stretch your legs if you need to. Now, then."

The Matriarch gave a cursory nod of her head, to which Iba bowed in return. It took a meaningful nudge from her for Arias to realize he should do the same, but the Matriarch had already turned and was leaving. He breathed out in awe. Brynne had been right about everything she'd said about Sheba. It was hard to imagine any creature being so mighty.

***

It wasn't long before night fell on the eyrie, and Arias lay happily in the soft fluff of the bedding in Iba's den. She'd lined it with bits of feather and down, and he even recognized a few of the types of mosses she'd tucked in. He couldn't believe his luck! Not only was he alive, but he'd be safe until he could return to Glendale. And not only that, but he was free to sit and observe what flock life was like for a bit.

Iba stretched next to Arias, splaying the razor-sharp claws in her hind paws as she did so. She gathered Brynne in close to her with a wing, and Arias was surprised when she raised the other, her tail waving amicably. "Don't be shy. Late summer nights can be chilly," she said.

Arias overcame a moment of hesitation before accepting the offer, snuggling in to discover how surprisingly warm it was to be nestled next to the bodies of two other Gryphons. He fell into a deep and satisfying sleep.

CHAPTER FIVE

Arias woke to the sound of Iba stuffing all manner of bedding into the den. She heaped it into high peaks that completely covered the hard-packed ground, and Arias soon found himself helping her to work it into the farthest corners. While a deep, soft substrate of mosses, down, and grass was comfortable to sleep in, its purpose here was more obvious. Amid the wall of material, Arias would be completely hidden from view. Anyone peering into the den through the branches above wouldn't see anything out of the ordinary, leaving Iba free to relax a little. The sky outside was overcast and heavy with the threat of rain, a good incentive to make Iba and Arias hurry in completing their work.

Brynne had been sleeping soundly nearby Arias, sprawled out on her back with her tail draped across her chest. She snored softly and murmured unintelligibly as she dreamed, and Arias trilled happily to himself, glad that she seemed to be doing better. His ears darted sideways at the sound of approaching paw falls, and he ducked low despite being concealed. One of the flock hunters had stopped nearby the entrance, and Iba cast him a warning glance to ensure he was out of sight before she walked over and stuck her head out to greet him. Arias could tell by the newcomer's voice that he was older in age.

"What are you up to, Iba? Making things cozy for your little one? If you stuff anymore into that den, there won't be any more room for you!"

"Just preparing for the cold days of leaf fall, Hengar," Iba replied, fluffing some down feathers especially high in the corner where Arias was. "You should be collecting some bedding, too. You know how the cold stiffens your bones."

"Hmph. These old hips don't favor the chilly season, you've got that right. Just hardly have time to do anything these days, what with the Primals trying to claw their way up here every other murm. Speaking of which; there goes a messenger with what I'm sure is more bad news now. Primals have been spotted west of here, so hunting parties have been pretty uptight. I guess I'd better get back to sentry duty. You be sure to stay warm, Iba."

Arias heard the old keythong shuffling away, and when he peeked his head up over Iba's body, he could see a gaunt figure moving away with a slow, rocking gait.

"What's wrong with him?" Arias asked, and

Iba's shoulders rose and fell in a shrug.

"Just old. Age catches up with us all eventually, even if you can't believe it now. I didn't used to believe it. With every year, I feel a little less spry, myself." She glanced at Brynne and then thought for a moment before saying, "I wouldn't feel right about sending you back to Glendale knowing Primals are so close by. You should stay here until they move on. I'm sure you're tired of sitting in here, though. Would you like to stretch your legs a bit after the storm passes?"

"Aren't you worried about me being seen?" Arias asked, despite the fact that he certainly was tired of being cooped up.

"You won't be. Just be very quiet and follow my instructions when the time comes."

Arias didn't complain. He watched the late summer rain rush over the eyrie for most of the morning, then jumped at the opportunity to do a little exploring when Iba gestured to him.

"Come on now," she said. "Hop on up!"

Arias wasted no time in climbing onto the hen's narrow back, pressing low against her sleek body, and closing his eyes as she covered him over with her wings.

***

Beautiful shafts of morning light penetrated through the dissipating clouds. The hazy glow was blinding to Arias, and he resorted to squinting at the ground to fend off the pounding headache that jabbed behind his eyeballs. He hurried to the nearest tree line, blinking gratefully as the shadows of the canopy spilled over him.

"Are you okay?" Iba asked with a note of worry, cocking her head sideways. She followed him at a distance, but not far enough away that she couldn't reach him if anything happened.

Arias nodded as he stretched luxuriously in the leaf litter, yawning himself to full wakefulness. "Bright light hurts my eyes, and I always forget how bright it is when I'm not underneath the trees in Glendale. The trees there are so tall that…"

A thunderous roar sounded overhead, and Iba instinctively moved to drape a protective wing over him. They both crouched low and froze as the sounds of distant wing beats grew closer and closer. Finally, the great Naugi himself barreled overhead on his massive, leathery wings. Arias gasped as the Hydra's serpentine voice cracked the heavens again, and he tried to stay hidden under Iba's wing as she stood up.

"It's okay," she said, prodding him to his feet. "It's Naugi, not one of his scale-kin. He's flying over to remind us that it's nearly offering time."

"What offering?"

"He only takes offerings from some beasts. In return, he protects us from other predators that would kill us and destroy our homes. I'm

guessing he doesn't take offerings from the
Alicorns, then? It makes sense, seeing as they
don't eat meat. And I'm sure they can protect
themselves, or they wouldn't have survived as
long as they have in the forest."

Arias nodded, still shaken. He'd seen Naugi
speaking to Xio before. But they spoke in a
language he couldn't decipher, and he'd been
eavesdropping to have even seen that much.

Iba was looking at him with a strange
expression. "It must be nice and… safe to live
alongside the Alicorns. What did you eat, though?
Surely you had to get preymeat from somewhere
to survive."

"Scavenging. Still do, usually."

Iba gagged before she could compose herself.
"I'm sorry, it's just… I've never heard of a
Gryphon scavenging before. Doesn't the meat
taste wrong after being left to sit?"

Arias shrugged. "It certainly tastes better fresh,
but I've never really thought about it." He tensed
as Naugi screamed into the wind again, his voice
distant now, and Iba gave him another reassuring
nudge. He eased away from her, embarrassed for
being so easily frightened. "What did you mean
when you said Naugi's 'scale-kin'?" he asked,
hoping to detract from his own skittishness.

"Have you ever seen a basilisk or a drake
before, young one?"

Arias shook his head.

"Well, one day, I'm sure you will. They come in all shapes and sizes, and they live all over this land, although some Gryphons go their whole lives without ever glimpsing one. It takes many murms for them to grow, but it doesn't take long before they are able to easily kill and eat even an ursos. They would freely hunt us, if Naugi didn't command them not to. That is the reason for our offerings to him; to protect us from those that would overpower and consume us."

Arias felt a chill run up his spine. The Alicorns had never told him that.

"Never approach any of the scale-kin if you see them. They are ravenous, and every now and then, they may choose to disobey Naugi in the name of filling their belly. After all, if no one is around to tell Naugi what happened, who is to say that it happened at all? Hunger drives beasts past reason all the time."

Arias fought with the conflicting feeling of being equally horrified and filled with wonder. "When is Skyhaven going to make an offering?" he asked.

"Soon, I suppose. I don't really know. Sheba is the only one who knows such things because she is the only one from this flock he will speak with. For the offering, everyone who is able is expected to contribute. Only the finest of preymeat will be stockpiled."

Arias pondered her words. It seemed that he'd learned more about Gryphons in a matter of murms than he'd learned in a lifetime in Glendale. A short lifetime thus far, but a lifetime nonetheless.

Iba curled her tongue in a luxurious yawn and closed her eyes in a moment of rest. Arias was grateful for her presence. She had a very affable personality, and he already felt incredibly at ease around her. Would his real mother have been this way with him? It was an alien thought. He thoroughly viewed Hlaena as his mother, although they were obviously different species. He wondered how hard it would be to assimilate into life here while also visiting the Alicorns in Glendale from time to time. He'd already won Iba over, hadn't he? And Sheba, the Matriarch herself, seemed fine with having him around... at least briefly, she did.

Iba shifted, sprawling out on the ground, and then suddenly was on her feet, snarling. "That plant again," she said, pointing toward a cluster of a vivid green plant with spike-like leaves. She'd accidentally lain on them, but the hardy shoots appeared no worse for wear. Arias immediately recognized the hardy lichthorn for what they were. While Iba made herself comfortable elsewhere, he carefully picked the topmost leaves with the very tip of his bill, excited to show them to her.

"Spit those out!" Iba demanded. "Those sting worse than biting insects, I don't want them anywhere near me."

Arias shook his head. "They can sting, which is why you can't let them touch bare flesh. But they can help your flock mate… his name was Hengar, I think."

The corners of Iba's mouth flicked downward at the suggestion. "I appreciate that you helped Brynne… but you must use discretion. I have no knowledge of what these plants do. It honestly sounds strange to me that you're suggesting stinging leaves can help anyone to feel better. I'm afraid that you can't go on performing your strange ways here if you're to remain undiscovered."

Arias's ears pricked forward at the mention of him remaining in the eyrie, and Iba gave a defeated sigh.

"I'm going to end up getting into trouble now that you're around. I can't help it. I'm grateful for Brynne, she makes me proud in ways I never could have imagined, but you're like the cub I'll never have an opportunity to raise. I've always wanted a little keythong."

Arias dropped the lichthorn and poked them thoughtfully with a claw. "Iba, can't you just say that you met an Alicorn in the woods, and they gave you the medicine? I know they make their way up here sometimes, and you know you can trust me because I already helped you once. I like it here, I won't make any trouble for you. And if you can gain a reputation for helping others, things can only get better for you and Brynne in the flock."

Iba blinked past the uncertainty in her dark eyes. "I suppose," she said, though it sounded to Arias more like she just wanted any reason to let him stay. "Come on, then. I'll give your 'lichthorn' to the sentry tonight when he passes by my den. For now, let's head back. The first hunting party should've returned by now."

***

Arias held his herbs carefully as Iba walked back to the eyrie. The hen lacked Sheba's girth, and he had trouble holding onto her slight frame. While graceful and lithe, Arias hadn't noticed until now that beneath her petite exterior, her ribs poked out from beneath her fine coat. Every now and then he had to dig in with his claws to keep from sliding off, and he could feel her tense as she winced.

"Sorry!" he whispered, but she didn't answer. Soon, the nearby sound of voices blossomed around them, gaining in volume as Iba cut her way through the heart of the eyrie. Arias was able to pick out one voice in particular distinctly addressing Iba.

"Hey Iba! Good to see you! What, too tired to use your wings these days? With that hellion of yours about to fledge, you must be exhausted! How is Brynne anyways?"

Iba sidestepped and laughed nervously as the owner of the voice swatted at her playfully.

"Brynne isn't fond of having to rest, she keeps

55

me up wanting to play all night. It's nice to enjoy some quiet every now and then. So, uh, how many peryton were caught today?"

Arias marveled at how well she managed to switch subjects.

"Six, if you can believe it! Sheba herself took two on the wing, and the rest were our junior hunters. The quicker they can learn to kill, the better in these uncertain times. Take whatever you want for you and your daughter today. I hope the little rascal is back to full strength soon enough. She still thinks she can beat me in a fight, and I can't wait to prove her wrong again."

A voice suddenly screeched across the eyrie, halting the exchange.

"Makith! Stop talking to that low born and come eat!"

There was an awkward pause as the other voice said, "Well… see you, Iba."

Arias nearly fell forward as Iba bowed her head, and after a few murms she was moving off again, toward a pile of assorted preymeat that had already had chunks of meat pulled and torn away.

"What to eat…" she said, before moving off to a more isolated carcass, asking more pointedly over her shoulder, *What to eat?*"

Arias realized she was addressing him, and blurted the first thing that came to mind, which happened to be, "Uhh… Liver?"

Iba obliged and took what she wanted as well, being careful to ignore the, "That's a lotta food for a hen in a drought who barely hunts for herself, eh lowborn?" that was shouted her way. She hastily moved away from the feeding area before she could attract anymore unwanted attention, and Arias could sense her prickling anxiety. He felt bad for her.

After being smothered for far too many murms, it was a relief for Arias to finally be back within the privacy of the den. While Iba preened and readjusted her wings against her sides, Arias stashed his lichthorn in his little corner. Brynne chirped a happy greeting to him, having just awoken. She wiped sleep from her eyes and let him eat his fill of the liver first, evidently not back to her typical ravenous appetite yet. Iba swallowed the chunk of meat she'd taken for herself in two gulps, then settled down to idly preen more. A hen of her size could easily have eaten three times more than that. Arias cocked his head.

"Why are some of the flock so mean to you? You're always nice to everyone," he said.

Iba finished plucking at a frayed feather. "It's simply my lot in life. It's what it means to be low born. Unfortunately, it transfers to Brynne, too, as she is my daughter. Or at least, it does until she's old enough to make her own way in the flock."

"Why you and not some other Gryphon?"

"Well…" She gestured to herself using her tail. "I'm small bodied, even for a hen, so I can only hunt small game if I'm alone. I'd never be able to defend myself against an ursos or a larger Gryphon, and I've never been any good at fighting anyway, so I can't hold my own. On top of that, I'm a young hen who no longer has a mate, so Brynne will be my last offspring. A hen that produces useful offspring for the flock is better regarded than deadweight. When my mate, who was a fantastic hunter, passed away, things got more difficult for Brynne and me. At least we weren't cast out, as some flocks may have done. Sheba is a merciful leader." She casually went back to picking at her feathers, and Arias felt very small for asking.

"I'm sorry," he said, feeling a twinge of anger at the way the others treated her. "It's not like any of that is your fault."

Iba's eyes rose and fell in a faux shrug, and then she stood. "I'm going out for a bit. Brynne, keep your friend hidden, please. No one should come by… but if they do, back him into that corner and don't let him be seen. I don't want either of you to cause any trouble while I'm gone." She vanished before they could reply, and Arias flattened his ears against his head.

"What?" Brynne asked.

"I don't know. I feel bad for asking. I guess that in all the time we've spent together, I never really grasped what it meant to be lowborn in a flock."

"Ah. It's just the way things are, Arias. In a flock, at least. Don't feel bad. Besides, it's safer here than out there with the Primals. We get food to eat, and we don't have to worry about being attacked in our sleep."

"I don't think your mom gets enough to eat."

"Well, that makes three of us, then!" Brynne jabbed him playfully in the ribs, but he didn't laugh.

"Oh come on," she said, sounding annoyed. "That kind of thinking isn't going to get us anywhere anyway, so quit it. It's why I'm going to be the greatest hunter this flock has ever seen." Her chest swelled at the thought. "Then those dumb *tucas* can stop calling us lowborn."

Arias didn't say anything. He curled up in his corner and closed his eyes, heedless to Brynne's insistent poking.

"Come on, let's play!" she said, but he only grumbled.

"I don't feel like it right now," he said. "Maybe later."

***

Sunset fell over the eyrie quickly. Brynne was asleep already, made drowsy by the blackroot she was still taking for her wounds. Iba sat quietly near the entrance to the den, staring at nothing in particular with tired eyes. Arias flicked his tail to try to drum it against the ground, but it wasn't long enough to even reach that far anymore. Sheba hadn't stopped by again, which was all the better for him, though if she had she wouldn't have spotted him with the excess of bedding in the den.

Arias now understood why Sheba had chosen Iba as the Gryphon he'd stay with; as a lowborn, she simply obeyed the orders of her alphas without questioning them. Despite their difference in rank, Sheba treated Iba with respect that many others in the flock didn't. It raised Arias's opinion of her, and gave him hope that he could win her over to the idea of letting him stay in the eyrie in the near future.

The sound of heavy foot falls crept nearby Iba's nest, and the hen threw a precautionary glance in Arias's direction before creeping out the entrance. Hengar's haggard voice sounded presently just outside, and Arias chanced to creep forward enough to take in the hulking figure, the scarred face, and a beak that was chipped, making it sharper at the tip than it should have been. He could see him perfectly in the low light, and knew that he must've been a mighty fighter back in the days of his youth.

"I was out in the wood and ran into an Alicorn, the same one who gave me the herbs to help Brynne. I thought of you when I saw him. I hope you aren't offended, but..." She reached back to retrieve the lichthorn, now partially dried out, and pushed the bundle toward him. Though the old keythong's face remained stony, his voice didn't hide his shock at the gesture.

"How very kind of you, Iba! The Alicorns don't leave Glendale very often. It means quite a bit to me that someone thought of me in the twilight of my life. We must stick together, those of us at the bottom of the pecking order… thank you again. May Halada shine upon you and your little one." He gave a shallow bow, and Iba hurried to return the gesture much more deeply.

"You are one of the few who regard me as anything other than a lowborn, Hengar. There aren't many who do that, so I suppose it's a small thanks. Oh, wait!" she said as he reached to take the herb. "You mustn't let the plant touch your tongue, it stings. Take it with the tip of your beak, and eat it with meat…"

Arias crept back to his corner as Iba recited instructions to the keythong regarding the herb. When she entered the den again a few murms later, she seemed star struck.

"I can't remember the last time another Gryphon bowed to me," she said, closing her eyes. "It feels nice to be seen."

It made Arias happy to see her so elated. That, and on a deeper level, he liked being able to help the other Gryphons, even if it was from the shadows.

"Iba."

The hen's eyes fluttered over to him.

"You said a Gryphon's rank can change depending on what they can give to the flock, right?"

She nodded.

"Well, what if I teach you the herbs I know when we go out during the day, and you can help your flock that way? Everyone loves the Alicorns because they can heal pretty much anything." His mind flashed back to the dying keythong that had attacked him and Brynne, but he shrugged away the intrusive thought. "Nearly anything," he amended with a spike of discomfort. "Everyone will love you for the same reason."

Iba shook her head. "No, that will just make them wonder where I learned everything. It's really sweet of you to want to help, Arias, but that's just not how things work."

"Come on," Arias said. "I know I'm young and I don't really know what the rules of a flock are, but it seems fair to me. Just tell them Xio the Alicorn showed you if anyone gets too curious... he wouldn't mind. I know he wouldn't."

"You do know the Alicorns better than any of us would, but still..."

"Are you really that afraid of a chance at a better life?"

Iba's crest raised as if offended, her eyes wide.

Then she snorted softly to herself. "Yep, I'm lowborn alright. Taking suggestions from a cub a fraction of my own age." She sighed. "I've trusted you twice now, and you've been right each of those times. Maybe Spirit Walkers are the opposite of unlucky. Maybe the tale just got passed along wrong somehow."

"There's a story about what I am?" Arias asked.

Iba nodded. "It's an old tale that often crops up during new moons. It begins when the earth was new, and Gryphons were just starting to inhabit it. Halada took favor on our kind, and gave us wings so that we could be a part of her heavens. One night, an adventurous yearling sneaked away from his parents, intent on trying to catch the moon.

"The yearling knew he'd have to fly higher than any Gryphon had ever flown before, and he did just that. When he finally was close enough, he took the moon carefully in his beak, intending to bring it down to his eyrie to show his parents. But on the way down, a terrible crosswind caught him, and in his panic, he accidentally swallowed the moon. The night went black, and his formerly brown coat suddenly bleached as bright and white as the moon itself.

"The creatures who lived in the night complained to Halada that her favored species had taken the moonlight for themselves, and she was incensed. The rest of the Gryphons wasted no time in blaming the yearling, and when he heard Halada was searching for him, he tried to hide. But his bright plumage was like a beacon in the darkness. Halada found him and took the moon from him, but left his color as it had been, so that every creature would know what he had done.

"Halada told him she'd let him live, but he'd be cursed. All the other Gryphons would live by day and sleep by night, but he would find the light of day unpleasant. No other Gryphon wanted to consort with him after what he'd done, and he lived an outcast life."

Arias waited for more of the story, but Iba had evidently reached the end.

After a bit, she added, "Honestly, I was surprised to see that it appears that some of the story is true. You're always squinting in the daylight. But whereas the tale says you're a cursed creature, you've brought nothing but good things."

Iba moved from her post and turned her back to the entrance of the den, gathering up her sleeping daughter with one wing and opening the other so that Arias could snuggle in. She closed her eyes and was soon asleep, but for long murms after Arias stared at his pink claws and his stardust-white feathers. He wondered if the story Iba had told really happened long ago. No one was alive from back then to tell anyone what really happened. Maybe Naugi. Maybe.

"I've never tried to steal anything," he

murmured pointedly. Then he closed his eyes, too. Iba was on board with his idea. He'd show Skyhaven flock that they were all worthy members of the flock, and then he'd come up with a way to win over Sheba. He wasn't sure how just yet, but he knew there had to be a way.

***

The following days were spent exactly as Arias wanted them. He was delighted to discover that Iba and Brynne were apt students; Iba was better at identifying the species of plants he described, and Brynne had the energy to find them nearly as quickly as they set out to look for them. Before long, they had a small stockpile drying in the corner of Iba's den, obscured by bits of twigs and grasses.

One chilly morning after tussling with Brynne, Arias was horrified to find that his fluffier feathers were strewn about the den. He and Brynne worked to clean them up before any other Gryphons noticed. It wasn't long before her feathers began to do the same thing. They stopped playing quite so hard, careful to keep the down that swirled in the air like snow and embers confined. Iba sat them both down that night and taught them the proper way to preen their feathers.

"You start at the root, like this," she said, taking the flight feathers at the tips of her wings in her beak. "And then you pull them through your mouth, as many times as it takes for them to lie flat. If they won't, or they're bent or crushed, like this one…" She grabbed a particularly frayed specimen that was sticking out at an odd angle on her chest. "You remove them and wait for them to regrow in the next molt." She yanked it out in a single, sharp motion, prompting both of the cubs to wince. Iba laughed. "You get used to it," she said.

Arias and Brynne had been grooming themselves beforehand, but not as meticulously as they could have. They spent the rest of the night preening fastidiously, plucking away any feathers that looked like they were keen to come out.

The molting of Arias and Brynne's first juvenile feathers was an exciting and deeply annoying time. Arias was frustrated by just how much the newly grown pinions itched, and found himself constantly scratching them at length. Likewise, Brynne dug relentlessly at the flesh on her chest and wing tips, to the point that she drew blood. Of course, Arias knew no remedy for such an event, and the two spent most of their time miserable and patchy, consoled only by the thought of how soon they would be flying in a brand-new coat of feathers. It was, after all, the only time in their lives when they would completely lose and replace all their feathers at once. Their adult plumage would bring the blessing of only shedding and replacing a few at a time.

As they grew, Arias and Brynne experienced an exponential growth in appetite, and Iba had trouble hiding just how much she was taking from the communal prey meat. Some nights she went without eating at all, and at other times

Arias and Brynne gave each other a mutual glance before insisting they weren't hungry. Their loudly grumbling stomachs betrayed them each time, but Iba was too ravenous to resist when she finally had a chance to eat.

To help offset how much was taken from the eyrie's daily stockpile of food, the trio began to hunt more seriously. On the off event when they hunted down and killed prey big enough to share, like the grunting tusker they caught early one morning, they all celebrated and ate heartily, too full to bother looking for herbs. Their momentary period of trying to stave off hunger was short lived, however.

Iba was growing quite a reputation for herself. Some in the flock began to call her a friend to the Alicorns, for clearly they must have favored her to share such bountiful remedies with her as often as they did. Her flock mates spoke to her in higher and higher regards, many stopping by to share their own kills personally with her. It wasn't long before she, Arias, and Brynne grew plump and glossy on the surplus of good meat.

Arias was happier than he'd been for a while. Thanks to him, Iba was given credit for treating everything from colds and runny eyes to infected cuts and arthritis; she nearly had to directly tell the other Gryphons to leave her alone at night just so she could sleep without accepting their heartfelt thanks or gifts. Most of the flock were amicable at the very least to her, but a few of the older elders merely huffed suspiciously whenever her name was mentioned, muttering hostilely under their breath. The worst seemed to be an older hen. She was increasingly keeping a closer eye on Iba than Arias liked. He wondered what her problem was, but then he decided that he didn't care. Things were going too great to be bothered by one ancient hen who would probably be dead by the next frost fall.

***

Arias wasn't exactly surprised when it happened, because he expected it to happen eventually. He was off to one side of a thicket, searching for a particular type of blue mushroom, when he sensed that he wasn't alone. He turned abruptly, and saw that Xio was in the thicket with him. The Alicorn stallion whickered to him in greeting, stepping forward to nose at his growing feathers in admiration. Arias wasted no time in crossing necks with him in a warm embrace, and after a time of seeming to wrestle with what to say, Xio said, "I had a feeling that you might make your way here eventually, especially when you started to spend time with that little orange hen."

Arias glanced across the trees to where Brynne was struggling to topple over a rotting log, totally unaware that there was now another being in the forest with them.

"I hope you're not upset with me," Arias said sheepishly.

Xio chuckled, using his magick to pull a few stray feathers from Arias's plumage. "No, not angry. I was more worried for your safety. I trust that Sheba knows about you?"

Arias nodded.

"Then there isn't much to worry about at all," Xio said. "Maybe things have changed. And maybe this is for the best. We were honestly wondering what would happen if we kept trying to get you to stay put in Glendale with us for much longer. You're a magnificent creature, Arias. You aren't like us. If the other Gryphons are accepting of you, I refuse to disturb that. I'll let Hlaena know that you're here, safe, and to leave you be." He draped his neck over Arias's in another warm embrace. "Don't forget to come see us in Glendale sometime."

Arias nodded, and the following silence enveloped him. Why did he feel like he couldn't speak past the lump in his throat? There was so much he wanted to tell Xio!

The Alicorn stallion's eyes looked distant. Finally, he said, "You know, Arias… the lifespan of most creatures seems very short to me. Only Naugi and a few others understand what it's like to see generations rise and fall. I know I'll miss your company. Still, it's also quite a treat to see how fast you're growing! You'll be a handsome keythong before long. The hens won't be able to keep their claws off you." He winked. "I'll try to come visit you, too. I know your life here will keep you very busy. I take it that you like it so far?"

Arias nodded again, unable to successfully navigate the conversation in the wake of Xio's somber attitude. "I can go back, you know," he blurted. "I loved my life with you and the other Alicorns! Maybe I can travel between Glendale and Skyhaven."

Xio was already shaking his head. "No. Your place is here. We will certainly see one another now and again. You know where to find us, and now we know where to find you!" He smiled briefly, then melted back into the woods, the dappled sunlight falling on his back like millions of stars.

Arias took a step, intending to follow him, but the Alicorn had already disappeared without a trace. He stood quietly, wondering what Xio would've said had he known the truth about his real role in this flock. It had almost come out, but he was glad it had caught in his throat. It only would've made the stallion worry. He'd done the right thing. And besides, he knew what he was doing. He trotted back over to where Brynne was beginning to dig into the rotten log, and lent her a second set of eyes in the search for mushrooms.

***

Arias curled up tighter, wishing he still had his tail to wrap around his body. It was cold, colder than normal, and he tried to move closer to Brynne for warmth, but she wasn't there. He fluffed his feathers and tucked his head under a wing instead, but before he could begin to drift off, he was poked hard in the side. He opened his eyes, and Iba gestured toward the entrance to the den.

"Come on," she whispered. "Let's practice

branching. Brynne has already started without us."

"Why so early?"

"Don't complain. Let's go."
***
Walking through the forest, Arias tried not to hunch his shoulders against the chill in the wind. Iba glanced back at him and chuckled.

"Don't worry, you'll get used to it. When the rest of your feathers finish coming in, you'll hardly feel the cold."

Arias straightened up, embarrassed that she'd noticed, but she was already cutting into the underbrush, edging past saplings that grew in tight clumps. Arias hurried to not be left behind, slipping easily through the gaps in the young trees, and finally emerged behind the hen in a clearing that was host to an enormous hardwood. It rose with twisting limbs high above the canopy of the other plants below it, the creases in its ancient wood deep and gnarled. High up in the branches, a smear of orange could be seen climbing up, wings flapping as the figure leapt from one branch to another.

Branching, Arias thought to himself excitedly. After receiving a nod from Iba, he ran to start climbing himself. The divets and notches in the wood of the old tree made it incredibly easy to scale, and he had nearly caught up to Brynne by the time he reached the first fork that made it necessary for him to jump across to another branch. He tried to judge the distance, grateful for the dull lighting of the early morning. Up above, Brynne had stopped moving and was looking down at him instead. He took a deep breath, dedicated himself to the leap, and forced his claws to release the wood beneath them.

The leap to the new branch wasn't nearly as far as the ones Arias would need to make further above, but the moment gravity took hold of him, he woodenly opened his wings and began to flap. He didn't really need to, it turned out. He landed dead-on where he'd intended to, and felt proud until he heard Iba's roaring laughter below. He looked down.

"Part of the secret to branching is to open your wings before you jump, Arias. You're just working harder with the way you're doing it."

Brynne smirked and resumed her activity without hesitation, fluttering to a thick branch opposite of where she was.

"Beat you to the top!" she yelled to Arias.

"That's not fair, you started before me!"

Brynne didn't look back.

Arias resigned himself not to be so immature as to partake in such silliness, but as he watched Brynne scramble up, a sense of competition awoke deep within him. He dug in and glided to the next limb with ease, amazed by how much easier–and how much more balanced—his movements were when he followed Iba's advice.

Brynne actually seemed a little startled by Arias's quick progress. He could see the panic in her eyes as he gained on her, navigating his way across the tree with ease. She wasn't used to losing, and he became eager to taste victory the moment he realized he could possibly beat her at something, even if that something was a simple game she'd just invented. She gathered herself hastily and made another leap, but the branch she'd chosen was slick with lichen, and she struggled to use her claws to secure herself. Bits of bark showered down as she struggled to no avail, holding on to the wood with only her talons, hind legs churning uselessly.

"Brynne!" Arias tried to hurry to reach her so he could help, but before he could make another leap, she lost her grip and slipped from the upper reaches of the tree. In a split moment, without thinking about it, he leapt after her.

***

Arias didn't have time to regret his actions. His wings cupped and released wind as he flapped, unseasoned in how to manipulate the air to promote flight. In an instant, he was tumbling after Brynne, and together they sped toward their deaths.

Arias squeezed his eyes shut as the ground rushed up to meet him, certain that the winding sensation that struck his gut was the final impact. But when he opened his eyes, he was airborne. It didn't make sense. When he looked down, confused, he saw Brynne held tightly in a set of claws. Iba had flown up with breakneck speed to catch them both, and he himself was pressed securely against her chest. The moment she landed, the mother poked at them both worriedly, afraid they were somehow injured even though they'd never touched the ground.

"I'm fine!" Brynne mumbled, snatching away a wing that Iba had been inspecting. Arias didn't say anything, but he still felt the same burning shame as Brynne. They'd nearly killed themselves over a game.

"It's okay," Iba said, withdrawing as she read their faces. "These things can happen when you're just learning. The important thing is that no one got hurt. Come now, let's head back. We'll try again tomorrow. You both have great form to just be starting out. Especially you, Arias. You'll be a promising flier."

The trio fell into line to travel back to the eyrie. Arias glanced over at Brynne hoping to make conversation after a while, but she wouldn't look at him. She kept her head down the entire way to the den.

***

Summer was making haste to end. Most mornings, Arias could see his breath hanging in the air, and the same again at night. He, Iba, and Brynne slept closer and closer together, packing in to conserve heat. The weather turned to favoring a chilly drizzle, and it kept them inside most of the time. When they weren't inside, they were hunting to put some meat on their bones. Learning to fly became a distant second to any other task.

The prey, it seemed, had suffered enough with the drought, and now was dealing poorly with the early frost. There was hardly any communal preymeat to be had in the eyrie. The older members of the flock had first pick at any that was scrounged up, and the gristle and bone left behind weren't enough to satisfy the rest of the population. Nearly every Gryphon set out to hunting, even the young and the infirm. Arias leaned into learning to hunt just as hard as Iba and Brynne, although his coat color was as problematic as ever.

Brynne was a fantastic tracker, quickly surpassing Iba in skill. It was an incredible feat considering that the prey was particularly on edge now. Iba coordinated their attacks, and Arias cherished his job as a flusher, stalking as close as he could to prey—which was never very close—before startling it into running toward the two hens, both of which had better chances of making a kill. They were their own little hunting party.

It was near sunset one evening, and Arias was stretched out lazily on his back, his paws resting against the dried mosses that insulated his corner of Iba's nest. He was talking with Brynne about their favorite meat to eat, when a sudden, piercing shriek rended the air, so loud and sudden that Arias feared someone was being killed right there in the eyrie. They both shot to their feet, with Arias poised to run for his life, but Brynne spread a wing to stop him from going anywhere.

"It's okay," she said, walking to the entrance of the den. "Sheba's called a meeting, an important one from the sounds of it. I'm going to go check it out. I'll be back." Arias slumped back down where he'd been standing to wait, taking a deep breath to slow his racing heart. He wondered how often Primals were startled, living a life unprotected in the woods. No dens, no true territory… even if he was here undercover, he was glad to be surrounded by a flock with sentries.

Arias closed his eyes for a few murms, and then he heard a very distinct crinkling sound. Assuming Brynne was back, he opened his eyes, and looked up at an unfamiliar face. He froze even though he slowly began to recognize the face, and he backed away in a flurry of motion. Far too soon, he was pressed up against the far wall of the nest, adrenaline pooling in his gut. Hengar didn't blink as he stared back, and the blank expression on his face only served to exacerbate Arias's fear.

"I knew that Iba was up to something," Hengar said in his gruff voice. Arias neither moved nor spoke, his heart once again slamming with purpose. His nub of a tail tried hard to press against his belly as he searched for an escape around the keythong. There was none.

"I'm not going to hurt you," the grizzled keythong said, glancing back to make sure no one was coming. "I didn't know what I'd find here, but I sure didn't expect it to be you. So it's true then? You're the one who helped me? Who has been helping everyone?"

Arias's voice came out as a small squeak. "She was the one who decided to give it to you… I-I just showed her what to use."

"Hmph." Hengar snorted and continued to stare at Arias, and his flat gaze reminded Arias again of the way the Primals had looked when they'd hunted him and Brynne. He swallowed dryly as Hengar reached into the bedding at his feet, pulling out a frayed white feather that had been missed in an earlier cleaning. "It's not exactly safe for your kind in these parts," he said ominously. "Been a long while since I've seen an adult Spirit Walker. But a cub… I remember a cub, not all that long ago, actually."

And then he was gone, his gait as smooth as that of a Gryphon twelve summers his junior. And for the first time in a while, Arias felt like maybe he was in real danger. Not directly. Hengar hadn't seemed like he planned to hurt him. But something would happen. He didn't have time to dwell on the way he felt for too long, however. Brynne burst into the den with news.

***

"The Primals have totally cleared out of the area for some reason," Brynne said. She'd found her mother and they'd both returned to the den, sitting side by side across from Arias. "Not a single one has been seen for a couple of days now. Sheba is going to cut back on the patrols to let everyone focus on hunting more for the upcoming winter, and for Naugi's visit. We should be able to wander more of the territory without worrying so much about the Primals at least."

"I think we should still be careful if we go any further than we have been," Iba added warily. "Who knows what the Primals could be planning? At the same time, we definitely need more fairywort, and we'll probably find it if we travel a little further south than we normally do. What do you think, Arias?"

Arias clearly hadn't been paying attention. He nodded mutely, and both mother and daughter shared a look. He hadn't told either of them about Xio… and now he was hiding what had happened with Hengar.

"Is everything alright?" Brynne asked, to which he nodded mechanically.

"Sorry, just… relieved to hear good news, I guess. Hey, why don't we go look for that fairywort now? It's a nice clear day, we'll probably be able to spot it easier."

The females nodded in excited agreement, and they set off immediately for a new patch of Skyhaven territory.

***

Before getting too far into foraging, Brynne had the good fortune to spot a lone peryton buck off dozing alone in a clearing. Arias took his cue as she tilted her head toward it, and he dipped into a crouch, slipping past yellowed shrubbery to close the distance to it. Any time the peryton looked up, he froze, but the beast was jittery and took to the sky after only the second instance. It didn't matter. Iba followed it up on the wing, intercepting it from the right just as it rose above the tree line. She dispatched it expertly, and the trio all ate heartily, leaving nothing behind. They sprawled out to rest a bit before rising to continue their search for herbs. There wasn't much to be found, and after gorging on preymeat, heading back to the eyrie for an early rest sounded like a much more lucrative plan.

Arias hopped up onto Iba's back, and she staggered sideways before righting herself with a chuckle. "You're getting heavy," she mused, fussing with her wings to try to make sure he wasn't visible. He squished himself as flat as he could against her back, but as fate would have it, they had hardly passed into the heart of the eyrie when Arias heard a statement that made his blood freeze in his veins.

"I didn't think that gray or orange hens could grow white feathers, Iba."

Iba took a step back as whoever made the comment evidently moved toward her.

"Is it true, Iba?" another voice said accusingly, almost disgusted. "Have you truly sheltered a Spirit Walker among us?"

The padding of steps painted a picture of a group that was slowly gathering, their voices coming from curious, angry, or scared Gryphons. Amid the growing crowd, Iba broke and did what any other low-ranking Gryphon would've done. She instinctively opened her wings to flee skyward, and a collective gasp ran through the flock at the sight of the albino fledgling perched on her back. Iba came to her wits, realizing what she'd done, and tucked her tail to try to pacify the group. Brynne hid behind her mother's legs, frightful.

Iba's eyes searched the sea of Gryphons fanning out. They came to rest on Hengar, and he shied away from her gaze.

"It's better for everyone that this no longer be a secret," he mumbled so quietly that his voice was nearly unintelligible. "What you're doing with this Spirit Walker, regardless of whether it helps us or not… it's not natural."

"Listen to what you're saying!" a speckled hen flanked by a runt cub said. "If he is the one who truly cured my hatchling of his cough, then I won't see any harm come to him."

Her mate, a youthful keythong of the same color, nosed his way in next to her and added, "She's right. No one here was alive to see the story of Halada cursing a Spirit Walker. Let him stay among us until we have a reason to cast him out."

Heads bobbed in agreement. One by one, other Gryphons that had been aided by Arias's deeds stood to his defense. Arias poked his head up, emboldened by the unexpected turn of events. But then the elder hen who had been watching Iba for days stepped forward, and his hope withered away. She took a rasping breath, and the entire flock quieted as she prepared to speak. Her voice was dry and crisp, like fallen leaves crunching under paw.

"It is my job as an elder of this flock to uphold our traditions," she started. "Such a one as this cub is not to be tolerated by any who follow the teachings of Halada. We all know this. It's bad luck, and has been ever since the dawning of our species. By all means, he should've been killed the moment he hatched out from the egg looking like that. But obviously he wasn't. It would seem that my sister has some answering to do."

She inched forward until she was just feet away from Iba, her wings half-raised threateningly. Even with her sinuous, infirm-looking body, she dwarfed Brynne's mother in size. "Give him over to be dealt with, and I won't punish you for your misguided decisions, Iba. As a flock, we will pretend none of this ever happened. You needn't be chastised at length for a moment of stupidity; all lowborn are subject to it now and again, I think."

Iba cowed for a split murm, then stood her ground, sizing the elder up. She shook her head without meeting her gaze.

"No."

With a horrifying shriek, the elder rushed forward, and Arias lost his hold on Iba as she reared up to meet her. He and Brynne darted among the crowd to hide, but the flock was backing away and thinning out, some even taking flight to avoid the white-pelted stranger among them. Feathers flew into the air as Iba and the elder hen plucked and grappled with one another, dark blood beginning to stain their coats as they dug in with sharp beaks and talons. With a mighty blow, the old hen clouted Iba to the ground and locked her eyes on Arias. Her grayed appearance betrayed her speed as she set off after him like lightning.

Arias couldn't keep up with Brynne. The sun was still too bright, and the shafts of light pierced his eyes like dazzling starbursts, disorienting him. He bumped into someone and immediately darted away, avoiding talons that both grabbed for him and tried to knock him away. It was impossible to tell which of the Gryphons were trying to capture him, hurt him, or protect him, and so he escaped away from them completely when he saw an opening.

Arias ran past the dens and set himself to the task of scrambling over the lip of the caldera, but the old hen was already upon him. She leapt up and swiped sideways at him, knocking his feet out from under him. He struggled to regain himself, but an ethereal mixture of pain and panic rushed through him as she clamped her jaws shut around his neck. He couldn't scream, couldn't breathe. It felt like his eyes were threatening to evacuate from their sockets, his throat burning as he struggled against her. He truly was powerless, like a fawn wrestling against a fully grown hunter. He felt the world growing hazy, and then a sudden and deafening roar caused everyone to freeze. Arias's attacker promptly dropped him to the ground, and Sheba swooped down in a cloud of dust. There wasn't a single Gryphon who didn't turn their attention to her. Iba caught up with Brynne and stood over her protectively, looking ashamed.

"What is the meaning of all of this?" Sheba asked. "Kayane, speak."

The old hen immediately pointed a gnarled claw toward Iba and spat, "This lowborn fool was harboring a Spirit Walker! Who knows how long he's been among us? Perhaps this is the source of the bad luck, of the drought—"

"Have you thought to ask me about these suspicions before taking matters into your own talons, sister?" Sheba asked. Incredulousness seeped into Kayane's eyes at the words.

"You can't possibly mean to protect this creature! You can't say that you'd be willing to risk the safety of an entire flock to protect such a cursed being, a wretch that the great Mother herself cast away? Have you become simple?"

"Enough!" Sheba said, lashing her tail. "No harm will come to him while he is here. If the thought enters anyone's mind, the perpetrator will answer to me. Any with a problem with this can depart from this flock immediately. Or they can face me right now, and we can settle things by way of the Old Law, with our claws."

"You're suggesting suicide, Sheba, on all accounts. You were never cut out to be Matriarch." Kayane's eyes were deceitful. "You waited until I was old and infirm to oust me, all so you could play leader. Why can't you see reason, sister? He'll never be one of us, and you invite destruction into our lives by keeping him here!"

Sheba hissed and flattened her ears, unsheathing long claws. "Question me again, Kayane, and I'll help you to see reason."

Kayane didn't speak again. The flock shifted uncomfortably. Eyes cut and then flicked away as if they had personally been verbally reprimanded. The only sound was of Arias struggling to force the air back into his lungs.

"I trust we have an understanding," Sheba said quietly, growling. "We've bigger problems than fighting amongst ourselves… or engaging in acts of cub-killing. Dismissed, all of you. I'll hear no more of this. Least of all from you, Kayane."

Kayane didn't reply. She had her eyes fixed on Arias, and they smoldered with hatred. Arias could still feel them burning into him as Iba gathered Brynne and him and turned to go. Kayane's gaze sent an ill message. It was a flaming promise of ill-will.

***

Arias slept fitfully between Iba and Brynne, jumping awake at even the slightest sound from beyond the mouth of the den. There was activity

84

just past the safety of the small hovel where he was nestled, hushed whispers that carried into the night. Kayane had wasted no time in whipping her flock mates up into a frenzy regarding the fact that a Spirit Walker was among them, and she'd already convinced a good number of the flock that their current misfortune was because of him.

By morning the division in the flock was clear. When Arias accompanied Iba and Brynne to the meat cache, walking on his own four feet for the first time in the eyrie, they were greeted by the sight of nothing to eat. The hunters were so busy quarreling over who they agreed with that they hadn't flown out to hunt yet. Their pointed remarks about who they would and wouldn't work with escalated until many were shouting at one another.

"I'm not having any of my preymeat go into the stomach of that thing," one of the more experienced hunters belted out. She stamped a talon decidedly against the packed earth. "I won't have the cursed nature of that beast spreading to my mate and me. Either you side with Kayane— the side of reason—or I'll no longer share my kills with any of you!"

The other Gryphons she'd been addressing didn't argue, just regarded her with a flat look. None of the other hunters spoke. Eventually, they all either flew off to hunt or returned solemnly to their dens.

Most of the Gryphons helped by Arias's medicines weren't capable hunters; if they were, they wouldn't have needed the herbal remedies in the first place. It would be they who would be most hurt by the deepening division in the flock. It was true that both the very young and the very old were indebted to him, and they certainly backed him accordingly, but it was also a harsh truth that they weren't worth much in utility.

Of the shoddily organized hunting parties that eventually flew out, two small peryton carcasses were produced. Fighting broke out over them quickly, and they were won over and strictly guarded by those following Kayane's lead. The elder hen promptly began to decisively pick and choose who would eat from the kills, showing no mercy as the flock's youngest members watched longingly after the succulent flesh, their small bellies rumbling. Even some of the older Gryphons, well past their hunting years, stared a bit too long at the meat before turning away. Kayane eventually yelled, "All who agree to banishing the Spirit Walker may eat freely from the cache."

"That's not fair!" a mother cried out. "Not all of us are proven hunters, and some of us have little ones to look after. Sheba will not stand for this!"

Kayane crooned with false pity. "I'll not be made to feel sorry for refusing to feed that abomination, nor any who would stoop so low as to aid him. You fools are all asking for the wrath of Halada to fall upon you! It won't fall upon me, or any of those smart enough to follow the ways that have protected our kind since its very beginning! If you're so worried about you and your cub eating enough to survive the winter, you know what to do."

She turned crisply and strode past the female, and the mother cast a wilting glance at Arias before slinking away.

"Let us not forget that Naugi will be here any day, looking for his seasonal offering," a hunter that had sided with Kayane said. "I'd hate to be part of the group that arrives empty handed before an expectant Hydra."

The tension in the air was palpable as the group dispersed. Arias ran through a thousand scenarios in which he turned things around for himself, but it was hard to ignore that circumstances seemed to be getting worse by the murm. Brynne saw the look of consternation on his face and threw her wings open optimistically.

"We're already pretty good at finding food, Arias. We don't need them! We can start hunting right now to get our portion of the offering ready for Naugi. Imagine how much more prey we'll be able to find when we can fly! Plus, Mom says that snow is white, just like you are. You'll probably be amazing at hunting prey when it starts to fall."

Arias tried to share her high spirits, but he was too busy watching the worried movements of the others around him. Even those who had been helped by his medicine nervously moved away from him now, their expressions guilty. He was losing them. He'd only just gotten them, and now they were reacting exactly how the Alicorns said they would before he'd arrived. He sighed heavily, defeated. Things would only deteriorate the longer he was around. He didn't want to admit it. He could see Sheba now, watching her flock from the depths of her den, her tail slowly winding and unwinding in deep thought. She was leader and her word was absolute, but the flock itself was a fluid thing. It could change—even break apart— at the slightest prod.

Arias's eyes met Sheba's from across the distance, and she gave an almost imperceivable shake of her head. It confirmed what he already knew. He couldn't stay. Not at a time as crucial as this, with winter and a visiting Hydra upon them. He didn't want to be responsible for the flock's differences tearing it apart. It would only endanger Iba and Brynne. He'd already done enough damage in that regard.

And so, in the silence of the night, despite any fears of the things that could lurk in the dark, Arias picked carefully over Iba and Brynne's sleeping bodies and stole into the night. A few guards noted him leaving, their crests raised in alarm, but they didn't call out. They gave one another long glances, but in the end, no one tried to stop him.

CHAPTER SIX

Arias experienced the stretch of forest leading
to Glendale with the same apprehension he'd felt
when he'd originally left it to travel to Skyhaven.
He nearly jumped when he crossed ursos tracks,
noting that they weren't fresh… but they weren't
old, either. Smaller scavengers were tracking him
from a distance, their eyes flashing reflectively in
the dark. He'd caught sight of them a few times
now. Sleek, social creatures that communicated
with barks and howls, their tails wagging
uncertainly to one another. They had probably
been prompted by the drought into hunting
unusual prey, and he was sure that he fell into
that category. He made sure to keep a decent
amount of distance between him and them.

Each sound was amplified by Arias's anxiety,
but in the end it wasn't the scavengers, the
potential ursos that might be nearby, or the other
dozens of unidentifiable sounds that bothered
him the most. He felt that if he raised his ears any
higher to listen, they'd sail straight off his head.

He tried to distract himself from the thought that something was following him… something large and sinister.

Arias sped up his pace, head snapping around as he detected movement to his side. His heart froze in his throat as he focused on the foliage, yelping as something broke away from its cover. Expecting whatever had been killing the Primals, he instead watched two longear dart across the narrow trail. His adrenaline ebbed away, leaving him feeling silly. He actually chuckled a little bit as he started to walk again, putting his mind toward what his reunion with the Alicorns would be like. Thinking of how overjoyed Hlaena would be to see him helped to set his mind at ease. He'd have to apologize to Xio and tell him the truth about his experience at Skyhaven flock. He didn't think he'd get into any real trouble. Somehow, his relationship with the stallion had shifted. He'd felt it. He was allowed to make his own decisions now.

Arias was so lost in thought that his ears didn't pick up anything amiss until he walked headfirst into something soft. Hissing with surprise, he tried to make sense of the strange face he found himself staring into. It was clearly that of a Gryph hen, but it was… wrong. Arias's eyes were immediately drawn to her eyes, eyes that were pure black, with no color to them. It was as if they were simply two huge pupils in her sockets. She had a flat, moon-like face, and her feathers were a stark white that contrasted against the rest of her body, which was mottled brown. Her bill was tiny and downward facing, mostly hidden by the feathers of her face.

Arias stared at her so long as to be rude, and she held his gaze without flinching. He backed away uncertainly, nearly jumping in his skin as an unearthly hooting sound rose behind him. It was two more of the weird Gryphs, these being two large keythongs with long ear tufts and amber eyes. They turned their heads sideways as they regarded him, plush tails swishing. The Alicorns had told Arias that there were other Gryphs in the world, but he didn't think he'd ever see them.

All the stories of Primals coming up missing and dead rushed back to Arias in a terrifying instant, and he shrank to the ground in fear. He probably would've been mystified by the strangers' appearances had he not been so afraid. But nearly as quickly as he'd crouched, the hen and the two keythongs bowed to him, their wings extended respectfully.

"Great Tsarine!" the hen exclaimed, "Forgive me for ever doubting you, Great One."

"And we, as well," the two keythongs echoed.

Arias paused, uncertainty clouding his senses. Were these strange Gryphs dangerous? He'd expected his innards to be strewn across the forest by now. And were they even Gryphs at all? They spoke the common tongue—maybe with a slight, clipped accent, but still the common tongue—so they must be.

"You know me?" he asked hesitantly, not sure

what else to say.

"Why, of course," the hen said, her voice jubilant. "But I suppose I can understand if you don't remember us. I wasn't sure how you'd come back to us… reincarnation is a thing that I have yet to fully grasp. You must not recall then that my name is Plithi?"

The other two keythongs didn't move to introduce themselves.

Arias blinked.

Nothing about these strangers seemed to hint at an imminent threat, although they were suspiciously overzealous. They all looked at him as if they were expecting him to say something, so he did.

"Well, uhh, it's good to be back? Now, if you don't mind…" he dodged behind the hen, the fur along his spine tingling as her huge eyes followed him.

"Your journey ends with finding us, Quarnar," the hen said with a laugh. "It's okay though, I'm sure Shadowbane can explain whatever confusion you may be experiencing. Come on! Off we go!" She moved so that she was beside Arias, and nodded toward the south. When she sensed Arias's hesitation, she frowned.

"Your home is with us, Quarnar, in Arborochre. I know you may not feel that way right now, but you will with time. Now, let's go."

The firmer inflection in her voice told Arias that resisting wouldn't lead to anything good. So he did the only thing he could think to.

"Okay," he said.

***

The processional of strange Gryphs began to make their way through the forest, with Arias being joggled into position between the three others until he was behind one of the keythongs, with the other and Plithi trailing him. Neither spoke, but each took turns staring reverently at him. The further he went off course on the unfamiliar path, the more uneasy he became. What were they going to do with him?

After a few murms of walking, the leading keythong stopped.

"The path grows narrow and tangled. Shall we fly the rest of the way, Plithi?" he asked.

Plithi nodded at the assessment and spread her wings. "Old enough to fly, Quarnar?" She asked hopefully, but Arias shook his head, as much in answer to her question as to the name she insisted on calling him.

"That's fine," she replied. "Let us continue the journey on claw."

Arias studied the brambles and thorns crowding the path up ahead and an idea sprouted into his mind. He gathered his courage for a flicker of a murm, took a deep breath, and darted under a mass of thorny creeper vines. He tucked his wings in close as he could, but even with his smaller size, the sharp thistles still scraped skin. He hardly felt the sting as he shot through the woods like a streaming comet, intent to escape. He had broken away in such a flash that he seemed to have confused his party, and it took a bit before he heard the cacophony of startled yells and rustling as they realized what he'd done.

Victory rose in Arias's soul as he found himself navigating the dark forest alone. All he had to do now was find a small, dark hiding place like he and Brynne had done when the Primals had hunted them down. The first potential spot he saw came in the form of a deep crevice between two trees, and he wedged his body into it immediately. Then he waited, swiveling his ears to see if the sounds of night would reveal his pursuers. When the insects resumed their droning hum, he dared to let himself feel a small measure of comfort. He'd lost them. He let a good quarter more of the night pass by just to be safe, then resigned himself to setting out again. The sooner he could put distance between himself and those disturbing Gryphs, the better.

Arias stuck his head out of the crevice he was hiding in and made his way out into the waning darkness. He picked his way gingerly through crowded plants, taking care not to so much as rustle a leaf. A different type of dread started to overtake him. He realized he had no idea where he was.

Could he backtrack? He had to do something. He couldn't risk travelling in the wrong direction for too long. Then he remembered the map left for all creatures intelligent enough to read it. Selecting a tree with lots of limbs, he scaled up and poked his head above the treetops, revealing the stars above. He hastily charted his course, suddenly grateful to Hlaena for forcing him to learn to navigate using the celestial bodies.

Climbing back down to the ground, Arias took care not to stray from the mental chart he'd created. It wasn't long before he started to recognize the more familiar flora that surrounded the woods he'd grown up in. Heart beating with anticipation, he increased his pace until he was outright sprinting, eager to enter the safety of Glendale. He promised himself that when he made it to that sacred territory, he'd abide by every Alicorn rule for the rest of his life.

The outer reaches of Glendale's calming magick washed over Arias like a welcome rain. Tongue lolling with exertion, he lowered his head and pushed into his stride, his breath catching in his throat. And then something heavy dropped on top of him, as solid as a fallen log. He'd barely seen the shadow when it fell, and then there was darkness. His mind didn't catch up to the situation until he heard an unhappy warble, and felt claws against his flesh. Plithi was pinning him down.

The strange hen wrested him onto his back despite him fighting with every fiber of his existence, and held him still while one of the keythongs carefully wound a length of something sinewy around his legs, crossing and knotting the material until he couldn't move. In a last-ditch effort, he screamed as loud as he could for Xio, but it was too little too late. His captors both stood back as the larger of the two keythongs swooped down on silent wings, and he was carried off into the milky dawn.

***

Arias had never known there were Gryphs who could fly silently before. It explained how he'd been tracked and caught so soundly. How long had they followed him before deciding to approach him? He made another attempt at convincing his captor to at least carry him right side up, but the long-eared keythong may as well have been carrying a chunk of preymeat. He ignored every plea and comment, but occasionally he looked down with what, confusingly enough, appeared to be genuine pity.

The world was dizzying to look at from the awkward angle Arias was stuck in, and so he eventually settled for closing his eyes and wishing fervently that this nightmare would end. He had been so close to Glendale… he couldn't believe it. Maybe he really was cursed.

The keythong carrying Arias started a long descent just as the sun was rising, and Arias opened his eyes to see a forest of humongous proportions. The trees were so large and moss encrusted, they easily rivaled the old growth giants in Glendale. He felt a jab of anxiety when he saw that they were landing nearby a small opening in the earth that angled down into pure darkness. Milling about on the ground were more cubs than he'd ever seen in one place before.

Most were dejected and whimpering.

The long-eared keythong placed Arias gently on the ground and flew off, to be swiftly replaced by another young Gryph. This male had no ear tufts and no crest, but his bright yellow eyes gleamed with excitement. He greeted him enthusiastically before beginning to untie him. After freeing his paws, he paused and looked uncertain.

"Please don't run off, Great One," he said. "I know you don't remember this place, but it really is quite alright."

Arias slanted his eyes. "There's nowhere I can run to," he said.

The moment the knot binding his talons was undone, he was ushered toward the hole in the ground. A dank air rose from the opening, stale and chilly, like the last breaths of a dying creature. Arias balked, then paused and watched as the cubs were directed forward into the same opening by a long-necked female. He hardly had a chance to gawk at her interesting appearance before she vanished into darkness. When the group disappeared and no horrific screams were heard after their passing, he gave a small sigh.

"It's really quite safe, I assure you!" the keythong offered. "Just stay close and you'll be fine!"

Arias watched as he dropped to his quarters and shimmied into the blackness, and he prepared to do the same with an anxious gulp. Before doing so, however, he craned his neck to scan the treetops. Sentries dotted every massive tree. It solidified his earlier statement that there was truly nowhere to go. He couldn't escape, but at least he wasn't in any immediate danger. He dropped to his forelegs and crept in after his exuberant guide.

***

"What's your name?" Arias asked the keythong leading him through the underground tunnel, more to stave off the nerve-wracking claustrophobia he was experiencing than out of interest. His voice shook, and he couldn't control it.

"I don't have a name," the keythong replied simply, as though that answered the question satisfactorily.

"Everyone has a name," Arias said, confused.

"No, not a True Name," the keythong said. "When I prove myself loyal and useful to the flock, I'll gain one. Plithi says I'm really close! You're lucky you already have yours. You've just forgotten it! Which is understandable, considering..." The lack of shuffling indicated that the keythong had stopped moving, and Arias nearly bumped into him in the dark.

"Shadowbane will explain everything to you, I'm sure. I-I don't think I'm allowed to talk about these things. We really shouldn't be talking like this, you and me. I'm sorry, Great One. Please, only consult me if you have a need for something

98

more immediate. One of my rank shouldn't converse so casually with you."

Arias tilted his head at the note of hysteria that had entered his voice. "What do you mean, your 'rank'? I must be younger than you, your rank should be much higher than mine."

"I'm sure that Shadowbane can answer all of your questions, Great One," the keythong replied.

"Who's this 'Shadowbane'?"

"Our flock Sire."

The lengthy silence that followed was all Arias was offered afterward. At certain points, the tunnel dipped down starkly, and Arias slid and struggled to keep his footing. He realized he'd been straining his eyes to see in the absolute blackness, and he finally closed them and focused on the sound of his guide clipping along up ahead. The tunnel opened up a bit after a few murms, and his guide began to take turns he'd no doubt memorized. At one point, brilliant shafts of light eked up through a jagged hole in the floor, and the keythong stopped before carefully stepping over the hole and turning around with difficulty.

"Here we are. We have to jump down," he said.

Arias peered down through the hole, trying to make sense of what he was seeing.

A cave floor with thousands of tiny stalagmites revealed itself below, and he squinted as he imagined free falling to land on all the sharp points.

"Oh!" the keythong said, reading his expression. "It's really very safe. I suppose you haven't fledged yet, but—well here, it'll be easier to show you." He looked up cheerily. "Ready?"

Arias nodded slowly, and watched closely as the keythong dropped through the hole, opened his wings to glide, and circled back into view. He dipped down low and reached a claw down, and the stalagmites rippled and broke apart at his touch.

Water.

It was simply a reflection that Arias was looking at! The knowledge was comforting next to the horrifying possibility of being sacrificed on points. That, and there was no way that he could back his way out of these tunnels. Even if he did, the guards outside in the forest would surely be waiting. The idea of trying to navigate backwards through the tunnel network bothered him a lot more than the thought of dropping into the water. At a reassuring call from his guide, he took a deep breath and convinced his legs to allow him to drop through the opening.

Remembering his training during branching, Arias spread his wings to slow his descent, cutting into the water with a chilly splash. The pool was a lot deeper than he thought, and the depths were a dark abyss. He paddled to the surface with haste, and heard awed gasps the moment he did. When he reached the shore, the eyes of a crowd of Gryphs followed him. He'd lost sight of the keythong he'd followed in the sea of new faces, but it didn't seem to matter. The moment he set claw on land, everyone fell into a hushed silence, and they all turned their heads toward a new source of interest.

The slow, tap-tapping of an approaching figure filled the cavern, and Arias couldn't tear his eyes away from the creature that separated from the crowd to stand next to Plithi. He, too, had a strange white, moon-like face, and eyes as dark as a peryton doe's. He was neither bigger nor smaller than any other average keythong, and yet everything about him screamed of regality. His pelt was crisscrossed with the scars of unseen battles, including a large, bare patch across one shoulder. His eyes narrowed with familiarity when he saw Arias, but when he boomed his welcome, it was in address to everyone.

"Greetings, my offspring," he said merrily, extending his wings. "The night has been wonderfully long, and you've all done well. May Tsarine bless all of us in our diligent efforts to bring her glory!"

"Tsarine bless us," Plithi and the others echoed in unison.

"Newcomers, my name is Shadowbane. I am the Sire of this flock, and I welcome you as my own. From this moment on, your lives will be very different from the ones you've led thus far. Always remember that you would not be here if fate did not allow for it."

Arias watched in awe. Even the keythong's voice was stately.

"If you show special promise at the tasks you're set to, you may even achieve an honorary position in this flock as a leader. In Tsarine's kingdom, ability is recognized even if you do not share the same blood as we, her preferred species, the Strigigryph. Consider, for example, this young Ardeigryph who has joined our ranks, and earned my respect as a fierce and loyal follower."

As if on cue, a stunning blue hen stepped up from the crowd to stand next to the Sire. Arias found himself staring again, just as he had been when he'd first seen Plithi. It was the same Gryph that had led the cubs through the tunnels here, the one with the longest neck of any creature he'd ever seen. Her beak nearly matched it in length.

She looked expectantly at Shadowbane, and he said, "Tell our new members where you hail from, and what you have done."

"I'm from Oceanside flock," she proclaimed. "I killed two of Shadowbane's best warriors when I was barely a yearling."

Sounds of shock ran through the flock. Even Arias couldn't suppress a gasp of surprise. Why would a Sire keep a killer of his own flock mates alive? And more so, how could such a creature be capable of slaughtering anything? Her neck was twig-thin. Arias felt like even he could even take her, and he'd done no more than play fight with Brynne.

"You may all be wondering why I'd keep such a Gryph alive," Shadowbane said as if reading minds. He turned his dark gaze back to the female. "Tell them."

"I had a vision from Tsarine herself," she said whimsically. "She instructed me to cease resisting Shadowbane's flock, and to carry out her glorious plan by aiding them instead of fighting against them. I threw myself at the mercy of his guards the very next night, pleading that they accept me despite my twisted Ardeigryph form. His suspicion was warranted, but I promised to do whatever I needed to be accepted, up to killing my own Sire. With his help, I did just that. His trust in me will never be in vain."

Shadowbane crooned appreciatively at her testimony. "I'm so pleased that such talent has been able to be utilized by Tsarine for good. It isn't often to see such a gifted hen at such a tender age. No less loyalty do I expect from each and every single one of you." His eyes shifted back to Arias, and he gestured with a wing tip for him to come closer. Arias sidled forward, aware that the attention of the crowd were on him again. When he got close enough to the Sire, he realized that the only thing he could see reflected in the blackness of his eyes was himself.

"And you. I've long awaited your return,

Quarnar. I thank Tsarine for your safe travel through the spirit world. We never once doubted that you'd find your way to us once again!"

Arias blinked. The keythong's brilliant jubilation seemed to falter as he waited, and Plithi hurriedly stepped forward to whisper something so quietly that Arias couldn't decipher the words even though he was mere feet away.

"Ah! My trusted children, leave us, please. Make sure that our newcomers feel welcome beneath Tsarine's loving moon."

The Gryphs dissipated almost as quickly as they'd come, many tripping over themselves in their haste to depart the cavern. The cubs were whisked away with them, leaving Arias alone with the keythong, his eyes gleaming in the dim light of the cavern.

"It seems I've some explaining to do," he said calmly. "You don't remember anything of your life here, do you?"

Arias hesitated, but the Sire lay down, twitching his tail as he crossed his forelegs.

"You need not fear me, friend! Speak freely. I won't hold you at fault."

Not like there was really a choice.

"I have no idea who you are or where we are," Arias said slowly. "I'm not Quarnar, you must have me mistaken for someone else. I'm Arias.

I'm from Glendale… and I really want to go home."

The keythong chuckled. Arias couldn't tell if it was a good or bad reaction.

"Well, Arias. My name is Shadowbane, and I rule this roost. In your past life, you were a great friend of mine. It was under your advisement that we travelled to this new land. I know the concept of not being a Strigigryph must seem strange to you… you're a Daywalker in your current form. I'm not sure why. If you'll permit it, I'd like to show you what your past life was like. Maybe it'll help your memory, and I can answer any questions you may have. Obviously you had a life before you were brought here to Arborochre. If you'd like to return to it, you certainly may. But please, first allow me to show you the life you used to lead here alongside me."

Arias hadn't expected to have the option of leaving presented to him so freely. He could leave in this instant, and probably should. This was a strange flock; he didn't belong here. But what was so great about this place that a Gryph—an Ardeigryph, she'd been called—had been willing to kill her own Sire to join it?

There was a slow pricking beginning at the back of Arias's mind. Curiosity. These Gryphs didn't hate him for his color, they actually seemed to celebrate him for it. The feeling was a welcome one after what had happened in Skyhaven. His interest overwhelmed him. Shadowbane himself, the flock's apparent leader, had told him he could leave if he wanted to. He didn't sense any danger from him. Even now, the Sire seemed to hold a bated excitement for his answer as he regarded him. Arias finally relented.

"Okay," he said. "I'll hear whatever you have to say."

***

The beauty of Arborochre eyrie washed over Arias like a wave. Just outside of the cave system was a forest of gargantuan trees that crowded around the eyrie like massive sentries, the trunks of the mighty plants thicker around their base than two Gryphons standing tail-to-tail. Gryphs of all ages were performing all manner of strange acts that Arias had never seen before. A trio of hens worked busily at a pile of preymeat, but instead of simply eating it, they meticulously pulled the hide free from the carcasses and organized the meat. A group of yearlings worked alongside them, dragging the hides over to a shallow sand pit, where they scraped every bit of fat off the hides with their beaks. Arias stopped to watch the strange act, and Shadowbane followed his gaze.

"You'll see the use of that when you bed down for the morning," he said.

Arias's ears pricked up. "Bed down for the… morning?"

Shadowbane nodded. "Why, of course! You'll be back to your old self in no time. You're clearly still Quarnar somewhere in there, you're just confused because you've returned to us in the

106

form of a Daywalker. We are creatures of the night, friend! The day is for lesser creatures."

Arias had to hurry to match his pace to Shadowbane's sweeping stride. Together, they passed along hordes of Gryphs carrying bundles of bedding or preymeat, and scores more heading in and out to sentry duty. They walked down a grassy hill where yearlings were clumsily learning the skills they'd need to fly, running up the slope and then gliding back down on untrained wings. An older keythong watched closely, instructing them on proper technique. It made Arias think of Iba and Brynne, and he frowned. Would Brynne go back to learning how to fly before winter set in?

Shadowbane leapt halfway across a small stream where several members were drinking and bathing, dipping his head down to take a sip before crossing over on his considerably longer legs. Arias sighed when he realized he'd have to get his feathers wet. He'd nearly dried after his dip in the cave pool, but the water was refreshing and tasted quite delicious. The Gryphs around him glanced up and bowed their heads respectfully as he and Shadowbane passed.

Shadowbane and Arias finally arrived at a jagged clay precipice. It seemed to be quite a long way to the top to Arias, but Shadowbane was able to scale it in three great leaps with the help of his wings. He waited for Arias to pick his way up, tail waving patiently. Arias tried to hurry so as not to look weak, and was rewarded when he came to the lavish den dug directly into the earth at its peak.

Inside, designs had been smeared on the walls in a smoky black substance. The space itself was cluttered with bones the likes of which Arias had never seen before. Beasts with huge, sweeping horns lay in skeletal form against the walls, interrupted by various severed claws, teeth, and skulls. Arias wondered if Strigigryph were collectors of some sort.

Shadowbane sat on a dried peryton hide, and gestured for Arias to sit on the other pile of hides opposite from him. When he did so, he found that the fur was surprisingly soft and lavish against his body. It was much better than the bits of moss and grass he was used to bedding down on.

Who knew that hides could be preserved and make good bedding? Arias thought. *Interesting.*

Shadowbane tapped a claw against the ruddy wall nearest to him, and Arias pricked his ears as he realized the markings there formed into intricate designs that had been painstakingly crafted, not just meaninglessly scrawled. His eyes went over the shapes until he realized that they looked akin to Gryphs. He gasped in surprise.

"We Strigigryph carry many traditions that are long lost to our sun-bathed brethren," Shadowbane said. "This is one of them… the ability to tell tales with more than just our voices." He extended a wing to point even further, to a figure that had been colored in with white clay. It was larger than the rest, its eyes marked with brilliant flashes of red.

"That's you," Shadowbane said.

Arias cocked his head sideways as he noted that the other Gryphs were depicted much smaller and more crudely than Quarnar was, and he wondered whether he actually had been that much bigger than everyone else, or if that was simply how everyone else saw him.

"Tsarine gifted her creatures with abilities that Daywalkers don't, and never will, possess. We can see well in the dark, our hearing is superb, and our flight is as silent as snowfall. But Tsarine gave you two amazing abilities in particular; the ability to communicate with her directly through your dreams, and the gift of immortality. She is so fond of you that she marked you by making you the same color as her grandest creation, the moon itself."

Arias nibbled a feather thoughtfully. "Immortality?" he said, half to himself. The story he'd just been told sounded like a strange version of the one Iba had told him about Halada and Spirit Walkers.

"The ability to rise and fall, and rise again," Shadowbane went on. "You've lived among us before, and you promised us that you would return to us again following your death. And here you are!"

Arias thought back to Plithi's comment about

his journey ending with finding them when he'd first encountered Plithi and the two other Strigigryph in the forest. He slowly connected the dots. These Gryphs believed he was one of them, and had returned to them following his death. Not even the Alicorns had ever mentioned anything as strange as this! "Who exactly was Tsarine?" he asked.

Shadowbane reeled back as though he'd been physically struck by the question. "What kind of uncivilized flock did you rebirth through? Tsarine is the rightful ruler of this world. She co-created it alongside Halada, but it wasn't long before the latter grew jealous of her work. Tsarine's beautiful creations of the night were infinitely superior to Halada's day-loving mongrels, and thus, driven by jealousy, Halada attempted to kill her. But Tsarine was wise. When Halada attacked, Tsarine scattered her body to the four winds, where they were eventually carried up to become the stars that dot the night sky. Halada couldn't gather all the pieces together to finish her off, and so she lives on… fragmented, but alive." Shadowbane shook his head. "In her broken form, Tsarine knew she wouldn't be able to look after her creations the way she needed to, so she made envoys like you in every race of creature. Only you can guide us to her amazing wisdom. Each time you die, you rise again, sometimes immediately, sometimes after the passing of many seasons. Regardless, you always come back."

Shadowbane paused to study Arias, seeming a trifle perplexed. "I just can't figure out why you've been rebirthed in the form of a Gryphon.

But Tsarine must have a plan for this. She always does."

Arias stared at the crude depictions on the wall. He'd never stopped to wonder what happened at night, when he and the rest of the Gryphons slept. And these Strigigryph… he'd never seen them before. But maybe, even if it was a small chance, Shadowbane was right. What if he and his flock carried the knowledge he'd been lacking about himself? What if this was the reason he never seemed to fit in anywhere else?

"I've always felt that something was wrong about my life," Arias said slowly. "The sunlight hurts my eyes, and prey sees me wherever I go. The other Gryphons shun me. They call me Spirit Walker, and say I am bad luck."

"There are many names for what you are," Shadowbane cut in quickly. "But unlucky is far from true."

Arias ruffled his feathers, wrestling with what to make of the things Shadowbane had said. The few items the Sire had shared with him were much more interesting than he'd anticipated, although the story itself had seemed a little outlandish. But the Alicorns had instilled him with a hunger for knowledge. He had to admit that the small amount he'd heard about Halada from Iba and Brynne had seemed equally as strange as what he'd just been told. He wanted to hear more.

"I can understand if you need some time to

take in what you've learned," Shadowbane said. "It must be a lot to take in for you."

"No… I'm glad I've found you. It may take me a while to… understand my role here, but I'm excited to learn about the life I used to have here. Or rather, the life I should have here, now." *Afterall,* Arias thought, *I can always leave later.*

Shadowbane's dark eyes lit up. "We're glad to have you back, Arias."

"Please…" Arias started slowly, looking up at the Sire. "Call me Quarnar."

CHAPTER SEVEN

Quarnar could scarcely sleep in his
anticipation for learning more about Arborochre
and the Gryphs that inhabited it, but despite his
eagerness, he was still unprepared to be nudged
awake at the first touch of twilight. Shadowbane
gave him a final poke to be sure he was actually
awake, then turned and nodded toward the
mouth of the den. Quarnar stirred to his feet and
shook his grogginess away, following with his
eyes to whatever it was Shadowbane had
motioned to.

"Look at them all," Shadowbane said,
encompassing the Gryphs working below the cliff
with a flourish of his wings. "All devout followers
of Tsarine, working tirelessly to carry out her
divine will. And they look to us for guidance! We
truly are blessed, aren't we, friend?"

Quarnar stretched and yawned before joining
Shadowbane at the entrance, nibbling a few
feathers into place before peering down to the

bustling eyrie below. The gentle light of the setting sun didn't dazzle his eyes like it did during the day. He was mesmerized by the moving tangle of Strigigryph, and was surprised when one of them met his eye, pointed, and called out to the others. Upon seeing him, a small cheer rose up from the flock. He shyly trilled a hello back down to them. Shadowbane didn't hide how pleased he was.

"You were mumbling in your sleep," Shadowbane said. "No doubt engaged in *fuhkrata* with Tsarine?"

Quarnar frowned. "Engaged in what? You mean dreaming?"

"Dreaming?" Shadowbane said, tilting his head. "I've no idea what that word means. *Fuhkrata* is when we see the things that Tsarine wishes for us to see in our sleep. It's a sacred way we can transcend ourselves and touch Tsarine's world. But only you, and those like you, can speak to Tsarine herself. Did she say anything to you?"

"No." Quarnar decided not to correct him regarding what dreaming was. Obviously, it meant much more to him and his flock than it did to the Alicorns or the other Gryphons he'd met.

Shadowbane was silent for a murm, and then said, "Tsarine doesn't always use a language we can understand. Sometimes, she shows us things."

"I drea—I mean, I thought of peryton when I slept," Quarnar said, retrieving the already-fading memory of his dream. "There were peryton everywhere, it was quite delightful. Especially after the drought and the early cold we've had."

Shadowbane breathed in sharply and closed his eyes. "What a beautifully clear sign. Fantastic. Why don't you go and mingle with your flock, Quarnar? They're eager to catch up with you."

Quarnar tilted his head. "What do you mean, 'clear sign'? Clear sign of what? And you want me to head out alone? You're not coming with me?"

"No," Shadowbane answered. "If your dream is any proper indication, there is work to be done. My duties will take me far beyond our territory tonight."

Quarnar threw him a wayward glance, but Shadowbane was no longer paying attention.

"A guide can be arranged for you, if you'd like," he said, sensing his hesitation. "You won't have any trouble, but I'm sure one of my flock would be happy to show you around."

Quarnar was grateful for the offer. He'd only barely learned how to behave as anything other than an Alicorn, and now he was expected to meet an entire flock… a flock with expectations of him.

"Sorry, it's just a lot to try to get used to all at once," he said.

Shadowbane waved a wing dismissively. "No need to apologize. Now, let's see…" After a brief murm, he took a deep breath and shrieked, and Quarnar's ears pricked up as the sound reverberated down the cliff and out over the eyrie, repeated over and over by the Gryphs who heard it and passed it along. It was an interesting method of communication.

It wasn't long before a blue streak appeared on the horizon, and the lithe hen with the long neck that Quarnar had seen earlier in the cavern landed just outside the entrance of Shadowbane's den.

"Your orders, Sire?" she asked formally, and Shadowbane pointed his tail toward Quarnar.

"Show him the territory, and allow him to bless those who've just returned from battle. See that no harm comes to him."

The hen gave a curt nod, turned, and immediately arched into a low bow. "Ratina, at your service. I will accompany you on your travels today. Are you ready?"

Quarnar had never heard a Gryphon with such a strange accent. Every word she said seemed to run into the other one, lazily, although nothing about her demeanor indicated such a disposition.

"Where are you from?" he asked her curiously.

She answered immediately. "I'm an Ardeigryph. I hail from the coast east of here. We are creatures of both the morning and the night. When I crossed paths with Shadowbane, I admired him, and it wasn't long after he visited the flock that Tsarine initiated me in a *fuhkrata* to join his flock. Shadowbane's first visit to a new flock is always peaceful. His second isn't so mundane. I'm truly lucky to have joined the most powerful leaders I've ever seen."

Ratina started down the cliff side, looking behind to make sure Quarnar was following. He eased forward, still a little put off by the steep grade of the cliff. Thankfully, his time adventuring in the forest alongside Iba and her daughter had bolstered his confidence in navigating questionable terrain.

"Want me to find an easier way down?" Ratina called up. "I wasn't aware that you hadn't fledged yet." The last part of her statement flustered Quarnar, and he shook his head.

"No, it's okay, I've got it."

Quarnar extended his claws and focused on a single point partway down the cliff, locking his eyes on a spot before he went for it. He knew that once he started his descent, gravity wouldn't allow him to stop, and so he scanned each section of the cliff for feasible landing areas as swiftly as he could, running down with quicker and quicker steps. The impact of each landing jarred his shoulders, and he flapped his wings frantically to create a bit of lift before he cast off again, bracing as he began to slide a bit. A few of the sharper stones cut into his paws, but he was too busy trying to keep his balance to focus on the pin pricks of pain.

When he finally stumbled next to Ratina amid a cloud of dust, he noticed he had a rapt audience consisting of the rest of the flock. The fact that he hadn't fledged yet was evidently adorable to a few, as he heard a number of coos rise up, and he composed himself as rapidly as he could.

"Well done," Ratina said. "I trust that you are not hurt?"

Quarnar shook his head, trying his best not to appear winded. "Oh no, not at all. So where should we go first?"

Ratina turned toward the heart of the eyrie, and Quarnar was surprised to see quite a few Gryphons like himself working closely and quietly alongside their Strigigryph counterparts. He didn't remember seeing any Gryphons when he'd first arrived, except for the cubs. He turned his head to eye one of them as he and Ratina strolled past her, but the hen took painstaking care not to meet his gaze. He flicked his stub of a tail and cleared his throat.

"I don't remember seeing any Gryphons the other day. Have they been here, and I just didn't notice?" he asked.

"They were not," Ratina said. "These Gryphons are ones who weren't injured in our most recent battle. Shadowbane will fill you in on the details of the skirmishes we've been involved in when he returns, I'm sure. Your first stop this morning will be to bless the recovery of those who are worthy of surviving their injuries."

Just as nearly as she'd said it, she and Quarnar crested a small, tree-lined ridge that dipped down into a shallow rocky area on the other side. Quarnar could see impressions in the cool, arid soil, and figured that it must have been dug out recently. It was lined with an assortment of leaves and moss; nothing as fancy as down or hide, but soft and warm enough to keep the ground habitable for the four Gryphons that were huddled there.

A single Strigigryph guard languished nearby the Gryphons, all of whom lay sullenly, their eyes closed. Even from the distance, Quarnar could see that they were in a bad way. Bite and claw marks crisscrossed their bodies at jagged, ugly intervals, exposing the red flesh beneath. At Quarnar and Ratina's approaching footfalls, the Gryphons straightened up as best they could.

"Here is where you must do your blessing, Glorious One," Ratina said. The expression on her face was always somehow remarkably the same, no matter what came out of her mouth. Without further explanation, she turned and closed her eyes. Quarnar panicked, eventually jabbing her in the side with a claw.

"Hey!" he hissed. "What do you mean, 'do my blessing'? What am I supposed to do? I'm new to all of this!"

What must have passed as surprise on the hen's face was quickly passing. "My apologies. I don't know how much you do and don't remember from your past life."

"None of it," he whispered, hoping only she could hear.

Ratina was quiet for a few fleeting murms, and then she mused, "Well, we won't watch or judge you. It isn't our place. Just tell Tsarine what you'd like from her regarding the fate of these souls. It's said that she listens more closely to her select chosen than the rest of us." And, as if that was satisfactory, she stopped speaking.

Even the most battle-worn Gryphons struggled to their feet out of respect as Quarnar prepared his blessing. He twitched his stub of tail, trying to hide his discomfort, and announced, "Okay. I… ah, I'm going to pray now…" Everyone around him immediately closed their eyes, which was a small relief. At least they wouldn't be watching. He wasn't sure whether he was supposed to say anything out loud or not, and in the end he felt that would be too awkward anyways, so he decided to say a few silent words in his mind.

"Okay," he said after a few murms, glad that he didn't receive any looks of suspicion. The Gryphons, exhausted, simply sank back into resting, and the guard resumed his vigil over them. Ratina rejoined him.

"Well done," she said, nodding. "Tsarine will

show us which are worthy to survive in the coming days."

Quarnar's eyes lingered over the sullen figures. "We don't have to leave it up to fate, though... I know how to save them. Am I allowed to go into the forest surrounding the eyrie?"

Ratina's eyes darted doubtfully. "I don't believe tradition allows for—"

"I'll be quick. And no one has to know. Just me and you."

Ratina struggled to retort, and then sighed. "My duty is to serve, Glorious One. Our surrounding forests are protected for miles. Let us go."

***

Quarnar loped between the immense trees that made up the forest surrounding Arborochre, eyes scanning expertly for herbs he could use to help the Gryphons he'd blessed. Ratina wasn't too far behind, though her reluctance was evident in her steps. She watched him pluck leaves from yellowing bushes and dig around rotted logs in silence. It was a long time before she finally asked, "Excuse me, Glorious One, but how is collecting bedding supposed to save the Converts?"

Quarnar carefully sat his cache down on the ground and eyed a tiny cluster of mushrooms, concentrating to try to remember with certainty whether the colors on their caps meant that they were the poisonous variety or not. "It's not bedding," he mumbled, distracted.

"Are you almost done, then?"

"Not yet," he replied. "Why do you call them Converts? They're just regular Gryphons, aren't they?"

"They are Gryphons who have accepted Tsarine's teachings as a way of life, just as I did. That's why we call them Converts. I technically am one as well. It's a shame that the rest of my flock was too foolish to see things similarly."

"You don't seem to hold your flock in very high regard," Quarnar said, though he balked a little at how sharply she returned his gaze. He hurried to add, "I'm sorry. I don't mean anything bad by it."

"It's fine," she said. "They wouldn't be the first ones not to see the sense in joining a worthy leader. But only the strong survive in this world. Anyone who criticizes an action done in the name of survival is a fool."

Ratina said the words with enough fire behind them that Quarnar didn't ask her any further questions. He couldn't imagine believing in power so much that he'd betray his own friends and family, but he didn't know her life, either. He turned his mind back to finding the rest of the ingredients he needed, but all he ended up finding that was truly helpful were tons of blackroot. They'd have to do.

"Can you help me carry them?" he asked. Having obviously become bored with watching him poke around for plants, she was quick to grab a few bundles and wait for him to pick his up.

With blackroot in beak, the two loped back to the eyrie together in silence.

***

The moment Quarnar and Ratina set foot back on the eyrie, a young Strigigryph hen cut across their path. She bowed to Quarnar, and hastily said, "I apologize for intruding, Glorious One, but Shadowbane requests Ratina's presence at once."

Ratina froze, but her voice remained calm as she said, "May I have permission to leave, Glorious One?"

Quarnar balanced his blackroot on a claw so he could open his mouth. "Of course. That sounds important. I hope everything is okay."

Ratina didn't reply, just assigned the young hen as his new guard, pushed the bundle of blackroot toward her, and launched into the sky in a flurry of feathers. Quarnar gave the new hen a quizzical expression, hoping for some information on this turn of events, but she gave him a puzzled look back in response.

"I'm sorry, I was just asked to deliver the message."

Quarnar nodded and took his bundle of herbs

back in his beak, motioning for her to follow as he headed back to where the Converts had been. He didn't bother asking for her name, somehow sure that she would reply similarly to how his guide who had led him through the tunnels to the cavern had.

Upon arriving at the Converts' rest area, he received a few curious glances at the bounty he'd brought. The Strigigryph guard craned his neck from where he stood a proper distance away, his moon-like face turning slowly as he tracked Quarnar's movements, but he asked no questions.

Quarnar explained how the herb worked and how to use it, though he received no response. He felt so awkward in the silence that he started to talk to himself about the plant as he distributed portions of it, just to fill the unearthly quiet. Talking, even if just to himself, made him feel better.

"I was always told that these are at their highest potency during the colder seasons, so… I don't want to say we're lucky to need it right now, but it'll be highly effective. It's not the easiest thing to eat on account of how stringy it is, which is why sometimes it's better to crush it up and use it as a poultice instead. It works very well either way, but—"

He cut himself off as he caught sight of something out of the corner of his eye, and he turned just in time to see a Gryphon gobbling down one root after the other. "Don't eat too many of those!" he cried, leaping forward to snag the remaining long line of purple roots away from the unwary Gryphon.

"How many did you eat?" he demanded, but the Gryphon only cowered in response.

"Blackroot will kill you if you eat too much of it!" Quarnar tried to remember how many he'd originally given this particular Gryphon, but he couldn't. "Did you eat three?" he pressed again to no answer.

"Do you not understand the common tongue?" he asked, exasperated. How long did it take for blackroot to kill? Had he ever seen it actually kill before, or had Xio just pounded the fact into his skull? Was there a cure for it?

"Glorious One," the guard began, the first time he'd spoken since being assigned. "The Converts can't—"

There was a long scratching sound as the Gryphon took a claw and made three scores in the earth. Quarnar looked at the markings and then back to him.

"Three?" He held up three claws to emphasize. "Are you saying that you only ate three?"

The Gryphon nodded, and Quarnar let out a sigh of relief. Three, while still quite a bit, wouldn't kill a creature of his size. Maybe a bit of an upset stomach, but not death. He divided what was left between the remaining Gryphons and let out a small chuckle as his fear dissipated. "Keeping me on my toes, I guess. Anyway, I'll be back tomorrow with more. You should feel a lot better by then. But please be wary, all of you. Herbs can heal just as well as they can kill."

The Gryphons all shared a glance with unreadable expressions, and then, one by one, they did something Quarnar had never seen before. They spread their wings, bowed, and then made a clicking sound. It seemed almost ceremonial in a way, and it made the Strigigryph guard visibly uneasy. The Gryphon that had eaten more blackroot than he should've clicked again, and though Quarnar only just barely saw it, he recoiled back in shock the moment he did.

"You—you don't have tongues!" he breathed in horror. He turned to the Strigigryph. "Is that why they didn't speak?"

"Why… yes, my lord."

"How? How does something like this happen?"

"It's part of being a Convert," he replied simply, frowning, still seeming to struggle to understand Quarnar's extreme reaction. "Every Gryphon you see here chose to have it done."

Quarnar narrowed his eyes. "No creature in its right mind would choose to have something so atrocious done to them. That's sick!"

Another hush descended as the words left

Quarnar's mouth. The Strigigryph squirmed before finally saying, "Every Convert must part with something before they can assimilate. Ratina killed her flock leader as a show of dedication, and these Gryphons chose to have their tongues removed. But I digress, with your permission, Glorious One. You must be tired after a long night of necessary duties. Would you like to be taken back to your quarters?"

When Quarnar didn't respond, the young hen who had helped him to carry the blackroot said, "We apologize, but we wouldn't be the best Gryphs to ask regarding customs we've long held as a flock."

Quarnar wrestled with his disgust, but in the end he slowly nodded. He let the Strigigryph hen lead him back to the den he shared with Shadowbane, too wrapped in his thoughts to regard the groups of Strigigryph who gestured respectfully to him as he went.

****

The lightening of the sky heralded the coming of morning, but Quarnar still lay awake on his pile of skins, picturing the stubby nubs that replaced what should've been tongues in the Gryphons' beaks. It explained why, despite all the chatter he heard out in the eyrie, he'd never seen or heard a Gryphon speak.

The night still felt unnaturally long to Quarnar, probably because he was still used to operating by sunlight. Did a creature of the day ever adapt to the night? The weak stream of dawn spilling through the entrance vanished behind a shadow, and Quarnar looked up to see the Arborochre Sire returning.

"I trust you've had a busy night, Quarnar," Shadowbane said, lying heavily in his nest of furs.

Quarnar leveled his eyes on the fresh cuts that crossed the keythong's face, his pristine coat mottled with patches of missing fur and feathers. Shadowbane curled his body until his tail was resting over his beak, closing his eyes.

"You've questions, clearly. Speak, Quarnar."

"Where did you go?"

Shadowbane's speaking was muffled as he spoke into his tail. "It is my duty as Sire to protect this flock. We've had a particular group of Gryphons that have been harassing our hunters for quite a while now. They refuse to listen to reason, and killed one of my flock mates in a particularly heated dispute not too long ago. Then they ran, like cowards. Well, tonight we finally avenged our fallen comrade by finding and putting an end to them. It took my trackers a long time to find them, but because of the vision Tsarine granted you last night, I knew that this was the time to strike. I know that you may still have doubts about your role here, but let this night be a testament to the power you hold, Quarnar."

Quarnar processed the information silently. So Shadowbane and his flock were the force that was moving against the Primals. They were the only group that he could've meant; no other Gryphons were having trouble beyond the typical issues regarding food and territory. Could he really feel bad if Primals were being hunted by Arborochre flock? They weren't anything more than a pain for flocked Gryphons, plus he'd been hunted as prey by them before. But perhaps even more important than all of this was the fact that Shadowbane had moved his warriors into action based entirely on a single dream that he'd had.

It was a strange feeling to have a Sire under his control, just by word of whatever he happened to say a dream he had was about. He'd never felt important before. He was surprised by how much he liked it.

"This is great news," Quarnar said with feigned excitement. "Tsarine has brought us a marvelous victory, then?"

Shadowbane nodded sagely. "I was hoping to rest, but our first victory together should be a special one. We should celebrate this night in Tsarine's honor!" With that, he walked to the den entrance, summoning a Strigigryph with a single call. "Have a feast fit for both Quarnar and me brought up. We'll start with ursos."

Quarnar gasped. Ursos? Who just hunted and casually dined on ursos? The towering beasts were deadly, their hulking bodies capable of pinning and crushing the life from their victims, their sharp teeth primed for ripping through flesh. Shadowbane noticed his reaction and almost seemed smug, as did the young Strigigryph hunter who had been summoned to procure the meat. He bowed and exited the den without comment, however, hooting into the night for the rest of a hunting party to join him.

"You won't find better hunters anywhere other than those I've got here," Shadowbane said. "Admittedly, the prey around here is ridiculously easy to catch. The ursos aren't even a challenge, which was surprising... half the time, it's like they don't expect to be attacked at all. It's only when you've already initiated the battle that they decide you're a threat worth considering."

"Well, I can't say I've ever willingly fought an ursos, nor do I want to," Quarnar said. He went back to the words Shadowbane had actually said, and his ears raised with curiosity. "Where are you from that something other than ursos is more of a challenge? That seems impossible!"

Shadowbane's eyes slid over to his. "Far, far south. So far that the trees are different, the climate is dry, and only the strong survive. Here, life is easy. Water runs in streams every few miles, the trees are thick and strong, and the prey isn't used to a predator that strikes at night as we do. But in the south, water is scarce. Predator and prey are nearly equally matched, if not in strength, then in skill. That skull over there," he said, nodding to a bleached, armored collection of bones tucked into a corner, "was a juvenile basilisk that I slew to feed my flock. I was alone, flying close to morning in desperation, when I came upon him.

"He was huge, stretched out in anticipation of the warm sunrise. I stooped into a dive before I knew what I was doing, and once I started the fight, I knew I either had to finish him or die. The beast had just learned to breathe its fire, and was spouting flames every murm. It's where I got this scar." He pointed to the patch on his shoulder where no feathers or fur grew. "It took me until the sun was high in the sky to bring that beast down. I was so exhausted that there was no way I could bring the meat back to the eyrie with me. I contemplated biting off its tail and flying that back, but my body refused to obey me any further. It was pure luck that some of my scouts flew by and saw me.

"Unfortunately, I was too late for quite a few in the flock. Hunger and dehydration were killing even healthy Strigigryph. My own mate and cub were among them. It had been nearly a moon since anyone had eaten a proper meal. How I wish that I had found that basilisk sooner." He shook his head. "I could've died that night, Quarnar. I could've died many times over, but here I am today. Tsarine blesses her select few. I can still say that with certainty even after she took my companion and my heir back to her dark domain. I'm glad you told us to come to this new land in your past life, dear friend. It is truly a land of blessings. We will increase our numbers, perhaps even to one hundred strong, especially after we gather more Converts. I've been watching Oceanside for quite some time now, too, and think it'll yield a good number of Converts. With Ratina to lead us, we can't fail. She knows every bit of that territory."

Quarnar stared into the hollow eye sockets of the basilisk's toothy skull. He was coming to simply accept and take credit for these deeds his past self had evidently done. He could only try to live up to the god-like image the others in the flock had of him.

It wasn't long before the hunter who'd originally set off returned with a hefty amount of meat, some of it still warm to the touch. It had been beautifully quartered, and Quarnar's mouth watered just looking at it. He took a chunk of the meat in his beak and held it there for a moment, savoring the interestingly sweet flavor, and then swallowed it before reaching for another piece. Ursos, it turned out, was delicious! Shadowbane joined him in eating after a bit, expertly snipping the meat away from the dense bones. After a while of munching away, he started to get full, and he realized just how odd it felt to eat until he felt he might burst. There was still plenty of meat left. Back in Skyhaven or Glendale, that would've been a rare occurrence.

Quarnar sighed, leaning back and closing his eyes, feeling a deep, surreal sense of calm come over him. This was amazing. Shadowbane seemed ready to fall asleep at any moment, his beak tucked into his chest, and Quarnar mimicked the action, feeling sleepy. He'd meant to ask about the Converts, so why hadn't he? He felt like it would cause trouble, and this… This was beyond anything he could've ever imagined. It felt right. This was where he wanted to belong.

***

It didn't take Quarnar long before he became accustomed to the schedule of events he followed in Arborochre. Each night he rose, and Shadowbane would ask him a series of questions, beginning with whether he'd envisioned anything in a *fuhkrata*. Quarnar didn't particularly believe in the power of the *fuhkrata*; he still saw his nightly fantasies as just meaningless dreams. But it was obviously expected of him, and it seemed to keep Shadowbane happy when he played along. In fact, the regal Sire was staring at him expectantly right now, dark eyes shining as he waited for answers to his inquiry about his most recent vision.

"I was hunting again. I never saw what I was after, though," Quarnar said. He'd noticed that whenever he mentioned hunting in his *fuhkrata*, Shadowbane immediately gave him his full attention. Tonight, the Strigigryph leaned in and cryptically asked,

"Did you catch anything?"

"I don't know," Quarnar said, "I jumped through some brush, and then I woke up before anything else." It didn't seem to matter what the actual content of his *fuhkrata* was, so long as hunting was the main focus. Once again, Shadowbane seemed excited, nearly too excited. He started to mutter to himself.

"So the battle will be fruitful after all... thank Tsarine."

Quarnar blinked. "Will you fight against the Primals again?" he asked.

"No," Shadowbane said. "This battle will be of much higher stakes, friend. We must plan carefully." A ruffle of excitement ran along the ridge of his back. "I can hardly wait to bring the pompous Matriarch to her end."

Quarnar felt a chill course through him. "What's the name of the flock?" he asked.

Shadowbane peered at him from the corner of his eye. The stare lasted just long enough to become uncomfortable, and Quarnar nearly questioned whether he'd asked something wrong just to break the silence. Finally, Shadowbane said, "I honestly do not know the name of the flock. But enough of this talk, you have far more to concern yourself with than the brutish business of fighting. Surely you must be hungry?"

The shift in conversation was so obvious that Quarnar found himself peeved by the blatant derailment. He managed to hold the Sire's gaze as he returned to the original topic. "Well, where is the flock?"

"Somewhat north of here is all I know. My trackers are the ones who pinned down the exact location, and they'll share the information with me later today. You're welcome to question them, if you wish, as they know more than I do for now." An edge crept into his voice. "But I'd caution you against getting too involved in the acts of violence we must commit to protect our flock, Quarnar. That's exactly how you lost your original life with us. It would be for the best if you left matters of war to me, and dedicate yourself fully to your role here: helping us to build the future Tsarine wants for us. But enough of this talk, dear friend! Why don't you try something more exotic with me for tonight's meal? It's a rarity, even in our homeland."

Quarnar didn't question the Sire further, feeling chastised. He figured he could discover whether the flock was Skyhaven through questioning some of his new flock mates, but if Shadowbane himself had shut down the conversation, he could only imagine the responses he'd get from the others.

Shadowbane called for one of his hunters, and upon the arrival of a young keythong, he told him, "Bring us the highest quality preymeat. Only the best."

The hunter bowed obediently and flew off, and when he returned it was with a heaping amount of… some strange meat that Quarnar had never seen before. When he tried it, he couldn't quite place the flavor or the texture. It had an initially pungent bite, and an almost sickeningly sweet aftertaste. He couldn't bring himself to eat more than a few bites, but Shadowbane was downing it like it was his favorite food, eating every last bite with haste. Wanting to get the disgusting flavor off his tongue, Quarnar rose to head to the stream for a drink, and Shadowbane called after him.

"I can have something more common brought for you to eat, if you wish. I hope you aren't upset by our earlier conversation, Quarnar."

Quarnar shrugged. "I'm not very hungry anyway. And it's okay, I understand." It was only a little bit of a lie, but he knew better than to force the issue. He scrambled down the cliff side without waiting for a reply.

***

The streambed was always surrounded by at least a couple of Gryphs, and today was no exception. A huge hunting party was busy washing themselves clean after a hunt, happily discussing the highlights of their chases. They made room for Quarnar when he came up, hooting amicably to him, and he trilled back. He moved upstream a bit and drank deeply before wandering back toward the hunters and clearing his throat. "Umm… any of you going to double as warriors in the upcoming battle?"

The hunters all shared looks with one another, then three of them nodded and stepped forward.

"We are. Why?" one asked.

"I was just wondering where you'd be headed," Quarnar asked. "I grew up somewhat north of here, so I might be able to offer some information about the terrain you'll be going into."

"Ah," the Strigigryph who had spoken replied, "I see. No, we aren't told the locations we'll be heading to. We just follow Shadowbane and his trackers when they lead the raiding parties. Sorry."

136

Quarnar nodded. It was clear that Shadowbane liked control. Lest he ask too much and be suspicious, he bid them all good luck in Tsarine's name—something they became quite excited about—and went on his way. He'd check on the Converts he'd been treating later, but for now, he wanted to explore more of the territory here. A trio of guards flew overhead as they started their patrol, calling out to him in greeting, and he returned the pleasantry. Warriors were never far off here. He had to admit that it was always nice to not have to worry about roving bands of Primals.

Quarnar picked his way past the caves he'd originally come to Arborochre through, walking into the overgrown forest beyond them. The trees breathed an icy breath in anticipation of a full-blown winter, their needles glistening with frost. A herd of startled peryton bolted from where they'd been browsing when they noticed his approach, flying skyward on soft wings, and he extended his own, frowning. He'd been so busy assimilating into life here that branching hadn't crossed his mind since he'd last done it with Brynne and Iba.

Quarnar sighed at the thought of the fiery orange hen and her meek mother. He hoped they were doing better now that he was gone, and that they would be safe, especially if Shadowbane *was* planning to raze Skyhaven. Could he just ask the Sire straight off what his plans were? Ask that his friends be spared? The idea seemed ridiculous. Shadowbane viewed him as a friend, but the edge

in his voice had been undeniable when he'd
questioned him. He was, after all, still the Sire of
a powerful flock. It was a miracle that he was
even on casual speaking terms with such an
authoritative figure. But he couldn't just stand by
if it was possible Brynne and Iba were in danger.

He needed to find some way to warn them.
Even if he did, how much safer would they be on
their own than in a flock? He hissed quietly,
frustrated. He was thinking in circles. Action,
that's what he needed. To do something. He
processed that the forest seemed newer here, the
trees having just started their long climb up to the
canopy. The remains of a few of their giant
counterparts littered the ground, their bark
blackened and stripped from their trunks. Here
and there, the heart of a fallen giant was split
open and dark with char. He'd never seen it up
close before, but Quarnar had seen a fire in
Glendale before when he was younger. He'd seen
the lightning that started it, too, but Xio had
never let him enter that portion of the forest to
investigate, not even after the rains had put out
the worst of the fire.

Quarnar heard a scratching sound, and he
instinctively ducked down, eyes darting toward its
source. It was hard to see with all the saplings
blocking his line of sight. He was, of course,
nowhere near camouflaged, and he quickly eased
his way behind a fallen log. The scratching
continued on indiscreetly, and Quarnar's ears
swiveled to register that it wasn't far off, just
beyond a small copse of live trees. He couldn't
will his body to move, and so he stayed put,

desperately hoping to hear for the reassuring call of a guard. Was it an ursos, sharpening its claws? What if it came this way? He hadn't seen any large predators in Arborochre territory yet, and had grown complacent with the knowledge. He'd also wandered further than he'd meant to, having been too lost in thought. *Stupid!* He scolded himself. He held his breath as paw falls started in his direction, and before long, a figure eased into view.

Quarnar's breath caught in his throat. It was Ratina! And her coat had traded its brilliant blue color for a chalky black. She gave herself a good shake, spraying the ashen ground with bits of charred bark, and clawed into a nearby downed tree. The charred wood yielded easily, and she stomped it into a powder before promptly rolling in the stuff. She shook again, then sat down to spend long moments picking at feathers until they were perfectly in place. Finally, she said, "Why are you hiding? And why are you out here anyway?

Quarnar climbed over the log he'd been crouched behind, feeling a smidge silly. "Getting a feel for the territory. What are you doing?"

She didn't reply as she rubbed more of the burnt char into her wings, using her long bill to reach the furthest feathers at the tips. "Preparing for a raiding party. Blue isn't a good color to hide in. I'm sure you can relate." She gave him a look that chastened him for being so far away from the eyrie, but he didn't relent.

"You're going with Shadowbane to fight later.

Where are you going?"

"I don't see how that information benefits you. You're not a warrior."

"I have friends in an eyrie north of here," he blurted out. "I want to make sure they'll be safe."

Ratina stopped picking at her feathers. She turned to face him. "I'm sorry to hear that."

"Where are you going?" Quarnar repeated.

"I can't tell you. It's for your own good. I don't know if the flock is the one your friends are a part of, but if it is, you'll only get yourself into trouble."

"You don't understand!" Quarnar said, working to keep a note of pleading out of his voice. "I'll blame myself if anything happens to them because I didn't warn them."

"I do understand," she replied. "Probably better than you'd know. Life isn't about what we want, Quarnar. It's about survival. Do you think I wanted to kill my own Sire? No, I didn't. But he was sick and weak and dying anyway. Shadowbane's warriors killed off most of Oceanside's warriors the second time they came through there. They left the offer to join or die. To this day, those fools in that eyrie are still thinking they can hold out. Like the danger Arborochre imposes will just disappear on its own one day. Shadowbane leaves them for the time being because he knows they aren't a threat.

At all. Ardeigryph aren't warriors, Quarnar. Look at us!"

She spread her wings and held up a talon. She was easily twice his height, but everything she had consisted of long, thin appendages, clearly made for soaring and catching water-prey, not for maneuvering and crushing enemies.

"I did what I had to do to live," Ratina said. "I forced myself to become a warrior. Most Gryphs and other creatures don't even know how to fight something with a beak and height like this, so it's an advantage I use quite a bit. I'll never rest easy knowing I betrayed my own kind. But I'll be alive, Quarnar. And you will be, too, won't you? Now, come on. I'll do you one favor. One favor, because I know how it feels to be where you are now. What do your friends look like, and what are their names? If I happen to see them during the raiding party, I won't kill them. I'll even try to make sure they escape. But that's the only thing I can offer you. At least then you can sleep in the morning. Now come on, let's start walking back. Someone will begin to wonder where you are."

Quarnar swallowed past the lump in his throat and fell into step with her. He told her about Brynne and Iba, even Sheba and Makith, the youngster who had spoken to Iba like she was an equal. He'd never even seen him, but he hoped if the raiding party visited Skyhaven, he'd survive. When he mentioned Sheba, Ratina set her jaw and didn't say anything. He looked over at her, but she avoided his gaze.

"I'm guessing that Matriarchs and Sires are the first target of a raid," Quarnar said.

Ratina gave a single nod in response. "They are the lifeblood of a flock. Break the leader, and you break the whole faction."

They didn't speak further, but when they reached the eyrie, Ratina turned and said, "Try to stay on Shadowbane's good side, Quarnar. Don't do anything stupid. And don't tell him anything that you've told me. Sweet Tsarine's hide, you honestly shouldn't have even told me these things. The Sire must believe that this flock and Tsarine are all you care about. Don't give him any reason to question that." And she flew away.

***

It hadn't even been a full moon yet, but all of the injured Converts were thriving under Quarnar's care. He'd been doing so well with them that he now had a small audience each and every time he carried herbs to them. Curious eyes watched his every move. During the days following his talk with Ratina, there hadn't been any marked difference in the flock. He didn't see Ratina at all, and he couldn't tell if she was just busy or if she was actively avoiding him. It probably wouldn't be too hard to hide from him in such a large flock, but he went about his business feeling like there was a pit in his stomach. The not knowing killed him. But her warning had been very real.

Don't do anything stupid.

No one in Arborochre ever spoke about the

raids, and he knew better than to ask. No new Converts joined the flock, and if they did, they wouldn't be able to speak, anyway. He treated the newly injured as he would've any other Gryph. It was no surprise that word of his healing abilities eventually reached Shadowbane. Upon hearing of his skills, the Sire requested his presence following one of his visits to the group of Converts one night. The breeze was calm and frigid as Quarnar walked with Shadowbane through the eyrie, their strides nearly matching. Quarnar had gone through another growth spurt just as winter had descended. The cold no longer bothered him.

"I briefly recall you said something about how you were from Glendale, Quarnar," Shadowbane said. "I've heard very little about the place, only that it is the home of rare and powerful creatures known as Alicorns. Winged beings capable of flight, reason… and magick."

"I grew up there," Quarnar replied. "I know a bit about healing from watching the Alicorns."

Shadowbane's incredulous expression remained. "We've never had an entire group of Converts injured in their first battle survive before. It's unprecedented, truly amazing. We have a rudimentary understanding of what some of the plants from our homeland are capable of, but to have a Gryphon who is familiar with the herbs here in this area is a welcome surprise. So… you say the Alicorns taught you all of this?"

Quarnar shook his head. "They didn't really

teach me, but I guess that when I watched them, I remembered, and it just made sense."

Shadowbane seemed almost giddy. Finally he said, "I understand, now. You were sent back as a Gryphon so that we could have access to this amazing wealth of knowledge. It would've been impossible for you to learn these things as a Strigigryph, since we don't have Alicorns in our native land. And the Alicorns themselves are supposedly elusive, impossibly-hunted creatures. I never thought they'd share their secrets with another species. Do you think it's possible they would ally with us?"

Quarnar's ears flared at the words. "Impossibly hunted? And no, of course not! The Alicorns don't get involved in the quarrels of other creatures."

Shadowbane tilted his head. "I simply mean that even the best of hunters couldn't land a claw on one, even if they tried to. Not that anyone would. You obviously have quite a bit of empathy for them, I see. I suppose it's only normal, if they truly raised you as you say." He seemed slightly amused before continuing on, "Alicorns aside, do you think it's possible that you could teach others here the ways of using plants to heal?"

"Maybe," Quarnar said slowly. "I'd have to be careful, because the wrong plants can cause harm."

"Ah yes, that's right, the dangers of poisons… I was told one of the Converts nearly killed himself with something called blackroot a while ago. Lucky that you caught him! Quarnar, why don't you take a couple of the Converts you've aided with you to collect herbs? Surely there must be something you can still collect, despite the onset of this colder weather?"

"I'll have a look," Quarnar said.

"Perfect. The Converts are quite indebted to you for saving their lives, and I'm sure more than a few would be happy to help. Most are really quite bright, despite what some in my flock choose to believe. If there's anything else you need to practice your craft, just let me know, and it will be procured for you."

Quarnar figured that it could be useful to have a few assistants. Even if those assistants couldn't talk. Even if the clicking sounds they made were a bit unnerving. "Shadowbane," he said carefully, looking up at the Sire. "Why is not having a tongue part of being a Convert?"

Shadowbane blinked. "Well, you are familiar with the Primals, are you not?"

Quarnar nodded. "They're part of why I'm missing my tail."

"Ah, I noticed that when you first came here. Figures it would be due to those worthless Primals! They cause nothing but grief for everyone here, it seems. They attack hunting parties, overhunt the land, and trespass freely. They only follow the Old Law, wherein Gryphs are simple beasts, following no master and being no different from any other unintelligent creature. So you see, they must be dealt with for our own defense. I know it sounds harsh. We had groups just like them in our homeland. The Primals are resistant to talk of peace, and entirely reject the idea of Tsarine. We Strigigryph would never kill cubs, but Primals are such savages that they won't even spare young minds. Still, even among such… uncultured Gryphs, we occasionally come across a couple who are ready to accept Tsarine's blessing and wish to join our flock.

"Tsarine has traditionally always demanded a great price of any would-be Converts, and thus is the reason initiates give up their voices. The choice to have their tongue removed is entirely up to them, Quarnar," he added, seeing his growing apprehension. "It's a way for them to show that they're dedicated to Tsarine. It's not a choice to be taken lightly. And Tsarine must be pleased with us for following this ancient rite, because she continues to send us victory after victory. It's a sacred ritual that has been in place for decades, long before my reign over this flock. I, too, was originally just as horrified by the practice, and I was raised into it! But these laws and traditions exist for a reason, and I must say, they have worked beautifully for us and our ancestors for as long as anyone can remember."

Quarnar winced at the thought, though it brought him a miniscule measure of comfort to know that even the Sire himself believed the action to be brutish.

"Why did you let Ratina keep her ability to speak, then?"

"Ah, young Ratina. She was a special case. Killing her own Sire, especially at her age, wasn't a simple feat, Quarnar. I can think of no better way to show her dedication to us and to Tsarine."

Quarnar swallowed. "Are flocked Gryphons more inclined to listen to reason?" he asked, thinking of Skyhaven.

"Our talks with the other flocks are… a work in progress," Shadowbane said. "You certainly hold a lot of curiosity for the other flocks in this land. I hope you understand that Arborochre is your home now."

"Of course," Quarnar quickly replied. "I'm just concerned with the number of Gryphs we've been bringing in to become Converts. I'd like to find a way to bolster those numbers, but you were right in our earlier conversation, Shadowbane. I'll leave matters relating to such things up to you."

Shadowbane nodded. "It's for the best, though I understand why you're worried. More Gryphs killed means less followers for Tsarine. But enough questions for tonight, young Quarnar. Dawn is nigh, and the morning chorus will begin soon. I must sleep, and so should you. The hunters will have left you some preymeat to eat; whatever you don't want, leave and they'll clear it later. I'm sure Tsarine, no doubt, is eager to see you in today's *fuhkrata*."

Quarnar didn't reply as Shadowbane spread his wings and flew off. Now he knew for sure that it was useless to ask him anything relating to other flocks. He wished he could talk to Ratina. He didn't agree with her views completely, but there was something comforting about the cut-and-dry way she put things. If survival was his goal, as it was of most living things, then he was performing brilliantly at it for now.

Quarnar's thoughts kept wandering to the other Gryphs in the surrounding land. What monsters the Strigigryph must seem to be to them. Flat-faced Gryphs that flew on silent wings, and killed in the night while the world they knew slumbered. And what was a flock leader supposed to do when a strange enemy visited them and demanded they surrender their territory, their beliefs, and their customs? There was no honor in surrendering before putting up a fight, and there was no way any Gryphon could expect an enemy to silently appear and slay them in their sleep.

Quarnar flicked his tongue against the roof of his mouth as he walked, imagining it not being there, just as his tail wasn't. Sometimes he still tried to use his tail as he used to. It was always a surprise to realize that it was gone, and it had been gone for quite some time. Did Converts try to speak with a tongue that was no longer there? What was it like to be able to only click, when before they could form entire sentences, call out to one another in greeting and in goodbye?

Quarnar shuddered as he climbed his way up

the cliff to the den, and just before he fell asleep, he decided that he wasn't okay with the taking of tongues, or the destruction of the other flocks. Shadowbane said that every Convert here had voluntarily chosen to become a part of Arborochre flock, but what choice had he given them? Shadowbane would never know his thoughts on these matters, of course… but it felt right to admit to himself that he was against the things happening here. He'd figure out what to do about it later. He drifted off uneasily to sleep.

***

Quarnar couldn't remember his *fuhkrata*. All he could remember was that there was an ominous clicking that seemed to go on forever, an inescapable din of haunting snapping sounds. It was a relief when he finally managed to jolt awake, a cry catching in his throat.

Gentle rays of moonbeam spilled into the cavern, striking his pelt with streamers of silver. His eyes adjusted quickly in the low light. He was immediately aware of another presence in the room, and he anxiously bolted to his feet. His heart slammed against his ribs as the outline of two Gryphons became visible. He felt his hackles rising, then shook his head at his own stupidity. These were the Converts Shadowbane had spoken of the night before. They clicked questioningly to one another, and he realized that the sound from his dreaming had been them all along.

A glance to the side revealed that Shadowbane had already taken off for the evening, no doubt enrobed in his own duties for the night. He was

gone more and more frequently, it seemed, and
Quarnar was secretly a bit glad that he hadn't
been present to see how flustered he'd gotten just
now.

There was nothing exceptional about either of
the Gryphons that were present with Quarnar.
One was black, and the other was tan. They were
both quite young, though not quite as young as
he himself was. Their eyes seemed tired. The tan
one yawned, stretching luxuriously, and the other
scratched absently at a spot on her shoulder.
Quarnar assumed that they weren't allowed to
wake him, and so instead they'd opted to patiently
wait for him to rise on his own, clicking softly to
each other as they passed the time.

The tan keythong made a sighing sound in the
back of his throat and lifted a wing with a quick
snapping sound, and the other tilted her head and
clicked once, dropping her tail and wriggling her
ears. Quarnar watched them in wonder, realizing
that they had a system for communicating with
one another despite their lack of voices. It was
nice to know that they weren't completely mute.
It gave him hope for learning more about them
later.

When Quarnar poked his head outside the
den, a hunter was already posted and waiting. He
didn't care what he was brought so long as it
wasn't anymore of Shadowbane's favorite exotic
meat, and he ended up with a whole side of ursos.
Quarnar looked from the meat to the hunter and
back to the meat. The hunter gave a bit of a shrug
and said, "Fruitful hunting today, Glorious One.

If it displeases you, I can bring something else."

"Oh no, this is… fine, I suppose," Quarnar said, wondering how he was expected to eat even a quarter of what was offered. He noticed immediately that the Converts had ceased talking and were both watching the food with rapt expressions, but they looked away the moment he met their eyes. He called them over to eat with him, happy to have a little company that wasn't in the form of Shadowbane asking him about his most recent *fuhkrata*. After a murm of hesitation, they sat down next to him and reluctantly ate from the shared meal.

Quarnar wasn't very hungry, and by the time he'd finished and sat to preen his feathers, the two Converts had gone from polite nibbles to ravenously attacking what was left of the ursos together. They tore entire pieces of meat free and choked them down, continuing until only bones littered the floor of the den. He blinked, and they seemed a bit embarrassed before dipping their heads in thanks. They were by no means starving—at least, they were nowhere near as bony as he, Brynne, and Iba had been when food was scarce—but he wondered if they ever got a chance to truly eat their fill. He asked if they were ready to go, and then led the way into the forest to show them the species of plants he was interested in collecting.

***

The surface layer of the ground was already frozen, and the firmness made digging more difficult than Quarnar was prepared for. He searched out the areas where the herbs he needed

151

were likely to still have a foothold, areas that would've been sown in bare patches of soil and shaded from above during the spring. He marked the ground with claw marks to show his two students where to attempt excavation, and they followed along behind him well enough, digging with gusto. The only thing to be found in the bitter cold, just as before, ended up being blackroot. Apparently the forests around Arborochre were prime habitat for growing it. All the other herbs he would've loved to find found couldn't survive above ground during the frost, or their withered remains were useless for medicinal use.

A slight commotion sounded as the Converts looked up from their work and saw a third mottled Gryphon sprinting to join them. A barred Strigigryph sentry wasn't far behind. He hardly gave the newcomer a warning before setting into him with fervor, sparing neither beak nor talon in his discipline. The Gryphon yelped and whimpered, but made no effort to fight back, simply cowering with his tail tucked as the Strigigryph plucked and clawed at his hide.

Quarnar struggled to find his voice in his bewilderment. "Stop this at once!" he yelled. "What's all this about?"

The guard looked surprised that his punishment had been interrupted. "Of course, Glorious One. This keythong was late to join your group just now, despite being instructed to be present at the same time as the others. Sleeping in is not allowed for Converts."

Quarnar looked from the mottled keythong to the other two Gryphons, then back to the Strigigryph. "We've hardly begun. Your punishment is… excessive."

"There are strict orders from Shadowbane himself that all Converts are to be prompt whenever called to duty," the guard pressed. "You'll learn from this experience and be more astute in the future won't you, Convert?"

The mottled male wasted no time in vigorously nodding, and Quarnar frowned. "I'll see to it that you not punish anymore of our flock mates so severely for anything so mundane ever again," he said.

The Strigigryph's already wide eyes impossibly opened wider. "I didn't mean to upset you, Glorious One! I was only doing my job. My apologies, I'll do as you wish in the future. I'll take my leave now, with your permission, of course!"

Quarnar narrowed his eyes before saying, "You are dismissed."

The barred guard bowed before flying off, and the Gryphons did little to hide their shock at Quarnar's actions. They all immediately did the same thing they'd done when he'd healed the other Converts, touching their wings together and bowing to him. Although he didn't know what exactly it meant, their sense of reverence was palpable. He waved his wings self-consciously at them to stop, then glanced at the mottled keythong. "Are you okay? I'm sorry I didn't react sooner."

The Gryphon gave a simple nod, meek again after his brief show of unity with the other two. Quarnar didn't want to drag the moment on any longer. "Let's not waste any more time," he announced. "There's blackroot to be found."

***

After a time, Quarnar eventually settled into the supervisory role of watching the Convert trio dig, but he didn't totally exclude himself from the activity, either. He was mostly satisfied that they knew what they were doing, but he still reviewed their findings as needed. Sometimes they pulled totally unrelated things from the ground to show him, ranging from bulbs of different species, oddly shaped rocks, and once even a strange hibernating creature that didn't appreciate being dug up. They seemed to enjoy his reaction to seeing them.

With the help of the Converts, harvesting went quickly, and Quarnar soon decided they'd found enough for the night, but the Converts were overzealous. They showered one another with frozen clods of dirt in their efforts, continuing to dig on long after he'd ceased and lain down to rest, feathers ruffled against the chilly wind.

"You know, we have to carry this all back to the eyrie to store it," Quarnar said. "With the way you guys are digging, I'm thinking it's going to take two, maybe three trips."

The Converts immediately froze and stopped, and he laughed. "I think that's enough for tonight. We'll get back to it tomorrow, I'm sure. I wish I had a terrapin shell to carry some of this in… or some Alicorn magick would be nice, too."

The black hen's head shot up at the mention of Alicorns. She opened her beak and waved her tail, looking for all the world like she was about to try to say something, but then she scrambled to pick up her share of herbs instead, realizing her companions had already collected theirs. Quarnar was confused by their focused attention on him for a split murm, then realized they were waiting for the command to depart.

"No need to wait for me," Quarnar said. "We'll store this in the initiate's cavern for now, there's plenty of room in there. You've all done a great night's work! Thank you for your help."

The Converts all bowed and headed off at once, with Quarnar lagging behind considerably. As they walked, he noticed the black hen stealing a couple of glances at him. She gingerly fell back in step until she was right alongside him and, receiving uncertain looks from her comrades, clicked hopefully. She crouched low and pounced as a playful cub might, but scattered half of her blackroot in the process. Quarnar laughed. "You seemed interested in the Alicorns I mentioned earlier," he said.

She nodded enthusiastically.

"Want me to tell you more about them?"

Another nod.

"Well, I don't know if you've ever seen an Alicorn before, but they walk on all fours like we do, and they have wings just like we do, but instead of paws or talons they have hooves…"

***

Quarnar watched day break over the sleeping eyrie. Although it was hard to appreciate in the rising wind, he'd forgotten how warm the sun could feel, how pretty it looked as it touched everything beneath the sky, bringing it to a different kind of life that he simply didn't witness at night. Night had its own unique kind of beauty, and while it was true that the bright light of day often hurt his eyes, he still missed it sometimes. He looked over at Shadowbane's pile of skins, empty and tossed aside from when he'd risen the night before. He was increasingly gone, though he made sure he maintained an active curiosity in any *fuhkrata* Quarnar might've had while he was away.

The reverence with which Shadowbane regarded anything related to Tsarine was both interesting and unnerving to Quarnar. What would happen if he found out that he didn't fully believe the teachings the way he expected? Shadowbane did anything that he believed was for the good of Tsarine and the flock. There was no way he wouldn't see a fraud acting in the place of his dead friend to not be a threat somehow. It made sense that the Sire of a flock would hold most strongly to the very things that bound it together… but Quarnar was quickly finding his zeal to be unnerving.

"I see you're still alive."

Quarnar glanced sideways from his basking and found Ratina standing not far away, feathers ruffled as though she'd been in a tussle, but nothing serious. She gestured with her beak toward the ground next to him. "May I?"

"Of course," Quarnar said, barely suppressing himself from asking her about the raid.

She stretched out next to him, a blue and black smudged blur against the earthy brown. "I'm sorry. I can't give you the answers you want. I was posted as backup in the forest surrounding the eyrie. I don't even know which eyrie it was. I didn't see much of anything. But the straggler I caught wasn't one of your friends. Listen—"

Quarnar felt like millions of tiny fibers that had been constricting him ever since he'd learned about the raid suddenly tightened more. Ratina placed a talon on his shoulder and shook him. As usual, the look in her flat, grey eyes didn't match the urgency in her voice as she said, "I know you're worried about your friends. That's normal. But you really should be more worried about yourself. You're being tested by Shadowbane, you know. You don't even realize it, do you?"

Quarnar stiffened. "What are you talking about?"

"It sure seems to me like you're cozying up really nicely to the Converts. You might want to stop doing that." She looked around to make sure they were truly alone. "Over time, I've noticed a slow change in our leader. He's gone from wanting what's best for the flock to wanting to turn every Gryph in this area into a follower of Tsarine. The Converts to him are just a means to an end, a source of willing labor that brings him closer to his goal. Everyone captured alive is offered the chance to convert. No one leaves here, though. Ever."

Quarnar shuddered as he recalled Shadowbane's words to him when he'd first been brought to Arborochre, that he could leave whenever he wanted. Why did it surprise him that his words weren't true?

"I don't have anything against the Converts. I'm one, myself. But you're putting yourself into a bad position with the Strigigryph here by befriending them so openly." She cast a paranoid sweep around before continuing, "Our Sire has a quick temper that few see, but I know that it isn't something you want to be on the receiving end of. I've seen it enough times when we're out on a raid to know how to hold my tongue. Word will have reached him about you preventing the beating of that Convert by now. If I were you, I'd try to make that out to be an isolated event."

"How did you hear about what happened with that guard? We were practically alone in the woods when it happened."

"Strigigryph talk, a lot. And I know pretty much every guard and hunter here. I should go," she said suddenly, standing. "Let's see one another again some night. Its growing early, and I should let you get some sleep. Good day, Glorious One." She stooped low to bow, but Quarnar scrambled to his feet to stop her from departing.

"You can't just leave after just offloading comments like that."

She leveled her eyes on him, side stepped past him, and then launched into the night, swooping down to the eyrie below just as Shadowbane flared his wings on the horizon, headed toward the cliff. Quarnar watched him until he finally banked to land, calling out a greeting as casually as he could.

"An early morning consort with the Ardeigryph, old friend? She's a bit of an odd sort to take as a companion, isn't she?" he asked, heading to his skins. "There are much better-looking hens among even the Converts. They are typically willing enough, I might add."

It took a moment for his words to register with Quarnar, and he had to work at keeping his face from twisting at the implication. "Oh, no! No, not at all! Just catching up with a flock member I haven't seen in a while."

Shadowbane gave him a disbelieving glance. "You'll be a yearling soon, and you're telling me that none of the hens in this flock catch your fancy? You've no curiosity at all?"

Quarnar shook his head vigorously. "No! No! Not in the slightest. I mean, honestly, I have much more important things to attend to than chasing hens around. There are herbs to be collected, skills to be learned, much more than following the tail of some… some longbeak, or of a tongueless freak." The last words were surprisingly harsh to his ears even though he was the one who had spoken them.

Shadowbane laughed much harder than he expected him to. "Well, it grows early. I'm going to turn in. You should, too. See you at twilight."

Quarnar waited until Shadowbane made himself comfortable before lying down. He was glad for the cover of his wing as he tucked his head underneath it. Who knew what may have happened had Ratina not seen Shadowbane in the distance? He hoped the Sire couldn't hear the frenzied beating of his heart. It was only with great effort that he eventually dropped off to sleep.

***

Naugi flew twice around the abandoned eyrie that once was Skyhaven. Old blood had frozen into the snow there, and feathers stiff with frost still littered the ground. Just as there were no Gryphons around, there was no offering, either. It seemed that the flock had met a grisly fate. Annoyance crept into his veins. His first thought was that some of his scale-kin had gone rogue and decided to go on a hunting spree without his permission, but he'd already heard from other creatures that there were intruding Gryphs causing an uproar. These newcomers seemed different.

Naugi circled the stricken eyrie one last time, skimming low to get a better look. It was odd that there were no bodies. Every den had been ransacked. The whole thing had obviously been quiet. There were hardly tracks leading in or out of the area, suggesting that the enemy force had mostly flown in. He bared his teeth and roared, rising skyward to depart. These strangers had disturbed his food supply by cutting off a source of one of his most abundant offering sites. Any force that could take out Sheba and her warriors was a force to be reckoned with. He'd need to find these newcomers and make sure they understood the laws of living in his territory.

CHAPTER EIGHT

Every day when Quarnar and the Converts went out to collect herbs, he thought of Ratina's warning. Shadowbane never seemed put off by his relationship with the Converts, and would even occasionally prod him for more information about them to make conversation. The Sire had placed more Converts into the harvesting group to multiply efforts in finding blackroot, encouraged by the fact that the plant could be dried and preserved. Quarnar longed for warmer days when he could forage for more varied plants, but digging for blackroot gave his days purpose when there weren't any injuries to treat.

Despite the growing number of Converts that accompanied Quarnar each night to their digging site, only one trailed him like a shadow. The black hen that had been excited to learn about Alicorns always worked closely beside him, and he appreciated the company. He was beginning to learn her mannerisms, and she tried to help him as best she could to understand the way that she and the other Converts communicated. He recalled what Ratina had said about being too openly fond of the Gryphons, but he figured that it wouldn't matter when there were no Strigigryph around to witness it.

Quarnar did notice that a few Converts stared after the black hen with jealous eyes when they noticed him paying more attention to her, and so he tried to increase his efforts to make sure he interacted fairly with all of them. Still, it was the first time since Brynne that he felt like he had a friend. Sometimes, the hen was so focused on whatever the subject of their conversation happened to be that she forgot to dig, which would always garner acidic looks from the others. Despite these developments, everything seemed fine. That is, until the night Quarnar called her to him and plainly asked,

"Hey, can I call you Larin? I don't know what your name used to be, but it'd be nice to be able to call you by something. If you don't like it, we can pick another I suppose?"

Larin immediately leapt in a huge arc, bounding lightly on her feet with excitement and nodding enthusiastically. He'd never seen her so happy before.

And that's where the trouble started.

***

The following night, Quarnar rose as usual and struck off to meet his growing circle of Converts in preparation to lead the harvest, as he'd become accustomed to doing. All were astutely present, save for one. He glanced around in confusion for Larin, and asked the others if they'd seen her. His question hung in the air without answer, and the other Converts shifted in the cold wind, waiting to begin their day's digging.

"We can't start without her," Quarnar said pointedly, noting with unease that the group that had seemed jealous of her had unusually smug expressions painted on their faces. Finally, the mottled keythong that was part of his original group stepped forward and nudged him as he passed in an invitation to follow. A few despondent clicks sounded from the others as Quarnar fell in behind him, but the keythong didn't respond back. After making sure that Quarnar was following him, he traded his walk for an urgent trot.

Curious hoots erupted from the flock as the Glorious One followed so desperately after a lowly Convert. The mottled keythong led Quarnar to the initiate's cavern, and his heart quickened as his ears made out the sound of frenzied splashing.

Quarnar ran ahead of his guide, weaving between stalagmites that jutted from the ground, and beheld the sight of four Strigigryph guards all standing at opposing ends of the pool of water in the cavern. They almost looked bored as they watched Larin's flailing body at its center. The water wasn't yet frozen, but had taken on the consistency of a slurry that glistened with ice, and Larin struggled to stay afloat in the freezing mixture. Her breath puffed into the air as she woodenly churned against the still water, slowly slipping underneath only to break the surface again a few murms later, choking. The guard nearest to Quarnar jumped when he saw him and, seeing his reaction, immediately threw out his wings and said, "by order of our Sire Shadowbane, Glorious One. Perhaps you should avert your eyes from the punishment of this scum."

"Scum?" Quarnar cried. "You'll let her out at once!"

"By order of the Sire—"

"At once!" Quarnar roared, pushing past the guard. He leapt into the frigid water, the shock of the cold rushing to his bones like a blow, winding him. He gasped as he swam furiously, grabbing the exhausted hen by the scruff of her neck. He felt as stiff as the ice itself by the time he dragged her back to shore. The guards all shared uneasy glances, unsure of whether to stop him or not, but he ignored them completely as he shook droplets of water from his coat and nudged his unsteady friend to her feet.

"Let's get you somewhere warm," he said, crossing a wing over her body to help guide her. "Come on."

The guards each attempted to retort, but stopped themselves before they could form words. In the end, they let the Glorious One pull the Convert away from her certain doom. Who were they to question the actions of one such as him?

***

Quarnar piled the hides and furs from his nest around Larin and, in his frenzy, even took a few from Shadowbane's bedding. Not knowing what else to do to help keep her warm, he crowded in next to her, pulling his wings tight around them to share warmth. Who knew how long she'd been in that pool, struggling to stay afloat? And how could those guards just allow something so terrible to happen to a Gryph from his group? He expected that the guard he'd confronted before about such punishments would have spread the word by now.

Something in Quarnar broke a little, because he knew the answer. The guards had already said it themselves. Shadowbane had ordered this. Ratina had told him the truth about the Sire. *It sure seems to me like you're cozying up really nicely to the Converts,* she'd said. *You might want to stop doing that.*

But surely he couldn't just let Larin die. She'd done nothing wrong. He realized that he needed to come up with something to say when Shadowbane inevitably found out what he'd done. His brain felt like mush at the moment, but he continued to think furiously anyway.

It took many murms before Larin's coat was only just damp, and even then she still continued to tremble uncontrollably, eyes closed. She clicked weakly to him, fluffing her feathers against the cold, and he squeezed her reassuringly.

166

"I wish you could talk," he said. "I know that you could tell me so much. You all probably could."

Larin suddenly sat bolt upright. She struggled to get to her feet, but Quarnar held her firmly into place. "You can't go out there, it's snowing for Halada's sake! That cold will kill you in your condition!"

Larin continued to struggle, insistent, a note of desperation creeping into her clicks. A smooth movement brought Shadowbane's form into the low light of the den a murm later. The silence was absolute as he took in the scene, and then a look of utter disgust blossomed across his typically serene features.

"Get away from that manipulative creature, Quarnar. I'll not tell you again. Just because you were raised by Alicorns doesn't mean that you can go around pitying every creature that cries for help. You're one of us now! We can't go picking and choosing who gets unwarranted privileges, it will upset the balance of the flock. This Convert crossed the line the moment she forgot her place and decided to do anything more than dig for herbs. I've been told of the way she croons over you to get out of work. I've seen for myself how she takes advantage of you because she knows you won't discipline her. Stand aside! I'll kill her swiftly. It's more mercy than she deserves."

The Sire loomed darkly as he took a step forward, and Quarnar rose to his feet, a hiss springing to his tongue. "You'll not lay a claw on her," he said.

Shadowbane narrowed his eyes. "You don't speak with reason. You're young and foolish; you'll thank me for this later. This worthless hen has tricked you into thinking that she deserves a name, and then had the gall to accept it after you chose one. Enough games, Quarnar. Trust that I know what's good for you." He rushed forward and threw Quarnar sideways with a quickness he was unprepared for. Before he could regain himself, the Sire had the young Convert by the neck. She offered no struggle.

"No!" Quarnar cried, pleading. "Please, don't do it, I'll do anything! It wasn't her fault, it was mine…!" His mind struggled furiously for a solution. "She's not just a Convert…" he went on. "She's my mate. I know, I'm sorry!" he added, seeing the new look of suspicion that was creeping into Shadowbane's eyes. "I knew you'd be disappointed. I didn't want to say anything. It wasn't Ratina, she's too different to me. It was this Convert. I swear it!"

Shadowbane slowly released Larin. His footfalls were heavy and deliberate as he crossed the space between him and Quarnar. Then, in a voice so quiet that Quarnar had to strain to hear it, he said, "Prove it."

A new flood of alarm coursed through Quarnar's veins. "You can't be serious! I mean, look at her! The poor thing is half dead, I—"

"That's enough."

Quarnar and Shadowbane both turned to see Plithi standing in the mouth of the den. Her voice was indifferent as she said, "If the Convert brings him happiness, then why don't you keep her alive, Shadowbane? He's learned his lesson, look at him. He knows not to treat them as anything more than what they are now."

Shadowbane didn't look at her. His eyes pierced into Quarnar like talons as he said, "Eventually... you'll prove it. Or I'll have her killed, slowly, while you and all of her kind watch. Do I make myself clear?"

Quarnar nodded, still terrified.

"Good."

Shadowbane turned to exit the den, and Plithi followed after him. Her eyes didn't meet anything other than the ground as she paused to say, "You were lucky. Strigigryph or not, my mate or not, he is the Sire of this flock. Sometimes the best thing to do is to obey." And she was gone.

***

Quarnar's ribs smarted where Shadowbane had dug in to throw him, but there was little to be done about it in the moment. Larin shivered quietly beside him. She'd glanced at him guiltily a few times, but he refused to entertain the thought that any of this was her fault. His understanding of the Converts' language was still rudimentary at best, but when a defeated rumble rose from her chest, the meaning was plain. Still, the more he thought about how trapped he felt here, the more a sparkle of hope arose alongside it. By pushing Shadowbane's boundaries, he not only knew his enemy, but he'd gained something of how he operated now as well. That had to be meaningful, even if he wasn't sure how at the moment.

"It's going to be alright, Larin," he said, as much to calm himself as her. "We'll figure something out. We'll do it together."

He had to believe that it was true.

***

Shadowbane didn't disturb Quarnar for the rest of the night. But the next night he was present as usual, acting as though nothing had happened the day prior.

"Anything interesting in your *fuhkrata?*" the Sire asked, stretching as he stood over the new pile of fur-lined skins he'd had brought over. Quarnar glanced over meekly from where he'd been preening Larin's feathers.

"Only of the hunt," he lied. He could feel the Sire's eyes lingering on him. Shadowbane wound and unwound his tail a couple of times, then said, "Take the day off, Quarnar. And keep her with you at all times. We'll figure out what to do with you tomorrow night."

"What to do with me? You don't want me to dig for blackroot anymore?"

Shadowbane laughed dryly. "You always did become a little too pent up whenever you just lazed around doing nothing. You need a job to do, dear friend! A real job. With the guardian Hydra of this region visiting soon, there are bound to be preparations you can help with."

"Naugi is visiting soon?"

"He sent one of his envoys to me. At first I was hopeful that I would get to hunt some real prey for once, but I wouldn't want to be rude to our host by slaying his messenger before we've even met, would I? I've actually never met any scale-kin that could speak our tongue before. This 'Naugi' seems to have control of all of them in this area, and he's noticed our flock. It would seem that he wants to make sure we abide by the rules of his land. Whatever those rules may be."

"But what about the Converts?" Quarnar asked. "What about harvesting blackroot? They need me to show them where to dig."

"Those you've trained are adept enough to know what to look for," Shadowbane said dismissively. "Now, stay out of trouble."

He brushed past Larin on his way out of the den, and Quarnar felt her tense at his touch. He stared after the Sire's departing outline, thinking again. Escape would be preferable at this point, but he couldn't just leave all these Gryphs to suffer here, either. Shadowbane had given him an idea without meaning to, though. How could he have just forgotten about Naugi? The Hydra controlled this entire region, and he had the power to oust Arborochre flock from his territory. He just needed to find a way to speak to the Hydra, and soon.

***

The night wore on as Quarnar preened Larin's feathers, watching the moon move across the night sky. The repetitive activity soothed his nerves as he entertained ideas of escape that made his heart quicken with anxiety. He frowned as he got to the end of one of her wings, noticing the abrupt end to feathers there. There were one or two that had just started to grow in, but the vast majority were missing. He unfurled his own wings, silky pinions unmarred in the delicate moonlight, and noted that all his were present, all the way to the tip. He reached over to check her other. It was the same way.

"What happened to your wings?" he asked.

Larin sighed and took one of his flight feathers in her beak, then made a pulling motion as if to remove it.

"Did the Strigigryph do it to you?"

She nodded.

"But, why?"

Larin seemed to have trouble explaining that bit. She motioned for him to follow her to the den's edge, where she spread her wings and flapped as hard as she could before jumping off. Quarnar could hear the wind whistling through the unfeathered portions of her wings. She didn't gain any lift at all, but instead glided gently down to the ground despite her best efforts. Quarnar

172

felt a genuine flame of hatred growing inside him. Was there anything the Strigigryph allowed those they'd converted to have? No voices, no names, no flight… only pure servitude. They were hardly Gryphs at all by the time they were through with them. And Shadowbane wanted his flock to continue to grow, which meant more and more would end up like Larin… or like the dying Primal he'd seen in Glendale.

"I need you to help me to do something, Larin," he said the moment she scaled back up to stand next to him. He glanced around and dropped his voice.

"I need you to help me find someone who can teach me how to fly."

CHAPTER NINE

The walk through the heart of Arborochre was eerily silent as Quarnar followed Larin. It was snowing enough that much of the flock was staying inside, but those that were out averted their round eyes when he looked at them. It was impossible not to notice the quiet murmuring that followed his and Larin's passing, the hushed whispers of how uncouth it was that the Glorious One should take such interest in a Convert. Quarnar felt the fur along his back raise as he followed just a little closer behind Larin.

Larin shouldered her way west, not changing course until she came to a deep ravine. A series of fallen logs roughly bridged the gap to the other side, and though the wood creaked under paw, Quarnar found them solid enough as he followed Larin across. At one point, she slid on the slick trunks and had to scramble to keep from falling over the edge, but before Quarnar could ask if she was alright, she was on her feet again, shaking lichen and snow from her dark coat. She pointed the way to just beyond the ravine, where a structure of massive proportions lay. Quarnar squinted and couldn't quite determine what it was. It was made of wood, lots of it, all heaped together into a massive pile that rose midway to the canopy. At the very base an opening had been dug out, and Quarnar spotted the glint of eyes watching their approach from within.

"Our Glorious One travels far from the eyrie on a day probably best spent near his den."

The voice rang out from the entrance, and Quarnar paused as a particularly plump brown and white Strigigryph hen stepped into the moonlight. Her yellow eyes were so bright that they seemed to glow against her face. She greeted Larin with a warm nuzzle, and Quarnar tilted his head at the gesture. It was the first time he'd seen a Strigigryph show any sort of affection for a Gryphon aside from himself since coming here.

"My name is Alissi," the hen said. "I'm sure you've seen me around the eyrie before, but we've never been properly introduced!" She bowed quickly, then added, "Please, won't you come in? We desert Gryphs are pretty crafty when it comes to building structures, but it's a little dark, even for my tastes!" She hooted a chuckle of laughter and disappeared into the darkness. "Just follow my voice and I'm sure you'll find your way just fine! No reason to be sitting out chatting in the cold!"

***

The hard earth disappeared beneath Quarnar's claws, replaced by a lining of soft dried grasses.

175

The Converts evidently weren't allowed to have furs or skins to sleep on, but the fragrant plant matter was nearly as comfortable. It reminded Quarnar of the time he'd spent with the Alicorns and in Skyhaven. All around, the sound of sleeping Gryphons filled the air, punctuated by the sharp cries of cubs playing somewhere in the darkness. Lots of chirping and squawking and clicking, but no talking. Quarnar wondered how early the removal of tongues began, and a chill ran down his back. Maybe cubs that grew up in the flock were allowed to keep theirs; he didn't ask. He listened to the rambling of Alissi ahead of him, grateful for the sound of constant chatter to follow.

"I must say, I believe it is so sweet you gave Larin a name! It can be difficult to get a Convert's attention around here, and we can't just go calling them nothing at all. There's usually a very strict process to naming any of the Converts that only Shadowbane can approve. You don't mind the name, do you Larin? I can only assume that he asked you first."

Larin clicked once and continued walking, and before the silence could even begin to envelop them, Alissi was back to talking. Quarnar had a feeling that this was how conversations with this particular hen usually went around here.

"Some of us Strigigryph are top-notch diggers, although I feel bad for making the Gryphons get to it alongside me. Of course, it only makes sense that my ancestors were fond of the earth since there are no real trees to be found in the desert.

We have tons of pokey plants and a few hard, gnarled trees, but you guys grew up in these handy forests and probably have never had to dig a hole in your lives!”

“Shadowbane mentioned you guys are from the ‘desert’ before,” Quarnar said, the first he’d spoken since following Alissi into the woodpile. “I gather that it’s really dry and not the easiest place to live in, but can you explain to me exactly what a ‘desert’ is?” He had to strain his senses to keep close to her in the low light.

“Ooh, the desert contains nothing but sand, dearie!” Alissi replied merrily, although a place with nothing but sand sounded the opposite of a happy place to Quarnar. “Sand, heat, very little water, and many, many scale-kin. Basilisks, drakes, there were even a few Hydra to watch out for. Right here is fine, by the way. Here’s my spot!”

Quarnar’s ears pricked up at the sound of more Hydra like Naugi. The idea seemed preposterous. He promptly walked into a wall of branches and small twigs and reeled back, stunned.

Alissi chuckled again. “I probably should’ve said to stop a little sooner.”

Quarnar shook his head and sat down somewhere beside the Strigigryph, sinking further than he thought he would into the fragrant bedding that had been heaped onto the floor. A rustle next to him heralded Larin sitting down.

"In some parts of this pile, we arranged the wood so that the branches would let in a little light, but it lets in cold air now that it's winter proper, so we've stuffed those holes up with mud. The structural integrity doesn't allow for too much manipulation anyway, so we decided it would be easier just to get used to being in the dark when we're in here instead of shifting the wood around every season."

A murm of a silence passed before she added, "Sorry, I tend to get a little carried away when I'm talking. Larin here usually shoots me a look whenever I go on too much, but I can't see either of you in here, now can I? I've always been this way though, long since before I joined this flock. When I was a cub, my ma used to tell me that if I talked too much at twilight, the prey would hear me from way back at the eyrie, and my pa wouldn't be able to catch anything to eat. Some nights, when we were hungry, I wouldn't speak for entire nights at a time, thinking I was boosting his chances of bringing back some meat—"

"Wait, you chose to join this flock?" Quarnar asked, cringing a little at cutting the hen off so bluntly. She didn't seem to care, or even to notice, as she answered, "Oh yes. Shadowbane and his band were big stuff back in the desert. In the desert, having a group as big as this flock was outrageous. We'd always lived in bands of twos and threes, and it turns out it was with good reason. It wasn't long before their huge group drove away prey. They were hunting the land into exhaustion, but Shadowbane kept bringing in new flock mates from who-knows-where despite it all. Then, one night, he and his closest friend started talking about this amazing place, a land with all the water we could drink, loads of prey so dumb that it practically walked into your open mouth, and no roving bands of scale-kin to worry about.

"I was just a yearling in my own band back then. We shared territory with Shadowbane's flock, and when the Sire himself came by one day to tell everyone about his plan to leave the desert, I was ready to join him. I was always the adventurous sort. It wasn't until I was far from the desert and my family that he started to change. It was… bit by bit."

Alissi's voice took on a somber quality, and it sounded so sad, it almost hurt Quarnar just to listen. "The fact that you are so close with Larin lets me know that I can trust you. And so I'll tell you that the amazing place Shadowbane spoke of obviously turned out to be real, but I would've never come had I known what the price would be. We always lived peacefully with our other Gryph cousins in the desert, and while most Strigigryph believe in the stories of Tsarine, Shadowbane breathed a sinister life into them. When he started to maim and kill those who believed differently than him, I knew I had to stay safe. He always said anyone was free to leave, but after we found the body of one of the first deserters shoddily covered in leaves, no one left again. So… My job is to maintain this pile, and that's what I do. I treat my Gryphon flock mates the same as I treat my Strigigryph ones. I just keep quiet, do as asked, and stay out of

Shadowbane's way while I'm at it."

Quarnar blinked in the absolute darkness. So Shadowbane's campaign had stretched much further than he'd thought. It explained why some of the Strigigryph looked so different from one another, Shadowbane himself least of all. He was the only one here who looked as he did, besides his mate Plithi. Quarnar still thought it to be odd that he'd taken another mate after the passing of his first. He'd mistakenly believed that most creatures were like Alicorns and Gryphons in that they partnered for life.

"Can you tell me more about his friend Quarnar?" Quarnar asked, and he could hear Alissi shaking her head.

"He was quiet. Never talked much. I can't really say much more than that, except that when he was dying, he apparently told Shadowbane that he'd see him again. Shadowbane took that literally. I mean, do you feel like… well, the real Quarnar? Because the last Gryph that looked like you that was brought here before didn't, and Shadowbane killed him right away."

Larin snapped her beak at the words and poked suggestively at Quarnar's side instead. He tore his mind away from the shock of processing her statement and said, "Alissi, I have a huge favor to ask of you. I know that you barely know me, but I'm hoping that you can help me. I need to learn how to fly. And Shadowbane mustn't find out."

"And here I was hoping that you'd come by just to tour my lovely pile." Alissi laughed dryly. "Why couldn't you have made him someone else's problem, Larin?"

The black hen squawked apologetically, and Alissi was quick to say, "I'm just joking. Let me think about it a bit. It's probably already suspicious that you've been here for so long, honestly. If I didn't have guards posted at the entrance, I wouldn't trust speaking like this. News travels fast in Arborochre, Quarnar. The moment you stood up for her—" she gestured in the dark toward Larin—"you made yourself an outcast. Be careful."

Quarnar ignored the implication of her words. "I'm aware," he said.

"Good. Then you'll do whatever it takes to stay in Shadowbane's good graces. And you," Alissi turned so that her voice projected toward Larin. "You must be prepared for anything. Shadowbane doesn't like Converts, least of all you after all of this. I'm sure he'll use you in whatever way he can to control him."

Larin rasped softly, then stood up to cross necks with the Strigigryph hen in farewell. Quarnar straightened up and stood as well. "If anyone asks, I was bringing Larin by to say goodbye to you, since it sounds like Shadowbane expects her to be at my side from now on."

Alissi crooned. "That's the way to think, yearling. You're just smart enough that you may make it out of here alive."

Quarnar followed Larin back out into the snowy night. It was time to start crafting a plan.
***
Quarnar sat on his pile of skins, forelegs crossed, waiting for Shadowbane to return to the den. Larin had taken it upon herself to sit in the far corner of the space, her head tucked underneath a wing as she napped. The black hen was incredibly good at making herself seem small and invisible, which was probably all the better for her when it came to Shadowbane. Their stomachs rumbled in the quiet, but neither outwardly complained.

A commotion from outside brought them to their feet. They ran to the entrance of the den, where Strigigryph were milling about, shouting excitedly in a din that was impossible to pick apart.

"Make way for the prisoners!" rose a cry from a group of warriors. Slowly, the mass of bodies parted to reveal a solemn precession of Ardeigryph, their long necks bowed in shame, their bodies marred with the wounds of battle. Quarnar reeled back in surprise. Weren't these Ratina's kin? What was going on?

Shadowbane flew overhead, calling out shrilly over the eyrie, and all the other Gryphs answered his call in earnest before taking off with haste after him, toward the initiation cavern. Larin took off at a run herself, and Quarnar followed hesitantly, joining her in the assembly that had gathered along the stalagmites.

Shadowbane had taken his usual place along the shore of the pool. The sight of the frozen water prompted Quarnar and Larin to stand a little closer together. They watched as the Ardeigryph prisoners were herded forward until they were spread out before those gathered, their backs to the icy depths of the water.

"Today we have torn away the heart of our scandalous neighbor, Oceanside flock, just as Tsarine promised us through Quarnar. With these heretics removed from the flock, it's likely that the rest of our Ardeigryph cousins will finally turn to Tsarine and ally themselves with us. We wouldn't have been able to do it without the efforts of our very own Ratina, whose familiarity of the territory won us an easy victory."

Shrieks and hoots of adoration rose from the flock, and Quarnar gasped as Ratina herself, her face bearing the claw marks of a brutal struggle, limped from the group to stand beside Shadowbane. She dipped her head in respect to him, and the flock rose into an even higher din of fervor.

"I had my doubts about her when she came here as barely more than a cub herself, bearing visions of grandeur about bringing glory to Tsarine. I originally believed it was impossible for a Gryph other than a Strigigryph to fully appreciate our master, but what greater show of allegiance could one ask for than this? We know where her loyalties lie."

Nods and murmurs of agreement followed. Ratina's eyes didn't search the crowd. She stared straight ahead the entire time, even as Shadowbane walked down to face each of the Ardeigryph, looking them over with interest. "They may not appear the same as us, brothers and sisters, but here we have a group of Gryphs who each will have a chance to join us, if they are willing to make the sacrifice."

More celebrating. Quarnar felt his heart quicken as Plithi stepped forward to question the first Ardeigryph.

"You can save your life by serving Tsarine in this flock, or you can die. Which do you choose?"

The Ardeigryph, obviously shaken, stammered as he looked at Ratina. She avoided his gaze, and finally, he screamed, "You traitor!"

A tension rippled through the space like static, so tangible that Quarnar felt it might rip the place apart. Ratina didn't speak, but the cavern descended into chaos in her defense, many rushing forward as if to slay the Ardeigryph that had spoken themselves.

Quarnar felt sick. He pushed past a wall of Strigigryph and Converts to reach the world outside of the cavern. Fluffy snowflakes brushed past his cheeks as he ran along the frozen stream, feeling as though he were trapped in a dream. He only stopped when he was well downstream of the cavern, and he could still hear the furor from the rest of the flock despite the distance. He wasn't aware that Larin had followed him until she sat down next to him and spread her wing over him, the partial feathering shielding him from the snowfall. She whistled reassuringly and nibbled at the feathers on his neck.

"How are you so cheerful, after all of the terrible things that have happened to you?" he asked. When he looked over at her, she was frowning, her eyes focused on him. Worried about him.

The sound of the stream burbling beneath the ice was a welcome distraction. It was many murms before the flock trailed away from the cavern, back to their lives. And then came the sound of crunching snow, growing nearer and nearer to the trickling water. Larin looked at Quarnar one last time before walking a distance away, and when Quarnar peered up through the falling snow, he could hardly make out the pale disk of Shadowbane's face despite his close proximity to him. The Sire rescinded his earlier statement that Larin stay near Quarnar by sending her away with an annoyed hiss, and she obediently stalked back to the eyrie.

It was harder to force down the ember of hatred that Quarnar had grown for Shadowbane. He was a disillusioned fool, but a powerful fool all the same. Quarnar had rehearsed this moment before in his head, over and over. He took a deep breath. "Shadowbane, I've spent some time thinking."

The Sire continued to stare at him, his expression unreadable. He didn't offer any comment in the quiet that followed, and so Quarnar went on, his voice gaining confidently in volume as he spoke.

"I realize that I've failed you and the flock. For that I'm sorry. I've given you reason to doubt me, and I accept the full blame for it. I know that my duty is to Tsarine first. I've selfishly thought too much of myself these past few weeks. I wish no harm to come to the Convert," he added in reference to Larin, "but I realize I've been quite foolish in my thoughts and actions. All of Gryph-kind needs to learn about Tsarine's great message, and I believe that I was sent back here to deliver that message alongside you."

Shadowbane nodded slowly. "I'm relieved to hear that you've pondered and accepted your role here in Arborochre, Quarnar. I couldn't be more pleased than I am in this moment, dear friend. Let us celebrate this glorious day... by seeing exactly how much I can trust you."

Quarnar froze, but Shadowbane's dark gaze was trained directly on him. He channeled all his energy into maintaining a calm façade as he nodded. He forced his tongue to form the words, "I'd be honored."

***

Quarnar's mind was already racing for ways to get out of whatever Shadowbane was planning. The Sire was leading him deeper and deeper into the forest, away from the eyrie. The further they went, the more of a sinking feeling Quarnar got in the pit of his stomach. They passed by a few Strigigryph guards posted high in the trees, unmoving sentinels that turned only their heads to follow their trek through the forest.

The forest eventually thinned out, and Quarnar's eyes were attracted to bright bits of bleached bone that glowed dully in the moonlight alongside the trail. At the edge of a clearing there stood a group of three Ardeigryph, the oldest of whom must have been ancient, and the youngest merely a cub. They were being guarded closely by half a dozen Strigigryph guards.

"These three are prisoners who wholly and violently reject the teachings of Tsarine," Shadowbane said. "No need to bother questioning them in front of the flock. They will only bring trouble to those who are striving to learn the correct ways. Their continued existence brings shame to Tsarine and her kingdom. They cannot be left to live. And so, Quarnar, you'll show your loyalty by dispatching the first of these agitators... humanely, of course. We aren't monsters here."

Quarnar took a step back, unbelieving. A couple of the guards jostled so that they were directly behind him, cutting off any chance of escape. The old Ardeigryph in the group gazed at him and growled,

"My time is nigh anyway, night-skulking heathen. I'll die and return to Halada this night, if fate demands it. There's nothing to fear in death." The cub, similarly bolstered, puffed his tiny chest.

"I'm not afraid!" he quipped, tail lashing. The other Ardeigryph standing near them didn't move or reply. She just stared unblinkingly at the ground.

"I'm not a killer, Shadowbane," Quarnar said, wilting as the Ardeigryph all turned spiteful stares on him. "I've never killed anything, not even a peryton! You can't expect me to—we can't kill them just because they believe and follow Halada!"

Shadowbane's expression turned dark. "Those sound like the words of a traitor, Quarnar."

"No! No, I'm just saying, there has to be another way."

Shadowbane ignored him. He eyed the group and pointed to the cub. "You. You're brave, I like that. Come here, youngster."

The cub shook visibly and made no motion to move, prompting one of the guards to scruff him and toss him forward. Shadowbane laughed. "I thought you said you weren't afraid?"

"What if he resigns himself to learning the ways of Tsarine?" Quarnar asked, to which the cub spat.

"Over my dead body!" he managed to sputter.

"Shortly, young one," Shadowbane said. "Time wanes, Quarnar, and my patience grows thinner. Either you kill this little one—you're

nearly a yearling, you can definitely kill a cub
cleanly without difficulty—or I send my guards
right now to kill that Convert you covet so much.
What's it going to be?"

Quarnar's mind spun at the sudden ultimatum.
"That's not fair!"

"So, you'd rather I do it?" Shadowbane asked.
He placed a talon on the cub, pinning him to the
ground, and paused before saying, "…But I can
promise you that if I do it, it won't be pretty. It's
either you do it quickly, or you watch me rip his
innards out in front of his mother and this elder."

The old Ardeigryph's eyes flashed. "You truly
are horrid creatures. I hope Naugi's flames burn
you eternally for the things you've done today."

Shadowbane didn't reply. He almost seemed
amused as he pressed into the cub's side, heedless
of the keening cry that peeled from the
youngster's throat.

"Stop!" Quarnar cried. Then, totally defeated,
he whispered, "I'll do it."

Shadowbane chuckled and moved aside,
watching carefully as Quarnar placed a talon on
the cub. The small Ardeigryph's body was soft
and warm under his claws, and he felt
helplessness rise inside him like bitter bile. "I'm
sorry," he said, reaching down to place the cub's
neck in his mouth. He closed his eyes. One sharp
movement, and it'll all be over, he told himself.

"Hmph," Shadowbane mused. "That's enough."

Quarnar's eyes snapped open. Shadowbane laughed and batted the cub toward one of the guards, who promptly snatched him and flew off with him. "We don't kill cubs, doesn't matter where they hail from. You think that fuzzball can really hold onto those bogus beliefs when he's away from heretics like the two still standing here? No! Cubs are valuable resources. But these older ones…" he bobbed his head toward the guards, and they all snapped into action, leaping onto the two Ardeigryph before Quarnar could flinch away. Feathers flew, bones cracked, and blood spattered his pristine white coat amid cries that cut off almost as nearly as they'd started. Quarnar looked away, but it was too late. He'd seen everything.

"Brilliant," Shadowbane said casually, shaking out his coat and spreading his wings in a grand stretch. "I'll take some of both for tonight's dinner. It's a shame Quarnar doesn't seem to have a taste for such exotic meats. Ardeigryph, for whatever reason, are simply delicious! I knew that Tsarine had guided us to this land for some reason. And don't worry, Quarnar," he winked. "Ratina will never know. I'm still disappointed in you, but I think I'll give you another chance. One of you—you, escort him back to the den. And Quarnar," he added, almost looking apologetic, "You'll get over it. Death is simply a part of life. I'd say you've done well today."

***

Quarnar's mind was blank as he trailed

robotically behind the guard. Ardeigryph. He'd eaten the meat of another Gryph. The memory of the pungent meat he'd shared with Shadowbane all that time ago made him want to retch. He couldn't believe that the strange flavor he hadn't been able to place had origins more unsavory than he could've ever imagined.

Shadowbane was a cannibal. Who knew how much more of his flock was? Now that Quarnar had eaten the meat of other Gryphs… what did that make him?

The instant Quarnar reached the den, Larin was waiting for him. She ran over to him, concerned by the drops of blood on his coat until she realized that they weren't his. She clicked questioningly to him. He didn't realize he was shaking until he sat down.

"He's going to make me do horrible things, and continue to do them, until he gets what he wants," he said. "I thought I could fight him, but…" Everything negative he'd ever heard about Shadowbane was slowly solidifying as true, like some kind of nightmare. Larin didn't move, just allowed him to nestle into the soft feathers of her neck. He knew that she felt as helpless as he did, perhaps even more so. She just didn't show it in the same way. He didn't know how long they sat together, feeling small and broken. He just wanted the horrors of this place to end. His eyes trailed down, to the spot on Larin's wing where her flight feathers were absent, grounding her as an eternal servant to Arborochre. There would be hundreds of other Gryphs that would befall the same fate if he didn't at least try to do something.

The ember of hatred he'd held had grown into a roaring flame. It was impulsive, totally alien to him, and in the moment, he invited the rage. It might've been ironic that he felt moved to save the very creatures that had so vehemently ousted him in Skyhaven, but his life here would end up being forfeit one way or another. Either he'd die by Shadowbane's claw, or he would mentally break himself. He straightened up, intent on acting before his nerve failed him. He still had his plan to see Naugi.

"Patrol will be gone in only a few murms, Larin," he said quietly. "I can't wait for Alissi to decide when to come to me."

Larin regarded him with dark eyes. She nodded.

***

Alissi shook her head under the rays of moonlight that filtered through falling snow. "I hadn't really assessed you before," she said honestly. "That, and I've never taught a fully grown Gryph to fly before."

"Grown?" Quarnar exclaimed. "I'm hardly a yearling!"

"Exactly," Alissi said. "All Gryphs learn to fly well before they're yearlings. You should've been practicing moons ago! I mean, look..." She poked despondently at one of his wings, tutting as she examined the muscle that connected them to his body. "They simply wouldn't know what to

192

do with the full weight of a yearling in flight."

Quarnar shook his head, incredulous. "There has to be a way."

Alissi jutted her head toward the cliff side. "If you went and jumped off that edge right now, I can guarantee that your wings wouldn't do a single thing to keep you from crashing. You simply haven't built up enough strength yet, dear. You've eaten and grown plenty—your body is exactly as it should be—but your wings are like playthings for looking at; you haven't exercised them at all."

Quarnar thought back to the way he and Brynne had practiced branching before he'd been kidnapped by Plithi and the other Strigigryph. He'd stopped even attempting to learn to fly after how unnecessary it was here in Arborochre. A regrettable decision. He'd allowed the idea to slip his mind as soon as colder weather had started to set in. "I need to learn, no matter what," he said.

"Then I suggest you practice flapping," Alissi recommended. "It'll help to build up those flying muscles. And then you can practice gliding. Do it as often as you can, and when I return, we'll try some real flying."

"I don't have that kind of time. I need to learn right now, tonight."

"Don't be foolish!" Alissi softened her voice. "Your haste tells me that you've realized what a dire situation you're in. I'm sorry for how things have turned out for you, but if we try tonight, you'll most assuredly just hurt yourself. I'd like to see you leave this place in one piece, Quarnar. Both you and Larin. But I'm also not willing to get myself caught and killed for helping you when it'll be moot. I'll see you after you've practiced like I said."

Alissi called out good naturedly to Larin in the den behind him before walking away, chatting excitedly with various groups of Strigigryph as she went. Seeing her talk to anyone aroused no suspicion from the others; she was obviously chatty and well-liked. Quarnar realized he should've spent more time building relationships with his flock mates here, since it would have made it much easier to gain resources. But the time for that was long over. Perhaps it was for the best that he hadn't, anyway. He was becoming increasingly paranoid about who he could trust.

Quarnar walked back into the den and plopped down next to Larin. After a few murms, he extended his wings, and experimentally beat them. Larin hissed at him and sidled away from the buffets of wind, peering at him from underneath the tail she'd draped over her face. Quarnar stopped flapping. What if Alissi was wrong? She'd only ever taught Strigigryph, and his wings felt fine.

He walked outside, fixed his focus on the cliff side, and started to run. Before Larin could do anything, he was soaring over the edge. He felt the air whistling through the pinions of his wings as a brief blanket of slowing descent engulfed him. Flapping furiously in the weightless moment, he willed himself to rise. The feeling reminded him of the way it felt to fall when he'd been branching with Brynne, right when the terrifying plunge of gravity had grasped him.

Quarnar was probably lucky that he collided with a boulder halfway down his fall. His ribs weren't grateful at all, but he managed to grip the crevices notched into the weather-scarred boulder with his talons, stopping his descent. He righted himself, groaning, as a few Strigigryph asked if he was alright in passing. He waved away their concern, and looked up as Larin neatly scaled her way down to meet him.

"I'm fine," he said, before she could shoot him an anxious gaze. "But this isn't going to work. I can't just sit here waiting for my wings to decide they're capable of flight." He struggled not to wince as he gained his feet. "I'm glad Alissi tried to help, but there's no time. I know where Naugi's lair is… Xio described it to me countless times in stories when I was a cub. I'll go to that Hydra on claw if I have to."

Larin frowned, obviously not liking the idea, but then she gave a slow nod.

"I'd like to bring you with me, but you and I wandering off too far from the eyrie would only attract attention. Plus, I don't think they can see me too well so long as enough of this stuff keeps falling." He held out a wing and caught a few snowflakes on it, and they seemed to disappear among the white feathers there.

Doubt crowded Larin's features.

"Come on, don't give me that look," Quarnar said, prodding at her. "It's probably our best chance. I'll be fine. But… If I'm not, I need to know you're safe, and I don't think you will be if you stay here after I'm gone. Can Alissi hide you, or help you escape to somewhere safer?"

Larin hooded her eyes and nodded again. She gestured to herself and then pointed to the forests beyond, crouching low as if she were stalking something. Quarnar let his eyes drift to the woods.

"I guess I never knew whether you were from a flock or if you were a Primal. But you probably lived in the woods somewhere around here before you were brought here, right?" he asked.

Larin looked up at the sky that was half concealed with clouds, then used her tail to indicate westward.

"I see," Quarnar said. "I don't know how far away you lived, but please be careful. If you disappear, I'm sure your old homeland is the first place they'll look for you. No matter what happens, I'll come looking for you when all this is over."

Larin leaned over to give him an affectionate nuzzle, and he crossed necks with her before watching her pick her way the rest of the distance down the cliff. He waited a few long murms before doing the same himself, sliding and leaping his way to the ground below. Like a good omen, the snowfall continued to drift down, blurring his vision. He headed off into the night due east, toward Naugi's territory.

***

It almost felt easy to slip away from Arborochre now that Quarnar had no choice. It wasn't really about just him escaping anymore. He could probably run to Xio, alert the Alicorns as to what was going on, and maybe they'd take care of it. But the Alicorns had always stayed well away from the conflicts of other creatures. He also couldn't risk them coming to any harm from Shadowbane. He could still hear his voice in his head, calling the Alicorns *unhuntable* prey.

Quarnar stopped moving as his ears picked up on the distinct sound of Strigigryph wings catching the wind over the dense treetops. It was incredible how he could pick out the sound of Strigigryph flight now, when before they had been undetectable. He automatically lay down and buried his claws in the snow, closing his eyes. The sound grew closer and closer… then veered off back toward the eyrie. With his white coat and feathers, Quarnar was virtually invisible to searching eyes, especially from above. He wondered if patrols were already out looking for him, or if the Strigigryph had simply been part of a small hunting party. It didn't matter. After determining that they were far off enough that he could keep moving, he continued east, keeping close to cover whenever he could.

Although he'd already decided that he

wouldn't, Quarnar secretly kept trying to figure out just how close he was to Glendale. With the calming magick over the forest there, it was possible the Strigigryph simply couldn't attack in the sacred land. The very idea of removing himself from the entire situation by taking shelter there was enticing over and over again. But he couldn't just leave all those Converts to suffer. Or the countless other Gryphs that Shadowbane would undoubtedly target as his influence grew. He forced himself to continue pushing further into unknown territory.

Eyes gleamed at Quarnar from the waning darkness. The snuffling of some hidden predator as it crossed his scent and crossed it again reached his ears. He even saw an ursos from just a few feet away, snacking on something it had recently killed. The creature looked up at him with a shaggy head beset with teeth, and then went back to its meal. His stomach perked up at the potential food source, but stopping to hunt or to challenge the ursos for its catch were the last things on his mind. He continued on cautiously, but without the fear he'd held when he was younger. Perhaps he'd grown. Or perhaps he'd realized there were bigger, scarier things in the world than other predators.

After a while, Quarnar no longer heard the cries of Arborochre's sentries. The terrain gradually changed as he travelled, with the giant trees slowly reducing in size and thinning out, disappearing completely as he crested the first of many hills. It took just as much effort to climb the gentle slope covered in snow as it took to

climb the cliff up to Shadowbane's den in
Arborochre, and he stopped to catch his breath
when he finally set claw on top. The sparkling
white domes of dozens more hills stretched out
before him, and he opened his wings, annoyed by
their uselessness. He imagined how quickly he
could make it to his destination if he could simply
fly from here.

It was enough that there were no trees on the
hills, but there was a massive flat plateau that
separated the hills from Naugi's lair. In the
dawning morning, it was impossible to see past
the hazy fog that had settled into the low area,
and Quarnar felt a chill run down his spine as he
wondered what dangers potentially lay in wait
there.

Quarnar took a deep breath, then started to
make his way down the hill at a trot. Momentum
slowly sped his pace up until he was at a flying
sprint, and an idea entered his mind. He took a
mighty leap, flapping his wings as he did so, and
the wind caught under them. Exhilaration
replaced the fatigue the journey had started to
instill in him. When he touched the ground, he
kept speed and launched himself skyward again; it
wasn't flying, but it was better than running.
Much better. He reached the bottom of the first
hill, and rested his wings as he started the grueling
climb up the next. He continued this process in
what felt like an immeasurable number of times,
until he finally reached the base of a hill and
touched down on craggy stones that poked up
above the snow.

Quarnar felt like slowing to rest a little, but the openness of the space urged him into continuing at a brisk lope. The land here seemed frozen in time, completely silent. There was no movement, no sounds from other creatures, just the stark padding of his own feet as he raced across the flat expanse. The sun crested the sky and then hung there lazily amid cloud cover, providing light but no warmth to those trapped in the winter below. It took many murms for the outline of a massive mountain to become visible in the haze.

Quarnar plodded along, wishing he could find some water to slake his thirst. He'd never walked so far or so long in his life. It was sweet, merciful relief when the mountainside eased closer and he finally arrived at its base. He allowed himself to stumble to a stop to catch his breath, unprepared for the climb it would take to reach Naugi's lair somewhere up above. The icy air felt good to his lungs as he allowed himself to lie down for a quick rest, the rock digging into his sides. It seemed safe enough. After all, there weren't any signs of any other creature around for miles. After a while, he looked up to select the best path to scale upward, and all at once, the section of the mountainside he was leaning against came undone.

***

Quarnar leaped back with a cry, his mind struggling to process what was occurring as a landslide of some sort. But the rock wasn't crushing him, it was moving *around* him. He scrambled back, but the mountainside was somehow taking deliberate movement toward him now, and he cowered as two eyes recessed

200

deep into the stony crags of the configuration fixed upon him. It wasn't the ridge itself that had moved toward him, but something even more terrifying. Its scales as gray and rough as the stones surrounding it, the massive basilisk opened its maw into a grimace and regarded Quarnar with disdain.

"What insolent creature wakes me from my slumber by resting against my tail?" the basilisk boomed in a voice so loud, the frozen earth quaked. Quarnar couldn't wrangle his tongue to speak. He struggled to break his gaze with the creature, but terrifyingly discovered that he couldn't. It wasn't until the basilisk blinked that he could control his trembling eyelids enough to shut. He took off at a mad sprint back toward the hills he'd left behind, but a massive tail was thrown before him, cutting off his only escape route. He turned to face the basilisk again, who was sniffing toward him with a gigantic pair of nostrils.

"Ahh…" the creature breathed, flicking a long, serpentine tongue against his cheek, "a small winter snack to send me back to sleep…"

Iba's warning about never approaching a basilisk rushed to Quarnar in a useless jumble. The basilisk opened his mouth, and serrated teeth that were browned with age glinted in the frosty air. His end would not be a pleasant one. He started to scream.

A sound that dwarfed even the booming of the basilisk swept across the plateau, and

Quarnar's oppressor immediately recoiled and backed away, folding into the cliff side until he was once again indistinguishable from the nooks and crannies that composed the ridge. A figure plummeted from the summit of the precipice, landing before Quarnar with enough force to leave a sizeable crater in the earth. The sight of the alpha himself took Quarnar's breath away. Naugi had come to him.

***

"What fool has wandered so close to my domain?" Naugi asked, his third head spouting a ferocious plume of flame. His voice was deep and brassy, filling Quarnar's head until there was no room for his own thoughts. Naugi's many eyes slanted at the same time. "I recognize you. I gave you to Xio to care for only a breath ago. Why have you come to me? Has Xio become so cavalier as to send you on his behalf, instead of gracing me with his presence himself?" The Hydra sounded disrespected at the very thought, and Quarnar forced his tongue to comply.

"No, great Naugi! I have come under my own power. I need your help."

The Hydra was not amused. "I concern myself not with the day-to-day activities of your kind. If you wish for me to attend to any matter, send your leader… if they dare to face me." He began to turn away then, and Quarnar stammered in his haste to stop him.

"W-wait! You don't understand! There are intruders in your land! They are trying to torture and enslave all of Gryph-kind!"

The Hydra's twisting jaws gave him the appearance of smirking. "You think that I don't know this, Gryphon?"

"You mustn't let the Strigigryph stay in your territory! Please!"

Naugi's already short patience had run out. "I will not speak with one so lowly as yourself, nor take the time to heed your warnings. I myself shall test the newcomers on their worthiness when I fly to their settlement anon. If you've a problem with your kind, you must sort it out among yourselves. Gather the other Gryphs and deal with it however you wish to. But do not come here again. Had you not been Xio's, I would have killed you by now… or let Simik eat you. Begone!"

"But-!"

Naugi rushed at him with a speed that belied his heft. Quarnar didn't know if it was fang, tail, or sharp claw, but something pierced into his hind end and tossed him, winding him as he landed some distance away. Naugi snarled in dismissal and dug his claws into the rock of the cliff and scaled the distance to the top as easily as Quarnar would have scaled a log. The Hydra disappeared into the heights of the clouds, and Quarnar shakily got to his feet. He could feel warm blood trickling down his belly, but he didn't have time to assess how bad it was. He was snapped back to his senses as the murderous eyes of Simik gleamed at him from where he'd tucked himself back into the cliff side, and Quarnar briskly backed away, turning to sprint back across the plateau.

Naugi wasn't going to help. That left one thing to do.

***

It was quite possible that Sheba was still alive. Ratina hadn't been able to verify whether Shadowbane's warriors had actually raided Skyhaven or not. If she was alive, as Quarnar dearly hoped, he was sure that she wouldn't take kindly to him returning and asking for her help against the Strigigryph, especially after the trouble he'd already caused. After all, hadn't that been exactly what the Primals had pleaded her for? And he needed to make sure that the Alicorns knew what was going on. Maybe there was something they could do that he wasn't aware of. At the very least, they would know what had been causing all the deaths in the forest.

Quarnar determined that he was closer to Skyhaven than to Glendale, making his decision to travel there first an easy one. By now Shadowbane would be aware of his desertion, and would be looking for him. He hoped that Larin was safe, but somehow he had more faith in her abilities than his own.

Quarnar had made it to the base of the hills, where he finally felt safe that Simik wasn't going to attempt feasting on him after all. With the fear of the massive basilisk gone, he peered at the wound in his flank, and though it had bled a worrying amount, the blood had already started

204

to clot. Evidently whatever Naugi had punctured him with, though it had hurt terribly, had hardly travelled into his flesh. It was obvious that the Hydra could've easily killed him, but had chosen not to. He silently thanked Xio for his association with the surly guardian, as it seemed to have been the only thing that had spared his life.

There was nothing Quarnar could do for the wound in his frozen surroundings, and so he forced himself to begin the journey up the first of many hills. He had to continue on; rest could come later. The longer he stayed in any one spot, the more time he gave Shadowbane to act on finding him and Larin.

The walk back to the forest had been twice as grueling as the original trek, and Quarnar's stomach growled loudly enough that he feared the wrong ears would hear it. It had been easy to ignore the gnawing pangs of hunger on his way to Naugi's lair. He'd been so wrapped up in his purpose that he'd hardly paid any mind. But now, combined with the growing weakness in his body from his wound, every step was draining. He could scarcely concentrate. He grunted, more in annoyance than pain. He needed to find something to eat, or he wouldn't make it past another night.

After finding and drinking deeply from the iced slurry of a slow-moving stream, Quarnar settled in to do what he did best. It'd been a while since he'd scavenged, but he still knew the tell-tale signs of a free meal. He remembered the ursos he'd seen the previous night, and started to carefully retrace his steps. The beast had to be done with eating its fill by now. He hoped.

The wood seemed unusually still as Quarnar limped as quietly as he could through the area he'd originally seen the ursos. It was impossible to make out any prints on the ground, as fresh snow had covered all traces of his earlier passing. He swept the same area twice over, keeping his eyes low and his ears high for any sounds that suggested danger. He probably wouldn't have been successful had he not noticed a spot where the surrounding foliage had been trampled and flattened. With a bit of careful searching, he was able to find drag marks under the newest layer of snow, and just beyond those, a heap of dead leaves, twigs, and shallow earth, all shoddily concealing what was left of a peryton carcass. It was definitely the leftovers of an ursos.

Quarnar felt anxiety prickle in his gut as he eyed the stowed cache, feeling like he'd be torn into by the owner of the hidden meat at any moment. After listening for what felt like eons and glancing in all directions, he chanced to move in. There was enough eaten off the carcass that he could easily move what was left of it if he had to, but that would make a lot of noise, and he wasn't sure that he wanted to. He uncovered the cache and started to eat as quickly as he could, unbothered by the chunks of grit and dirt he ingested along with the meat. It had already long since frozen solid, and it took a few solid tugs to get even small chunks to pull free. From the first bite, he gluttonously consumed all that he could. Any smaller bones, he ate whole. Nothing else seemed to matter except getting the meat inside his belly.

A loud snap shot through the silence.

Quarnar's ears flicked in the direction of the noise. He started a low hiss in his throat. And then he wheeled around just as the ursos sow began to charge.

*****

Injury or not, Quarnar had never moved so fast before. He dug his claws into the nearest tree and drew his body up in a fluid heave, letting his good legs take the brunt of his weight. He watched the ursos circle below, snorting and pawing at the base of the tree. Her fangs glinted maliciously as she pointed her beady eyes up at him, and to his horror, she thrust her long claws into the bark and strained upward, her ugly face contorting into a grimace with the effort. She planted both hind limbs into the trunk and heaved, looping a paw around a thick bottom limb, her small eyes flicking to him and then back to her task. Quarnar knew from his time with the Alicorns that any ursos not hibernating this late into the season was probably mad with starvation, too skinny to sleep the whole winter through. The determination of this one confirmed the prognosis. Quarnar let fear take him until he could feel the sow's sour breath huffing up to his paws. And then something clicked in his mind.

How can you save anyone if you can't even survive an encounter with this dumb beast? Quarnar couldn't place where the whispered thought had come from, but it took him like a storm. Ursos were powerful, yes, but they were also simple creatures driven almost purely by instinct. This one obviously felt like defending her cache, and so she was expending all of her effort into doing that. Was he not smarter than this remedial creature? He probably deserved to be eaten if he couldn't even save himself from being treed by another predator.

Quarnar drew himself up and stretched his wings as wide as he could, raising the fur along his back until it stood on end. He let loose with a screech the likes of which he had never made before. The ursos, undaunted, roared back, but instead of being frightened, the challenge awakened his defiance. The sow seemed to find hidden strength, pulling herself further up the tree trunk, placing herself directly below him. The frozen tree groaned under her weight. A probing paw equipped with claws that tripled the length of Quarnar's own swiped at him, and he surprised even himself by first snapping at the paw with the intent of tearing off digits, and then throwing himself ruthlessly down onto her.

The beast's shocked cry filled Quarnar's ears as he ripped and tore mercilessly at whatever he could find: an ear, the fur above an eye, lips, a wet nose. The ursos flopped on the ground in anguish, intent to unseat the demon that had planted itself firmly onto her back, but Quarnar held on with the strength of pure desperation. He no longer felt the pain in his hind leg. That meat would be his, one way or the other.

The ursos, now sporting her own newfound

sense of desperation, rolled completely over, momentarily crushing him under her weight. The air pushed from his lungs, Quarnar let go, managing to stumble back just fast enough to miss the brunt of the sow's huge paw hurtling toward him. One blow from that deadly weapon easily had enough force behind it to eviscerate him. She threw another knife-edged paw at him, spittle flying from her long lips as she roared, and the tip of her longest claw painted a bright gash across his chest. Quarnar was already advancing forward again, wings open, hooked bill aiming at anything that would elicit the most pain from the beast. He managed to connect with an eye, and the sow screamed at him with fury, rearing up so that she towered over him. He shrieked back, and she faltered, landing on all fours again. There was a tense moment as the two stared each other down, huffing in the cold, and then miraculously, the ursos's roar transformed into a plaintive whimper. She took a step back, beaten.

Quarnar watched the sow's lumbering hulk move off through the trees, and it took him a few murms to realize he could let the hiss die in his throat. The weight of his victory only sank in as he went back to tearing semi-frozen chunks from the peryton carcass, feeling the huge flakes of falling snow numb his wounds.

He had gone up against an ursos—one of the most fearsome beasts in the region—without training and without flight. And he'd won.

CHAPTER TEN

Quarnar shifted his course to head in what he hoped was northwest. Billowy white sails of snow were beginning to drift high, tucking against the base of tree trunks and coating tree limbs high above. He hadn't been able to see the sun well enough to recalibrate his course for the majority of the day. It would be night again soon. His shoulders ached from his tireless loping, and he'd tripped over his own clumsy paw falls twice now. The wound in his flank reminded him regularly of its existence. A headache was beginning to start between his ears. He hadn't drunk deeply enough from the stream he'd crossed earlier, and he quickly learned that eating snow didn't quench thirst the way he thought it would. But every step was precious. He couldn't give up.

Quarnar pushed forward, panting in the frigid air, head down and eyes closed except for when he needed to take in his bearings or weave through a particularly tight clump of trees. Sunset was threatening the horizon when he finally

stumbled, wing tips brushing the ground, down
the side of an embankment. He tried once to rise,
but his muscles betrayed him and he quivered
back to the earth. It was all he could do to tuck
his head under a wing and to fluff his fur and
feathers against the cold. He unwillingly let sleep
spirit him away.

***

Quarnar awoke to a soft crunching sound, and
he was immediately alert. A pair of quizzical eyes
peered at him from above stilt-like legs and a long
beak.

An Ardeigryph!

It cried out in alarm before he could speak,
flying off despite him yelling that he only wanted
to talk. Then he winced. Every fiber of his body
protested to his sudden rise, and even taking one
step took a gargantuan amount of effort. He
forced himself to stretch, ever so carefully.
Despite the pain, it seemed to help. He surveyed
the area around him and noted that aside from
the tracks the Ardeigryph had made, everything
else was undisturbed. He'd been lucky. He
couldn't afford to sleep so carelessly again.

Examining the sky initially confused Quarnar.
The sunset he'd fallen asleep to had been replaced
with sunrise, and the colors were nearly identical.
The clouds had finally cleared out, and the moon
and stars were a dim backdrop to the rising sun.
The Ardeigryph had flown northeast. Was it
possible that Oceanside flock was nearby? It had
to be. And despite everything Ratina had said
about the flock, he had to see if they would be

willing to provide any help, especially after what Shadowbane had done to them.

The going was slow. Quarnar had eaten enough the previous day that he wasn't at all peckish, but that was probably the only good thing about the way he felt. The slash the ursos had given him made it feel like the skin on his chest was being pulled too taut with each step, and his flank had gone numb where Naugi had struck him. The cold helped, as at least there were no flies to pester the wounds. As Quarnar limped along, his ears kept catching a sound he couldn't place. It was clearly something big, and the further he traveled, the more volume it gained.

Quarnar plugged his way to the top of a small incline, and was met with the source of the roaring. The largest body of water that he'd ever seen undulated in the distance, its sparkling depths unhindered by ice. Near the shore, the waves were small and peaceful, but he could see how much larger and more vicious they became further out. And there was something else he could see as well, in the form of movement along the cliffs that tumbled out partway into the sea. Oceanside flock.

Quarnar wasn't sure exactly how best to approach Oceanside, but his message was important enough that he didn't spend too much time thinking about it. It was thankfully daytime, since he assumed that coming in the night after what the Strigigryph had done to them would be particularly unwise. And then there was the fact that he was… well, himself. He didn't know how

Ardeigryph viewed 'Spirit Walkers', but most of him was too tired to care.

Quarnar ambled along the beach looking for a way up the cliffs, keeping an eye on the waves that slapped and reached up the sand toward him. They dragged whatever was caught in the current back into the water, very unlike the lazy ponds, lakes, and streams he grew up around. He didn't like it, but his thirst tempted him closer and closer to the current. He waited for the crescendo of water to rush up again before darting his beak down for a sip, and he instantly gagged and spat as an intense salt flavor coated his tongue. Choking and spitting, he was grateful he hadn't attempted to gulp more from the brine.

Quarnar had hardly made it a fraction of the way to the cliffs before he heard a cacophony of wild shrieks. A dozen Ardeigryph flew toward him in an arrow formation with their crests held high and tails lashing. It clearly wasn't going to be a friendly reception. Quarnar dropped and rolled over onto his back, hoping that the show of submission would stall them from immediately trying to kill him. It seemed to work. Instead of stabbing him to death with their sharp bills, they instead surrounded him and demanded him back to his feet.

"On all fours, stranger!" a gray keythong ordered in an exotic warble. "Any suspicious moves, and we'll spear that pearly liver of yours out!"

Quarnar complied, trying to decide whether it

was in his best interest to remain silent or to plead his case. The Ardeigryph all towered above him despite lacking any real bulk. Everything about them was long and thin, from their graceful tails that undulated like the water itself, to the long crests on their heads that reached down to curl against their shoulders.

"That's him, Bala!" one of the Ardeigryph cried out. "That's the one I saw out in the wood! Probably a spy for those monsters!"

An obvious wave of paranoia rippled through the group.

Bala, the apparent leader, narrowed his eyes. "He could easily be one of the enemy's flock for all we know. We'll take no chances. Cast him out into the sea… watch him to make sure he drowns."

Quarnar yelped as a tangle of beaks and claws reached to scruff him, vying for who would personally deliver him to death. He snapped at a few of the offenders before managing to belt out, "I'm not a spy! Ratina is a traitor to you! I've seen it with my own eyes!"

The Ardeigryph all paused as Bala raised a single wing, and they dropped their hostility.

"Take him back to the cliffs!" he growled after a brief murm. "We'll question him there."

***

The wind gusted around the high cliffs with a vengeance. Quarnar sensed he was no longer in immediate danger, but the Ardeigryph were all still rightfully untrusting. He rubbed the back of his neck where he'd been snatched and unceremoniously hoisted up onto the rocky heights of the cliffs. The flock had quickly learned that he wasn't much of a flier.

"Let's start with the basics," Bala said. "What's your name?"

"My name is Q-" Quarnar let the name die on his tongue. It had been so long that he'd almost forgotten that he'd had a name before he'd joined Shadowbane's flock. The name of Quarnar seemed sullied, like a curse. He hoped he'd never have to be associated with it again. "My name is Arias," he finished, eliciting the Ardeigryph to glance among themselves.

"So you say she's alive, with certainty?" Bala asked, eyeing him with a hard glint. "I'd hoped she'd been injured enough in that last scuffle to lie down and die someplace. Pity. Next time, I'll put her down myself if it's the last thing I do."

Arias eyed him with interest. *That's the kind of spirit we'll need to take on the Strigigryph*, he thought. "She's alive, and was quite clear in that her loyalties lie with whichever party is winning. I can't speak for whether that is right or wrong, I just know that I can't allow what is happening in that flock to spread any further."

Bala spat. "I'd rather die a good death ten times over than be a filthy traitor."

"If you don't mind me derailing a bit," Arias said carefully, "what's been happening around here? I can imagine that it's the same as what must be happening to all the flocks in the area… Shadowbane has been taking prisoners and killing any who stand against him. Have you heard any of Skyhaven flock?"

"Shadowbane," Bala said thoughtfully, rolling the word on his tongue in his strange accent. "The name of the enemy. And you think I'll just trade information with you, white one? How do I know that you're not here to collect what you learn to take back to your precious Nightstalkers?"

"I already told you, I'm not one of them," Arias fired back. "I'd appreciate it if you would stop referring to me as such. I hate Shadowbane's flock just as much as you do for the things they're doing to other Gryphs. Keep me prisoner here if you'd like, if that's what it'll take for you to stop thinking I'm in with his lot."

Bala studied him. He was clearly a younger keythong, though all the others looked to him as leader. Finally, he said, "How can I know that I can trust you?"

Arias shrugged his pale shoulders. "I don't know how to answer that. I'll tell you whatever you'd like about the Strigigryph if you'll help to rally with me against them. I already met with Naugi, and he won't have anything to do with ousting them. It disgusts me to think that he might give them his blessing to stay in this territory."

A trill of shock rose up in the group. "You went to see the great Hydra himself?" Bala asked incredulously, "And lived to tell about it? Bah! Your tales grow too tall!"

Arias pointed with his beak toward the north and scoffed. "He lives clear that way, on a ridge that makes this one look like a dirt clod. And a creature almost as ferocious as he himself guards it. It had eyes that you couldn't break your gaze away from." A shudder ran through his body at the remembrance. "It takes away your ability to control your movements. Only Naugi stopped it from killing me right then and there, but then he sent me off with a warning I won't soon be forgetting."

He lifted his hind leg. "How do you think I got this? You probably wouldn't even believe that this one on my chest came from an ursos."

The Ardeigryph all looked doubtful, but no one said anything. Finally, Bala said, "Oceanside flock doesn't believe in the silly superstitions of you Gryphons regarding so-called 'Spirit Walkers'. But how have you survived this long? Is it not their custom to exile or to do away with ones like you from birth? You mentioned Skyhaven, and so I assume that is where you hail from."

Arias wasn't sure if he wanted to bring up the Alicorns. His audience already seemed not to believe much of what he'd said so far. But what other choice did he have? There was no lie that could accurately take the place of his story.

Arias sighed, feeling tired. "Can I please tell you the entire story, from the beginning, without the threat of being thrown to my death?" he asked.

Bala gave a single, curt nod.

"I was born in Skyhaven, but I was never made privy to who my parents were," he started. "When I hatched out looking like this, the Matriarch took it upon herself to end me, but for some reason, she went to Naugi instead of doing me in herself. And when he vowed to kill me, an Alicorn named Xio stepped in and saved me…"

***

Arias was exhausted. He'd been left to rest at the top of the cliff under the watchful eye of three sentries while the rest of the Ardeigryph debated his tale. He'd told them everything he thought relevant, pushing through with confidence at the more fantastical portions despite the rumbles of dissent from his audience, and ending with emphasis on Shadowbane and his plans for the other flocks.

The Ardeigryph had brought up tough, woven mats of dried seaweed for him to lie upon, and a shell of some sort filled with fresh water. He'd drained the water and was just dozing off when the wet thud of something slimy being thrown to the ground in front of him jostled him awake. He opened his eyes to see a scaly creature with fins, and a further glance showed him that the

Ardeigryph who'd dropped it was choking down another one of the scaled beasts with gusto. He recoiled without completely meaning to.

"Thanks, but I'm good," he said, trying to hide his disgust.

"Bala's orders," the Ardeigryph replied. He was bigger than the others, much bigger, but that didn't stop Arias from denying his offering.

"I don't care whose orders, look at it! I'm not even fully convinced it's food to be honest."

The Ardeigryph didn't budge. "You're no good to us if you have no strength. It won't kill you, I just ate one, didn't I? That's probably why you Gryphons have such dull coats, none of you know how to enjoy a good wriggler. Stop being such an insolent cub and just eat it!"

"I'm not a cub, I'm a yearling," Arias said, as though it made a difference. "And you can't make me do anything."

The Ardeigryph seemed to take up the challenge. "Can't I?"

"Stop!" One of the trio guarding Arias said, rolling his eyes in annoyance. "Would ya please just shut up and eat the darn wriggler, young one? We have better things to be worrying about than whether you're starving to death at the moment… no offense intended, of course."

Arias looked down at the wriggler again, and

he jumped as it reflexively took a gasp of air, fluttering its gills. "It's not even dead yet!" he snapped.

"So? Never eaten anything that still has a kick or two still left in it? Just means it's fresh."

Arias shook his head. "No!"

"What kind of Gryphons are Sheba raising up over there?" one of the Ardeigryph muttered, and another corrected him quietly by chuckling and saying, "Alicorn, remember?"

"I don't care what you all say, I'm not eating that thing. Especially when it's still moving like that," Arias said.

The Ardeigryph who'd originally brought the wriggler reached down and nipped its head off in one fluid motion, and Arias watched the tail of the wriggler flop unceremoniously a few times before it finally twitched and lay still.

"Well?" the Ardeigryph said. His companions seemed to lean in as one.

Arias sighed, mostly resigned to eating the thing so that the rest of the long-bills would leave him to some peace and quiet. He grabbed it by its tail, and was immediately slapped in the face by a wing.

"Not that way! You've got to eat it the way the scales run. Go on now, flip it."

Arias narrowed his eyes and picked the wriggler up by where its head would've been, downing it in one gulp. He was initially repulsed by the slimy coating on the outside of it, but wasn't prepared to be pleasantly surprised by the mild flavor.

"It's not as bad as it looks," he murmured.

Despite their haughty behavior, the Ardeigryph all looked smug.

"Maybe there's some hope for Gryphons yet, if they can recognize good food after all," one of the guards mused.

Arias didn't bother to reply. He was just about to tuck his head under his wing to get some rest when the Ardeigryph who'd caught the wriggler poked nonchalantly at the wound in his flank. He yelped and hissed in response, but the keythong paid him no mind and started to speak with the others.

"Looks way worse up close, eh?"

The other Ardeigryph nodded in unison, tutting.

"Better get some sea water on that, it'll help him right out."

"It'll be fine," Arias said. "I've encountered enough injuries to know that—"

The Ardeigryph who'd brought the wriggler

cut him off.

"Right then, hold him down! I'll bring up some water."

***

Arias was in no mood for conversation. He'd been restrained by a number of gangly limbs while ice-cold sea water had been poured into his wounds, and then he'd been tossed, as gently as he supposed anyone could be tossed, into a den in the cliff side facing the sea. Years of erosion had left natural pits in the hard stone, and the Ardeigryph had lost no time in moving into those that were large enough to inhabit.

It was a bit terrifying at first, being able to see nothing except the shining black movement of the ocean under the moonlight. Some Ardeigryph had placed bits of colorful stone and seashell into this particular den, indicating that it had been lived in before Arias had taken it. The hard ground was made marginally softer with the addition of the woven seagrass mats, but not by much. The amenities did little to detract from the knowledge that there was no escape except via flight or swimming past the turbulent depths to the shore. The rock around Arias was unyielding to the heavy waves that pushed and pulled against it, so at least it felt stable. The worst part was the sound. It was almost impossible to sleep through. Almost. He was too tired to be picky.

"So what's an Alicorn like anyways? Must have interesting personalities after being alive for so long. Did you ever feel weird, living with creatures like that?"

It wasn't just the sound of the ocean that kept Arias awake. The Ardeigryph who'd originally brought the wriggler was crammed next to him. Arias shot him an irritated look that wasn't heeded. The cheeky keythong was his guard for the night.

Arias was beginning to feel worse and worse with each passing murm. He didn't know anything about venom, but he knew that Naugi was certainly capable. Would the Hydra have subjected him to a slow death on purpose? He shivered and buried his head deeper into the ruff of feathers at his neck. It seemed that he couldn't get warm no matter what he did. "I'm tired," he declared, hoping to somehow quiet his den mate.

"And I'm curious," the Ardeigryph responded.

Arias ignored him and tucked his head under his wing instead. He could still sense the Ardeigryph's eyes on him.

"Ey, you're probably coming down with something, huh?"

Arias squeezed his eyes shut tighter and tried to plunder more comfort out of the thin seagrass mats. They offered none. He longed for the deep furs he'd slept on back in Arborochre. He supposed the Ardeigryph wouldn't have anything like that, out here on the ocean. Not even anything close.

He dug his talons into the crispy seagrass.

After a few murms, he felt the Ardeigryph next to him shuffle closer, and he stiffened at the violation of personal space. He was just about to give him a piece of his mind for bothering him again when he found himself relishing how much warmer it was with another Gryph so close by. Not that he really liked cozying up next to a stranger, but it beat feeling like he was freezing to death. He opened an eye to peer skeptically at him, but the keythong only shrugged and said, "No use to us if you aren't alive to question, you know. My name's Tybrake by the way. Try to get some sleep."

***

The overcast sky set a pale, ghostly hue over Oceanside in the morning. Arias didn't even truly rise, just roused enough to watch Tybrake drop out of the niche in the cliff and vanish from view. It felt weird to wake up to daylight again. He watched Tybrake reappear and sail over the ocean, calling out in a shrill screech before folding his wings and dropping into the waves like a spear. Arias blinked twice, the visage of the Ardeigryph seeming blurry. He thought he remembered Tybrake asking if he wanted anything to eat, but he couldn't really remember. He wasn't cold anymore, but the burning heat that had replaced it was no better. He didn't recall drifting back off to sleep.

The sun was absent when thirst dragged Arias into wakefulness. To open his eyes fully felt like it took too much effort, and he had to squint to determine what the objects next to him were. There was a wriggler, with the head expertly bitten off, and a shell of clear water that he wasted no time in downing. His blood felt like fire in his veins, and the cold liquid was a welcome relief. He disregarded the wriggler, commanding his sluggish gaze to drift over to a figure that was directly beside him.

It wasn't Tybrake. He could make out that much. This was a hen, her coat and feathers a beautiful marbled black and white. Her eyes were as milky as the round stones she had spread before her, all of which she was lightly picking at, cocking her head this way and that. Her bill was moving, but Arias's ears couldn't strain hard enough to make out any words. He thought he could see movement outside, but the blistering light was too difficult to stare directly at, especially with the way the blood was pounding in his head. He closed his eyes, but the hen was bothering him again, pulling at his crest and whistling to him. He opened his eyes again and she shoved the wriggler closer to him, but the idea of eating made his stomach turn. He turned away from her with some effort, and after a while she left him alone. The sea returned to being the endless lullaby he slept to.

Arias had lots of visitors, but he remembered none save for the Ardeigryph who spent the most time with him, the white and black hen. She offered him another wriggler again the next day, and the day after that. She managed to force him to eat it on the latter attempt, but his body suddenly and violently rejected it, and she stopped trying. In his fevered sleep, Arias couldn't think. All he knew was that something was very, very wrong.

Arias eventually became aware of a hunger that grew into a gnawing pain in his gut, but the effort it took to even open his mouth to eat seemed like an impossible task. The white and black hen continued bringing him wrigglers, but he had no taste for the strange sea life. The very thought of eating one made him gag. At some point, she lost patience and shoved something into his mouth that was more familiar to him, and he ate gratefully of whatever it was. She dripped cool sea water through his feathers to try to help drive down his fever, and though it seemed to help, it was uncomfortable to endure. The water was frigid as it contacted his skin, and he fought against her; it was a battle he lost without fail, because she had no problem with calling Tybrake to come sit on him to hold him still.

These activities went on for a seemingly indefinite amount of time, until suddenly, one morning, he awoke with some sense of clarity. The hen was next to him, where he'd come to expect her to be by now. The moment he shifted, her milky eyes fluttered open.

"More water?" she asked gently, rising in one fluid motion.

It took Arias a bit of wrestling to create a sound with his voice, and when he did, the rusty sound of it surprised him. "No… thank you, though."

The hen's sightless eyes grew wide. "You're present, then," she said. "This is great news, I must tell Bala immediately!"

"Wait," Arias said, clearing his throat to see if it would help his voice to return to normal. "Who are you? You've been helping me. I know that much. Thank you for that. Also… I've never seen eyes like yours before. Why is that?"

"Ah," the hen said, settling back down. "My name is Nanchu. The others tell me that I'm blind. I've no idea what my eyes look like to you, nor how they should. I've always been this way. There are things I suppose you are able to 'see' that I simply can't?" Her tone took a lighter sound. "I see plenty, however. I've never felt any different."

"What do you do with those white stones?" Arias asked.

"Pearls," Nanchu amended. "They simply help me to focus. You were sick with a venom the likes of which no one here has ever had the misfortune to encounter. We were sure you would die, actually. When Tybrake grew weary of attending to you, I took over. He didn't want to be here alone if you died. Most Gryphs shy away from the presence of death, but the concept of it has never bothered me, as odd as that may sound." She brushed a talon thoughtfully over the spheres. "You're quite strong to have pulled through. Gryphs have died to less."

Arias blinked and turned to look at his flank. The flesh around the puncture was dark in color, and it was still quite painful if he moved carelessly, but it wasn't as bad as it had been. He closed his eyes against a wave of dizziness and lay back down. Evidently, movement took too much effort.

"As I understand it, there has been a worrying series of events while you were resting," Nanchu said. "I must go find Bala now."

Arias lifted his ears at the cryptic parting message, but Nanchu was already gone. It took mere murms before Bala swooped up to speak with him, Tybrake on his heels. There was hardly room for the three of them in the small space, but Tybrake dug his claws into the cliff side and snaked his long neck into the den to be present.

"You were right, Arias," Bala said. "The Strigigryph will stop at nothing. You are weak still, yearling, and I don't mean to push you too hard too soon. But there's something you need to see. I have a feeling what has happened is the work of the enemy."

Tybrake's voice was tight with fear. "I couldn't believe my eyes when I flew guard duty a couple of days ago." He glanced nervously at Bala. "There's still time. Can't we just fly away and re-establish the flock elsewhere?"

"No, you dally fool!" Bala said quickly. "These creatures will not simply leave us in peace if we give them our land. They want blood. They'll hunt us down until nothing is left. Arias, do you think you can be moved?"

Arias nodded, though when he attempted to stand the world immediately reacted by swaying nauseatingly. He crawled to the entrance of the cavern, feeling pitiful, but the fresh air was refreshing and cleared his head a bit. Tybrake released his grip on the cliff side and flew by, hovering just long enough to pluck him carefully from the ledge. He didn't have to fly far over the beach for Arias to see what he, Nanchu, and Bala had been talking about. His heart withered in his chest at the sight.

The beach was peaceful, hauntingly quiet save for one spot where the sand was ruddy with old blood. Saltwater faes rustled their wings and flew away in alarm, calling loudly in their crude, unintelligible language as Tybrake gently dropped Arias nearby the soiled sand.

The body itself was nearly unrecognizable, twisted in death as it was. The eyes had been gouged out, and every feather plucked away. No tongue was left in the long beak that was parted wide as if still screaming silently. The worst part was that the carcass had clearly been eaten from, and not by any simple beast. Select cuts of the body and organs had been removed, and Arias yet again resisted the urge to retch. It was clearly Shadowbane's doing... and a message that he'd be back for more.

Arias had resisted telling the Ardeigryph about the cannibalism because he hadn't wanted to take the chance of frightening the fighting spirit out of them. But now...

"We need to prepare to defend ourselves," Arias said. "We can't just let them continue doing things like this."

"Fight with what?" Tybrake cried desperately. "We haven't got the numbers. We haven't got the skill, Arias. We're made for spearing wrigglers and flying long distances, nothing else. Our ancestors moved us here because it was peaceful… but it was only a matter of time, wasn't it? Maybe the end will come quickly. Poor Presida. I should've never let her go on night watch alone. What if they took their time killing her? What if—"

"How dare you!" Arias, half dead though he felt, was overcome with disgust. "To simply give up like that. When I first came here and saw your entire flock heading toward me, I thought I was going to die. I was maybe even as afraid as I had been when I faced Naugi. But I still had a mission, and I was going to see it through. You get faced with a real threat, and you just crumble and give up? I didn't come all the way here for this. I won't see Shadowbane win." His sudden anger was replaced with fatigue, and he slumped down in the sand, taking a steadying breath. "You think Presida wants to be left dead in the sand without the knowledge that her flock has revenge in their hearts? She deserves at least that, I think."

Tybrake swallowed, feeling chastised. "Well what, then? As I said before, we can't face them alone. There aren't enough of us."

"There are enough of us," Arias said. "The rest of our help just won't come in the form that you probably expect."

Tybrake tilted his head in puzzlement, and Arias went on, "You trust me now, don't you? Otherwise you would've killed me by now."

Tybrake didn't answer.

"There's no time for buts," Arias said. "Our lives are literally at stake. Our enemy is the same to all of us. We have to find a way to work together if we're going to banish this threat before we all end up tortured, imprisoned, or dead."

"You're talking about the other Gryphons? How do we know that they won't just kill us before we even get a chance to speak? We honestly almost did you in, until you mentioned Ratina. You're a Spirit Walker, bad luck to them, and I'm obviously not a Gryphon myself. What makes you think they'll listen about an unknown enemy to them?"

"The Strigigryph aren't an unknown enemy to them. They've suffered just as much as your flock is now. It's possible that the Strigigryph already attacked Skyhaven. We need to see if the flock has survived at all, and after that, we need to get the attention of the Primals."

***

Arias was hoping to see if Sheba was still alive. Any news about the eyrie, or about Brynne and her mother, would be consoling to him. Even bad news. At least then he'd know.

Arias silently wished he could see Xio and the other Alicorns, but the time for that had passed. He'd just have to trust that the sacred protection magick that surrounded Glendale was enough to keep the Strigigryph away… and that they hadn't left their forest for any reason.

"We can reach Skyhaven easily in perhaps two days' time," Arias said, trying to rally the small group of Ardeigryph that surrounded him on the cliff top.

"That's ridiculous," Bala said. "You're in no shape to travel."

"I'll manage," Arias said, but Bala opened a wing to silence him. "No. You'd risk your life traveling in your state. The nights are cold yet, and warmer days are still a long way off. Whoever travels west will be too busy keeping guard during the night to see to it that you're fairing. An Ardeigryph can make that distance in a single day, easy. We fly high and fast. Besides, you can't even fly yet; the idea of sending you out is… frankly insane."

Arias wanted to argue, but Bala was so correct that he agreed with everything he'd said. How many times had he escaped death and been lucky? It would be pure stupidity to expect that track record to continue. "You're right," he admitted.

Bala snorted. "Right then. Let's choose who among us will be carrying out this task. I have no problem with volunteering to go myself. Who else with me?"

"No," Tybrake cut in, "We can't risk you. You're the best leader we have here." He cut his eyes sideways to Arias and took a deep breath before saying, "I'll go. And I'll take Lue and Brint with me, if they're willing." Two other young Ardeigryph stepped forward from the crowd, puffing their chests and nodding.

"We'd be honored," they said in unison.

"Right then," Bala said again. If he'd felt any relief in not having to go, he didn't show it. "Travel at first light, as early as you can. We know that the enemy doesn't typically operate in daylight." He looked to Arias for confirmation, before adding, "Make sure they know exactly what to look for, Arias. We'll probably only get one chance at this. We're counting on you. What you've told us is all we've got."

"I understand," Arias said, taking in Tybrake, Lue, and Brint with his pink eyes. "The place you're looking for is Skyhaven, a flock you haven't contacted in generations by the sound of things. By the way you read the stars, it's dead northwest of here. The leader's name is Sheba, and she'll have her guards on you perhaps even before you can approach the caldera. She's pale, battle-scarred… and massive for a Gryphon hen. If you say my name, perhaps mention the abominations that have been attacking you, she should give you an audience…"

***

Arias instructed the Ardeigryph trio on their mission enough times that they knew what to do by heart. He had each of them repeat what he'd told them back to him twice to be sure. They would weather the night at Oceanside, then set off at first dawn by the course he'd charted for them. Tonight, everyone was holed up in their dens facing the sea, trusting the guards on the clifftop above to keep their eyes sharp. If the Strigigryph attacked at night, the Ardeigryph would try to draw them out over the sea and then drive them down into it, hoping to drown them. The turbulent depths had even taken Ardeigryph lives occasionally, so it wasn't a stretch to believe that the desert-dwelling Strigigryph would perish to the waves if they fell in. Arias definitely couldn't imagine being able to brave the heart of the brine and survive for any length of time.

Arias ate of the small bit of preymeat he'd been supplied with, grateful for a familiar taste that wasn't wriggler. The source of the meat was some type of rodent, brown and furry, and he probably could've eaten eight of them before he'd even begin to feel satisfied, but he didn't complain. He felt his strength finally beginning to return to him, and just as well. He didn't like the idea of not being able to help the Ardeigryph out in whatever capacity he needed to in the coming days.

"I was raised on wrigglers, in the way that all Ardeigryph are," Nanchu said next to him, "but these furry 'preymeats' you enjoy aren't so bad, either. They were the only thing we could get you to eat when you were ill. Tybrake had the idea to leave a few big fish to turn under the heat of the sun, and to catch and kill whatever came to feast on them. Sure enough, lots of these little scurrying beasts came out to investigate. Enough that we each decided to snack on a few as well. Quite tasty."

Tybrake chuckled softly to Arias's right, though the unease in his voice made it a mirthless sound. When the three of them relocated to a spacious den later that night, they spent most of the time trying to lift one another's spirits.

"I guess we can all learn a little from each other, eh Arias?" Tybrake said.

Arias nodded, but his thoughts were centered on the best way to make sure the Skyhaven journey would be successful. It had been a long time since any Ardeigryph had journeyed to Skyhaven, so long that no one in the flock had even remembered exactly where the eyrie was. "It's the best chance we have, Tybrake," he said confidently. "I'd go if I could. I'd feel better if I was there along with you honestly, but I'd only slow everyone down."

They sat in the quiet for a little while, listening to the waves. Arias couldn't stop thinking about the irony of his situation.

"You know, I never would've thought I'd end up in a place like this," he said. "When I was a cub, all I wanted was to know what it would be like to be what I was supposed to be—a Gryphon—instead of doing whatever the Alicorns raised me to be. Now I feel like I know a little too much about Gryphs in general. I'd probably do anything to go back to my blissful, naïve life."

The other two laughed, but it was a forced sound. A laugh that indicated they just wanted to fill the silence of the night with something other than their own worried thoughts. Tybrake's eyes studied Arias in the dim moonlight, but Arias had nothing else to say.

"I wanted to be the greatest caster this flock had ever seen," Tybrake eventually said. He raised his talon and pinched two toes together. "I came this close to achieving just that, actually, but then I kept growing and growing. When I was larger than all my peers, our late Sire noticed and placed me into guard duty. Said it'd be a waste to not use my size for something useful. He must have forgotten that I was a total coward. I'd rather be out over the ocean with nothing to worry about aside from my next catch instead of flying sentry duty. But I guess every Gryph has to do what they've gotta do. Right?"

Arias and Nanchu nodded.

"That's true," Arias said. "Very true."

"I never really fought more than a scuffle, if you can believe that," Tybrake went on. "I always counted myself lucky because of it, but I don't really feel that way anymore. I wish I had the experience in fighting for when I end up in a serious scrap. You look like you've seen your fair share of battle for being just a yearling, Arias. Got any advice?"

Arias flattened his ears as he recollected how he felt fighting the ursos to scavenge the remains it had been eating, or how scared he'd felt as he ran from Kayane, from Arborochre, from Naugi. He shook his head. "No. But when you're fighting for your life, something else wakes up and takes over. If you find Sheba and she speaks to you… she probably could give you better advice than I ever could."

The silence weighed in. No one spoke further. The three Gryphs eventually all tucked their heads under their wings and waited for elusive sleep.

***

Morning came uneventfully. Tybrake and the other two Ardeigryph had left early and silently. They'd already been gone for quite a few murms when Arias opened his eyes. He wished them luck as he stared out over the glassy ocean, starting slightly as Nanchu stirred as well.

"Jumpy, aren't we?" she said, stretching and beginning to preen. Arias opened his wings and was appalled by the condition of his feathers. How long had it been since he'd groomed? He picked fastidiously at the stray feathers that had multiplied under his unwatchful gaze, only feeling satisfaction after he'd picked and smoothed the vast majority of them out.

"Today would be a good day for you to learn to fly," Nanchu said. "If you feel well enough, that is."

Arias glanced up at how casually she'd said the statement. "I feel as good as I probably will for a while. But my wings are too weak to support my weight."

Nanchu's blind gaze had a knowing sparkle in them as she regarded him. "You'll like what I have to show you, watch this!"

She took a small hop out over the sea, and for a moment, she sank as expected. But then, a few murms later, and for reasons Arias didn't understand, she rose up into view again, very slowly. Arias watched, fascinated as she rose without beating her wings.

"How are you doing that?" he asked with interest.

"I guess no one ever had a reason to teach you about air thermals since you never actually learned to fly," Nanchu said, still riding the current with a lack of motion that was almost eerie. "I can't explain why they happen, but every now and then you'll find a perfect thermal like this, one that you can ride for quite a distance without working to keep up your altitude. We Ardeigryph typically hunt deeper waters on a day like today, when we don't have to tire ourselves out to travel so far. Thermals shift, though, so you have to be selective. Come on, give it a try!"

She spun further out over the sea, and with only a couple of flaps, she rose until she was just a pinprick in the sky. Arias watched as she streamlined her body and dipped, and then reopened her wings to float easily again. The air seemed to be buoyant.

"You've got to want it," she called out, "or else you'll be a fledgling forever. Are you the same Gryphon that said he faced death countless times to achieve his goal?"

Nanchu was the last Gryph Arias expected to call him out on anything. He scoffed and gathered his courage long enough to approach the edge of the cliff. The rocks down at sea level snarled hungrily as the waves slapped against them. He tried to pry his talons free from their death grip on the cliff side, but they seemed to have grown a mind of their own and wouldn't let go.

"Jump far enough and I promise you'll miss those sharp rocks," Nanchu said. "And you can trust me to help you before the surf can take you under."

"How would you know if I needed your help?" Arias called out.

"I have extraordinary hearing," Nanchu said. "Now, jump!"

Mechanically, Arias forced his legs to bend. After all, once he jumped and was outside of the cave, all he had to do was open his wings. The worst he could do was fall. It wouldn't kill him.

Arias jumped. The air rushed by for a split murm and he prepared to plummet. Instead, a pleasant, if chilly, wind rushed up to cushion under his wings. He gave a couple of good flaps, and to his surprise, he rose as lightly as if he were a feather. Nanchu gave a trill of excitement as she heard him join her in the sky, and together they dipped and rose, tasting the salt off the ocean spray. It wasn't long before the commotion drew the rest of the flock from their slumber, and soon there were dozens of Ardeigryph ascending skyward, their shrill voices overtaking Arias's own.

Arias ignored the dull thudding of pain that flashed across his flank and chest, reminders that his injuries weren't totally healed. He felt an awesome sense of unity as he heard the wings of the entire flock flapping around him, travelling out over the sea for their morning casting. And then a voice cut through the sound, and he was drawn from his brief reverie.

"Arias!" it yelled, "Don't go too far!"

Arias frowned. He heard most of the group cut sideways in direction, and before he could fully react, the updraft ended. The full weight of his body dragged on him, and he immediately sank. The ocean seemed to rise up in anticipation of him falling in, gravity acting as its eager helper. Arias started to flail his wings, but they'd returned to their former status of being useless, and his wounds cried out in protest with the added effort. Panic flooded his brain, until a set of claws grabbed him by the scruff, steadying him.

"I've got you!" Nanchu said. "Your

movements have to be calm and controlled in the air stream. Cup the wind, and let it go. It's like swimming, only you're stroking with your wings."

Arias's eyes were still frozen wide as he stared down at the ocean that had been ready to swallow him alive, and it was only Nanchu's chuckling that broke him away from it.

"The ocean looks fearsome, but it wishes only to give you wrigglers, Arias! The waters only drown those who are foolish, and you are not foolish. Want to try again, without the help of the thermal? You seem to be in some measure of pain… we can go back, if you want."

"I'm fine," Arias said quickly, stretching his wings wide. "Let me try again."

Nanchu didn't wait for him to change his mind. The instant she released him, he fought against the urge to panic and instead poured his strength into lengthy, smooth wing beats. He ignored the pounding in his flank and chest, and though he still slowly lost altitude, he'd gained a sense of how to manipulate the wind with his efforts. He managed to turn back toward the cliff, and the thermal took him again, guiding him along like a river flowing upward. The moment he perched on the ledge of the den, a rousing cheer rose up from the flock. He hadn't realized that they'd been watching the whole time. Embarrassment flushed through him, but he dipped his head in thanks and disappeared to hide his face.

Nanchu joined Arias after a short while, and she was positively beaming. "I knew you could do it," she said. "You're something else, Arias."

"Heh." Arias allowed himself to experience a bit of pride. "I surprise myself more and more, you know. I'm alright with that, though."

***

All day, it was clear that though the flock stayed busy, everyone was really only thinking about where Tybrake and his companions were. Everyone cast incessantly in a hunting contest that sought out the largest wrigglers, but once caught, most of the meat went uneaten. No one had an appetite. Bala had organized more patrols, and a surprising number of Ardeigryph were beginning to volunteer to fly the perimeter. They stayed to groups of at least three for added safety, and always included a young, fast flier that could alert the eyrie to danger if anything happened.

Nanchu spent a great part of the afternoon rolling her pearls under her talons, her sightless eyes concentrating on something far away. Arias couldn't take sitting uselessly any longer. He stood, and Nanchu swung her head in his direction.

"Do you cast for wrigglers, Nanchu?" he asked, to which she nodded.

"I can hear them as they cut through the water with their fins. I even know exactly what size they are," she added.

"Can you teach me?" he asked.

"I'd love to!" she said. "Come, let's head down to the beach."

***

The beach was mostly deserted, save for a few Ardeigryph who were downing a catch or sunning themselves in the meager winter sunlight. Arias couldn't understand why he and Nanchu were spending time on the sand instead of over the ocean as he'd expected. "Why are we looking here?" he asked. "I thought wrigglers only live in the water."

"They do," Nanchu replied. "But we need something easy for you. Every now and then, an unlucky one gets itself trapped here inland. That's what you should start with."

Arias didn't believe Nanchu about inland fish, not until they came upon their first tide pool. He looked at the glistening bodies flashing across its depths with wonder, and tilted his head sideways, perplexed.

"See what you can catch," Nanchu instructed.

Arias snorted. "Hardly seems fair for the poor things. Nowhere to run to." He hunkered down at the edge of the pool and aimed for the nearest wriggler he saw, but when he made a jab, he came up with nothing but saltwater. He shook his surprise off and ignored Nanchu's chuckling. A few of the other Ardeigryph on the beach looked their way, and Arias tried not to feel the heat of embarrassment. He tried again unsuccessfully, and again after that. As if to prove a point,

243

Nanchu cocked her head for a murm and made a well-calculated thrust toward the center of the school of wrigglers, and came up with two of them. She tossed them down her gullet and clicked her beak happily. "Tastes delicious," she said. "I love these ones."

"That's hardly fair," Arias said. "Your beak is like three times as long as mine."

"And?" Nanchu said nonchalantly. "Life isn't fair. A young Ardeigryph can catch wrigglers almost from the egg, and their beak must not be much longer than yours."

Arias forced his tongue not to form an argument. He heard wings fluttering, and knew he had an audience again. The sun glinting off the tide pool water dazzled his eyes, and he squinted, annoyed. The wrigglers couldn't exactly get away from him, so he moved closer and used his wings to block out most of the light. The wrigglers stopped darting so fast, seeming comfortable in the dark.

"That's a good method," Nanchu said with approval. She must have heard him open his wings.

Arias picked one wriggler out of the entire group, and watched it for a few long murms. It came to rest, and then drifted forward. Came to rest, and then darted sideways. Came to rest…

Arias reached forward and snapped without closing his eyes. He felt something meaty in his jaws, and knew he'd succeeded. He clamped down instinctively and dropped the wriggler onto the sand, and a now-familiar cheer rose up from his newly assembled audience. He gave the cursory dip of his head, then looked down. The wriggler twitched reflexively a couple of times and then was still. Its dead eyes gleamed up at him. A strange sense of horror coursed through his body. Were wrigglers really that easy to kill?

"Go on!" one of the Ardeigryph in the flock shouted to him, "Eat it! It's only a small one, but you've earned it! Your first caught wriggler is always the tastiest!"

Similar sentiments were put forth by other Ardeigryph, but Arias couldn't help the feeling of revulsion that consumed him. What was wrong with him? It was food, which meant it was for eating. Was he somehow ruined by the way that the Alicorns had raised him?

Nanchu was staring at him with her sightless eyes. Her wingtip brushed against his, and he jumped.

"You don't have to eat it if you don't want to," she said. "But the day will come one day soon when you will have to kill to eat. You are a Gryph, dear. Unfortunately our food doesn't grow out of the ground. The prey eats the vegetation… and then we eat the prey."

Arias blinked. He felt silly. He contemplated simply flying back up to his den and waiting for everyone to forget this moment ever happened, but Nanchu seemed to sense his thoughts.

"The best thing you can do is to eat it now that you've killed it," she said. "Letting it go to waste would be… well, a waste. You seem to be a problem solver, Arias. I believe that you can deal with whatever problem you have now, even though I don't understand it."

The crowd of other Ardeigryph were staring curiously and silently at the scene unfolding before them. Was there something wrong with the wriggler? Had the white Gryphon somehow hurt himself during the catch? A couple edged closer, but Nanchu turned toward them and hissed, and they immediately departed in a flurry of long legs and feathers. And then she sat there, in silence, for as long as it took for Arias to say, "I don't know why I can't eat it. It just seems wrong."

"How is it any more wrong to eat than the headless one you were given when you first came here? It was once living."

"I don't know. I wasn't the one who killed it, I guess."

Nanchu lay down and flicked her tail lazily in the cool sand. "I've heard that Alicorns are amazing creatures that can impart life to other beings," she said. "But what creature ever thinks about death? What makes a good death, Arias?"

Arias didn't expect the question. He knew what death was—all creatures were gifted with a knowledge and a fear of it—and he struggled with the thought for a while.

"A swift one, I suppose," he finally said.

"That wriggler died a pretty swift death just now."

"I see what you're trying to do here," he said.

"Well, then. If you don't eat it, it'll rot out here in the sun, and its life—however long or brief, meaningful or meaningless—will have been for nothing. But if the thought of going hungry and wasting food doesn't bother you, then by all means, don't eat it."

Arias's ears flicked, and Nanchu didn't speak more. Eventually, she took off, flying in a spiral back up to the peak of the cliff. Arias stared into the wide eyes of the dead wriggler for a long time. He even picked it back up and placed it carefully back into the water, where the rest of the school promptly darted away from it. He fished it back out. He still felt bad.

As a cub, Arias had tried eating grasses and leaves for enough days that he'd made himself sick, and Xio had to enlist the entire flock in convincing him that it was normal to eat carrion. If even creatures as ancient and wise as the Alicorns believed it to be fine, then surely there was nothing wrong with the decision to eat what he'd killed. He took the wriggler in his mouth. Today, it seemed, was a day for new things. He swallowed the meat and forced himself not to think about how happily it had swum just a few short murms before.

With a running start, Arias managed to clumsily fly back up to the den. Even with the help of the vestiges of the vanishing air thermal, he still winced with the motion required to soar upward, and he decided he wouldn't try flying again until he felt a little better.

Nanchu was waiting in the den, and he successfully ignored the smug look on her face as he lay down.

No applause this time… but he could still feel Nanchu's pride beaming across the space between them.

***

Night came and went without event. Most of the next day went by similarly, but tensions rose as everyone prepared for Tybrake and his two companions to return. What if they didn't? It was a silent question that hung oppressively in the air.

Night fell. Bala and the rest of the flock were clearly resisting the urge to question Arias as to whether he thought they should scout after them. The number of Ardeigryph who were beginning to volunteer for guard duty increased until nearly all were involved in some form. Arias didn't shirk his chance to help out, and he took turns scanning for threats as well. The Ardeigryph didn't bat an eye at his presence anymore. It seemed as though he was one of them.

Everyone's back straightened as an alarm rent

the air, clear and loud. Eyes and ears strained, hackles rising. Was this the night it was to happen, then? Arias quietly vowed to go out fighting. If he saw Shadowbane, he didn't care what his chances were. He'd take him on whether he could hurt him or not.

Ardeigryph were beginning to creep past the beach, their bodies rigid as they moved up to the trees where the alarm was first sounded. Their hesitance was obvious in their movements, but they pressed on nonetheless. Arias dropped down and joined them, trusting the snow-dusted trees to make him disappear. They had hardly made any headway when they all caught sight of Tybrake and his two companions streaking through the sky, flapping like their lives depended on it. And they heard before they saw the sound of many wings and hurried feet tearing past frozen underbrush in pursuit.

The Ardeigryph rushed forward like a wave against whatever challenge the forest was bringing them, Arias among them. He met claws with one of the offending Gryphs without thinking, and didn't hide his surprise that it was indeed another Gryphon and not a Strigigryph. The keythong he'd engaged was an adult, a good measure larger than himself. He could already feel himself being pushed backwards under his opponent's weight.

"Why are Gryphons attacking this place?" Arias grunted, but the big male only sneered in response.

"I hope you're ready to taste death," came the

reply. Arias felt his center of gravity beginning to shift despite him straining forward with all he had, but before his grip was broken, an Ardeigryph leapt onto the keythong, biting into his neck and twisting. The male howled and turned to address his new attacker, and Arias stumbled sideways, stunned.

The Ardeigryph easily outmatched even the largest of the Gryphons in size, but it wasn't hard to see that they were already slowly being beaten back. They were concise in their attacks, but lacked any brute strength, and were too slow and fine boned. Their long limbs made them easy to topple, and Arias tried to think of a way to turn the tide of the battle, dashing out of the way as a Gryphon attempted to engage him. He disappeared easily in the flying snow that was kicked up, grateful for his cloaking ability.

The Gryphons that were present were all heavily scarred. In fact, they looked like Primals. A lot like Primals. The more Arias looked at the group, the surer he was that it was them. "Stop!" he yelled, running past the scores of skirmishing Gryphs. "We don't have to fight each other!"

Before he could get out another word, a Gryphon swept his legs out from underneath him and pinned him to the ground. Every muscle in him tensed as he prepared to fight back… but something in the intense eyes glaring down at him gave him pause. The offender had the same response. A brilliant orange coat, half hidden by the filth of a hard winter, blazed dully under the weak moonlight. Arias took a deep breath, unbelieving.

"Brynne!"

CHAPTER ELEVEN

Arias couldn't believe his eyes. Brynne was alive! The hen released her grip on him and backed away slowly, her mistrust apparent in the way the ridge of fur along her back continued to bristle. A keythong ran toward Arias, battle cry rising in his throat, but Brynne shot him a look, and he stopped short. A number of Ardeigryph had noticed the strange encounter as well, and turned their attentions toward Brynne, their bills poised like spears ready to come to Arias's defense.

"Stop!" Arias said, gaining his feet. "Just… just wait."

"Arias! why are you here with these longbeaks that were intruding on our land?" Brynne's voice didn't seem to belong to her, cold and monotone. "Give me one reason why I shouldn't kill you." It wasn't a threat, but an honest request.

The Gryphs that were watching the exchange formed a barrier around the two, and the activity brought others to stop fighting as they tried to determine what was going on.

"Just hear me out," Arias said. "Get yours to stop fighting, and I'll call mine off."

Brynne's eyes narrowed. "You first."

Arias wasn't sure exactly how to do that, but the Ardeigryph were already calling one another to submit. Faced with an enemy that wouldn't attack, the Primals backed away, confused. A few tried to take advantage of the situation by going for the neck of a defenseless enemy, but Brynne shrieked once, and every Primal froze. The opposing groups stood quietly in the forest, the only sounds being the panting of warriors who would've fought to the death if not interrupted.

Arias looked at Brynne in disbelief. "They answer to you as leader?"

Brynne didn't respond. She tilted her head, waiting.

"I'm trying to get help against the Strigigryph, the same Gryphs that have been torturing the Primals and every other flock. We sent Tybrake and a couple of others to Skyhaven territory to ask for aid. That's why I'm here, and that's why Ardeigryph were travelling so far northwest."

"Skyhaven no longer exists," Brynne said in the same flat voice she'd used before. "It's just us now. The Pale." She gestured to all the other Gryphons who had heeded her.

Quarnar frowned. "It was the Strigigryph, then?"

Brynne nodded. "I assume you mean the ones that came in the night. Not even Sheba was a match for them. You left at a good time, but many believed you were the cause of the slaughter that came after. They arrived not long after you vanished. That old fool Kayane had it coming, but not even she deserved the end they gave her. Iba, she…" She broke off abruptly and she jerked her head toward a nearby male. It happened to be Tybrake.

"You," she said, changing the subject, "Why would you and your flock take a Spirit Walker in?"

"We have no ill beliefs about his kind in our culture. He's been advantageous to have among us. We have a single enemy. It doesn't matter what species our aid comes in at this point. I understand your hostile response, as we did the same when he first arrived here." He pointed with a dubious wingtip toward Arias.

Brynne was unconvinced. "How can I be absolutely sure that you're not working with the Night Runners somehow?"

Arias felt an unjustified stab of betrayal that his old cubhood friend didn't take his word when given, but he shook the feeling away as quickly as it had come. Why should she take his word when she hadn't seen him for so long? Anything could've happened between then and now... if anything, she was smart to question his motives further.

Tybrake's eyes turned somber when he regarded her question. "The most convincing argument I have lies dismembered on our beach."

***

The gathering of Ardeigryph and Gryphons bundled along the coast, eyes darting over the remains of the hen once called Presida.

"It's definitely the work of the Night Runners," Brynne said, flicking her tail. "I'm sorry for doubting you, but one can never be too sure of anything in these times."

Tybrake shrugged. "I would've done the same thing. Have you had any success in fighting against the Strigigryph?"

"Strigigryph." Brynne said the name experimentally. "That's the same word Arias used earlier to describe them. Yes, we've had a bit of success in battling them."

"Strike hard and strike fast," one of the other Primals said, squinting past an eye that was mostly scabbed over. "Kill before the flat-faced *tucas* can have any idea of what you're capable of."

"How many have you killed?" Arias asked, hopeful.

"Three since this summer," the same Primal replied.

The silence was palpable. Three wasn't very many, not nearly enough for what they were facing. Arias forced himself to remain undeterred. "How?"

"Always go for the eyes and ears first. Instinct will tell you to go for the neck, but these things are like shadows in the night. If they can hear and see you when you're nearly blind in the dark, you're done for," the hen explained.

Arias nodded thoughtfully. He found Bala in the crowd and locked eyes with him. "I propose that we transition as many of the flock into operating after dark as possible. Being sleepy during a raid is suicide. I'll be the first to volunteer for night guard... it'll be easy for me. The sunlight hurts my eyes anyway, and I've been rising at sunset for long enough that it shouldn't be hard to slip back into."

Bala agreed, and heads looked toward him as he began to give orders, dividing his flock up into necessary duties. "We must have at least a few casters catching wrigglers full time during the day to feed those at night," he said. "We can rotate who starts and..."

Arias watched as Brynne began to similarly sort out her group. He wasn't sure if they were a flock or not... but they all stared at her and listened intently as she gave orders. He picked out the female with the scabbed over eye, and a plethora of others with various maladies. He wished he had useful herbs with him, and he realized that it had been quite a while since he'd actually practiced medicine. Not since Ratina had helped him to gather plants for the Converts. He wondered if he could find any useful items around here… it was chilly and there wasn't an abundance of vegetation, but it could boost their chances of survival if everyone was healthier before battle. He figured it was safe enough to comb through the bit of forest that grew along the coast, although he was sure that Bala would hear none of it if he learned he was planning to go alone.

Arias backed away from the sizable mass of Gryphs and walked back up toward the forest. He gave a couple of backward glances to be sure that he wasn't noticed. Everyone was evidently too deep into their strategizing to care. He disappeared into the tree line.

***

The assortment of available plant life was as sordid as Arias had expected. He'd gathered a few withered stalks of whisktail and some dried leaves of lichthorn, both of which were far past their prime and probably ineffective as a result. The Alicorns would frequently dry useful plants for later use, but frost burn was a different story. He wondered if he could reconstitute them with seawater, but they weren't even the right color anymore. He dropped the entire beakful and sighed. Maybe if he went deeper into the woods… he sure missed Glendale and its everlasting spring.

As Arias walked, paving a fresh path through the pristine snow, he began to wonder about Brynne's life after he'd left Skyhaven. It seemed not to have mattered whether he'd stayed or gone; misfortune had fallen on the eyrie anyway.

Arias froze and crouched as something moved nearby, and his mind conjured up the worst possibility. He prepared to sound an alarm as loudly as he could, but then made out the creature that had caused the disturbance. Nervous ears held high, a dainty snout that glistened darkly, and thin legs that ended in sharp, cloven hooves could only be a peryton. It ruffled its feathered wings as it browsed twigs and dried foliage, munching. This one was a buckling, and had already lost one of its antlers.

When was the last time Arias had had fresh peryton? It had been ages! He slowly dropped into a crouch and took careful step after step, closing the distance between himself and the flighty creature. The buckling stopped eating, flashing its bright eyes to and fro, then went back to eating, and Arias crept forward again, his mind consumed by his singular task. He could kill it. He'd done it before. *The Primals could use a good meal, even if I can't stomach eating it,* he told himself. And, as if it sensed his conviction, the peryton called out in alarm and took off.

Arias's legs propelled him after his quarry. He wouldn't take flight unless the buckling did first, and even then, he'd probably lose it. The thrill of the chase as he'd experienced it with Brynne in cubhood returned to him in full force as he dashed across the frozen landscape. Every time he gained on the creature, it changed direction with breakneck speed, and he had to dig in to catch up, breath puffing. He focused on the peryton's fluffy white tail flashing back and forth, and soon he was so close that he could feel the wind coming off his prey from the speed of its escape. He extended his claws just as the peryton leaped skyward.

Without missing a beat, Arias followed the buckling up in a mighty jump that sent pain lancing across his flank. He reached high with his talons, unfurling his wings and beating them to give him a few extra feet, and he felt soft flesh in his grasp. His hind legs touched earth, and he tumbled sideways, sending fresh powder up in a great cloud. He shook the buckling's life away, only having just relaxed to catch his breath when a voice sounded behind him.

"Congratulations."

Arias sat bolt upright, but immediately recognized the voice despite how it'd changed. Brynne crept from around a tree, and it was amazing to see just how well she'd hidden herself in a bone white forest. "Wouldn't give you much praise for the landing, but I never thought you'd make a true hunter. And yet here you are."

Arias pushed the peryton toward her. "For you and… yours," he said.

Brynne ignored him as she leaned in close and

inspected his pelt. "Even a few scars, I see."

Arias didn't stop himself from feeling the pride that flowed through him at the comment, but it was nothing compared to Brynne's battle-scarred pelt. "I see that you've got me beat in experience still, though," he replied.

"Easily," Brynne crooned, and for a moment it seemed like old times. "At first I didn't know why you left, Arias," she continued wistfully, "but it didn't take me long to be glad that you did. I guess we all have our stories by now, and clearly you have quite a harrowing one to tell. I'd like to hear it one day."

He nodded, and she squinted at him.

"You know, I never thought I'd see you again," she said. "Kayane wasted no time in blaming you for everything. She was slain screaming that our upcoming deaths were retribution for giving you shelter." She snorted. "Maybe she did deserve to die the way she did."

Arias grimaced. It didn't matter because they were dead, but it didn't feel good knowing that dozens of Gryphons had died believing he was the cause of their deaths.

Brynne preened a few stray feathers on her left wing before adding, "Sheba killed two Night Runners by herself before they all converged on her and killed her. I didn't see how she died, I was too busy running after Iba. For nearly half a season, those monsters trailed after us. We ran ourselves ragged trying to escape. Each night, it seemed like they tirelessly covered ground to meet back up with us. Sometimes they'd let us see them so we would know they were there. Waiting. It was like a game to them. They have tremendous endurance. It's otherworldly."

"They're from someplace known as the desert," Arias said. "Apparently it's pretty harsh. It must be nothing short of energizing to be surrounded by food and water at all times when you're from a land of nothing but heat and no trees."

"How do you know that?"

"Let's just say that I've studied them very closely," he said.

Brynne gave a tart grunt. "You always were smart in your own way. It's definitely a boon to have you on our side. And your coat... you'll make a good ambusher if we clash in this snow. You're a little clumsy, but that hardly matters if you land your weapons in the right spots."

She flexed her talons and allowed her eyes to drift into the landscape. "You know... Sometimes I think back to when Iba and I were trying to escape. We were so tired, we could scarcely hunt, drink, or rest. If we went for two days straight, it seemed like the Night Runners did, too. I wore out before Iba did... I was still too young, too inexperienced at flying. So she sent me downstream to cover my tracks, and she made enough of a convincing target that they must have peeled off and gone after her instead. I never found out what happened to her, but even so, I'm certain of the answer."

She frowned. "I've never been so eager to face something and kill it. Iba's sacrifice means I got to grow strong enough to serve up revenge. It didn't take me long after losing her to run into a small group of Primals. They were just as terrified as everyone else of the Night Runners. But not me. Not after what had happened."

Her eyes glinted, and it was almost a look of amusement. "It didn't take too long to unite the Primals. They were being decimated, and they took hold of whatever hope they could. It was easy to rile them up, to get them bloodthirsty. When we came across our first Night Runner, we broke up and let it hunt us until it realized we were actually hunting it. And by then it was too late." She looked directly at Arias, and the darkness in her eyes gave him pause.

"When we finally have the opportunity to kill, we take our time," she said. "We enjoy it, every bit as much as I'm sure they enjoy their unjustified raids on the flocks."

"You've changed," Arias said quietly, but Brynne only laughed.

"I've changed? Look at you! Here I am leading a warring group at barely a year old, and I had no idea the Spirit-Walker-Alicorn-Cub was doing the exact same with some long-beaked wriggler-eaters." She clapped him across the shoulder and nodded vigorously. "We can do it," she said excitedly. "Together, we can beat them. We'll reclaim these forests as our own, and send a message to these invaders who believe they can just take over our land and do whatever they want." She took the peryton in her beak and beckoned for him to follow her back, but Arias stayed put. Brynne sensed that he wasn't following after a murm and she half turned, her eyes questioning.

Arias quickly went over his thoughts. The way she'd spoken of killing the Strigigryph just now reminded him of how the Primals who'd hunted them as cubs had spoken. Finally, he said, "They aren't all the same, you know."

Brynne dropped the peryton, immediately indignant. "Well, they sure weren't selective in which of us they slaughtered, were they? There's no way I'm going to afford them that comfort when I have the chance to put them down."

"You don't understand what I'm trying to say," Arias said. "I've—"

Lived among them, his mind silently filled in for him, but he stumbled as the words rose in his throat. Brynne's hatred for the Strigigryph was a palpable energy, clear and pointed. All the way to her core, she had no sympathy for them. He wouldn't either, after what Shadowbane had done to her flock. But he'd seen otherwise. Not everyone had an easy choice in these matters. If Larin was still in Arborochre, she would be made to fight, same as all the other Converts. Alissi wasn't a bad Gryph, she had simply decided to stay with the flock after they'd left their homeland. How many others like them were there in Shadowbane's flock, scared Gryphs who didn't want to face the consequence of leaving?

Brynne's glare didn't soften. "Well? You've what?"

"When we were cubs, you didn't judge me based on my coat color like the others did. Why not?"

"Don't try to reason around it. It's not the same," Brynne snapped. "If they throw their lot in with that tyrant, then they all should expect the same fate. I'm disappointed to be having this conversation with you, even. Maybe I should watch you more closely after all." She grabbed the peryton before he could respond and took off back toward the cliffs.

Arias sighed. No herbs to return with, Brynne now distrusting of him, and the wisdom he'd hoped to glean from Sheba erased from all possibility. Gryph-kind's hope lay in a combined flock of the bloodthirsty Pale and clueless-at-battle Oceanside.

It would be a miracle if any of them lived to see spring, probably.

***

When Arias returned to Oceanside, the peryton carcass had already been reduced to bones. A few of the curious Gryphons from the Pale were tentatively trying out some of the wrigglers that the Ardeigryph had caught. One boney young hen was downing one after another, going on and on about how tasty they were, while a keythong ran to the edge of the cliff to empty his stomach of the sea fare. It might've been an amusing sight, under different circumstances.

Bala saw Arias return and immediately materialized beside him. He started to go into the dangers of going off alone when Arias cut him off.

"I'm sorry, Bala. Can we speak somewhere more private?"

The acting-Sire blinked away his surprise and nodded, and the two wove their way up to one of the furthest dens in the cliff side. Arias had scarcely folded his wings before he said, "We're not going to win, Bala. And the Pale—Brynne's flock—may fight with us, but I'm not sure what to expect from them if we're successful in battle. I don't see them going back to peacefully living in Skyhaven territory to begin anew."

"Are you saying we should view them as enemies? Where is all this coming from?"

"I met up with Brynne when I went off to look for herbs," Arias replied, ignoring Bala's look of disapproval upon mentioning going off on his own again. "I tried to explain to her how not all of the Strigigryph are the same as Shadowbane, but she wasn't having it. I didn't tell her that I lived among them, but I tried to explain that maybe some of them could be convinced to see things our way. She was hostile to the idea. Very hostile. It's gone beyond personal for her. I believe she wants to torture each and every one of them just for the sake of it." He dropped his voice as he heard a Gryph flying past outside. "I have an idea, Bala, and I'm afraid that she's going to ruin it."

Bala's eyes lit up upon hearing he had an idea. "Go on," he said.

"I know a lot of the Gryphons that are being kept prisoner in Arborochre. And I know enough about the Strigigryph there to know that not all of them agree with what's going on there… there are perhaps even more of them than I imagine. If we could start an internal revolution there and then strike the eyrie before the Strigigryph can attack here, we might stand a chance."

Bala was already nodding furiously, and Arias couldn't tell if it was because his plan was a good one or the Ardeigryph keythong was just happy to hear an alternative to waiting for their enemy to visit them in the night.

"Excellent Arias, your mind is brilliant! But if defenses in Arborochre were reasonable before, I'm sure they're much more fortified after your departure," he said.

"I have a good idea of the best way to try to slip in unnoticed," Arias said. "Plus, only I can recognize which Gryphs might help us and which will have us slain. I'd be the hardest to spot in the snow. You already risked some of your flock with

the mission to Skyhaven. It's about time I did
something to contribute to this plan."

Bala frowned. "If anything happens to you,
this all falls apart anyway. These two flocks listen
well to their respective leaders, but you've
managed to somehow wedge yourself into a
position where both Brynne and I are willing to
lend our ears to you. I know you said Brynne sees
you with suspicion, but what's going on here isn't
a common thing, Arias. Let me send three of
mine."

"No. Only me. The more we have, the more
likely we'll be noticed."

The doubt etched into Bala's face didn't fade.
"I see that your mind is made up, but mine is as
well. I insist that you take a couple of my guards
with you. They can trail you at a distance to back
you up if you need it. You've very quickly
become a friend to my flock and to me, but I
have no problem with telling you that my reasons
for seeing to your survival are just as practical as
they are sentimental. I have no idea what we'll do
if you're killed or captured and the Strigigryph
attack. To let you take the risk of going into
enemy territory alone would be a definite end to
this flock."

Arias was frustrated by Bala's stubbornness,
but he relented. "Fine. Let me know who you
have in mind as soon as you know so I can work
on filling them in on the details. I want to leave at
first light."

***

It would've been wise to spend the day resting and preparing to infiltrate Arborochre, but instead Arias found himself pacing along the cliff edge, closing his eyes against the chill wind that blew up over the ocean. He kept going over the pros and cons of accepting the help of Bala's guards, but there seemed to be an equal number on both sides. On one claw, obviously he'd have more eyes and ears to detect danger... and more defense if something bad were to happen. The Ardeigryphs' skills at fighting were negligible, but still. On the other, he didn't want to be responsible for the deaths of any other Gryphs. While not directly his fault, he felt guilty for what had happened at Skyhaven. He kept telling himself that had he moved quicker, perhaps Sheba's flock wouldn't have fallen to such a horrible fate. What if Shadowbane had specifically taken one of his *fuhkrata* as meaning to attack the eyrie? It was incredibly possible. He knew it was useless to think such thoughts, but his mind wandered to the same topics again and again.

Arias blinked as he picked out the shape of Brynne soaring over the sea. She looped and dove over the vast watery abyss, dancing across the waves. She was remarkably confident for a Gryphon who'd never been over such a large body of water before, and he marveled at what a strong flier she was. She zipped past a couple of casting Ardeigryph, her shorter wings allowing her to turn and dip with much greater accuracy. It wasn't long before she sensed and returned his gaze from across the distance, and he watched as the orange blip grew larger and larger as she approached, until she finally landed just to his right. She'd gotten so close to the waves that the saltwater had peppered her coat like dew drops.

"You're every bit as much of a flier as I expected you to turn out to be," Arias said.

"I could say the same of you, but that wouldn't exactly be a compliment." Brynne wagged her tongue at him, and he was disappointed that it took him a murm to realize that she'd taken a stab at him. He rolled his eyes. He'd already decided not to tell her about his upcoming venture into Arborochre. She'd probably ruin whatever stealth he was hoping to use with a full-on assault instead. "What do you plan to do after this is all over?" he asked her, and she side eyed him.

"Does it matter? The Pale never looks too far ahead. Reaching tomorrow is enough for us. I should like to see what you decide to do after this is all over, Arias. Will you stay with these sea-faring Gryphs? Or will you seek out your own kind? Provided you survive, you're welcome to join us."

Arias shook his head. He couldn't see himself being a part of the war-like Pale. "I appreciate the offer, but I think I'll end up going back to Glendale, at least for a time. I'm not like the Alicorns, but I find myself being homesick for them."

Brynne's face didn't register anything; she just gave a short nod and stared out over the sea. The two of them watched the waves together until one of Brynne's flock mates nervously called her aside to put an end to a scuffle that had erupted between two of her warriors, and Arias went back to being alone again. The isolation did nothing to soothe his anxiety. He practiced flying to work out some of his tension, but when he tired, he returned to the cliff edge. He sat there until nightfall.

***

Arias dozed and awoke on his own just before sunrise. His timing was impeccable, as a little while later, three Ardeigryph followed Bala up to see him. He immediately recognized Tybrake and his two companions from the earlier mission to Skyhaven.

"We insisted on going," Tybrake said upon seeing the look on his face. Arias simply nodded and raised his wings. No pleasantries were exchanged. Bala bade them good luck. They took to the air.

***

Arias skirted just above the treetops, charting his course for Arborochre. It should have felt insane to willingly return to such a place, but instead he felt a stirring within himself. It was as if it were another version of his being that had taken charge of his body. He wasn't the gentle cub raised by Alicorns that healed others and spent long murms trying to decide what his future would be. He was now Arias the warrior; his future didn't matter as much as the task at hand. Maybe he partly understood Brynne's outlook after all.

He felt alive.

The closer Arias and his party got to the border of Oceanside territory, the lower they banked. Arias had made it clear early into the flight that they couldn't risk being detected by Shadowbane's scouts, not even to save time. As they reached the neutral boundary that marked the Ardeigryph's land, they landed among the trees and started to trek on claw.

The deeper the party pushed, the more grateful Arias was that he had decided not to eat the day prior. He felt lighter on an empty stomach, and despite his best efforts, a twinge of nervousness had taken up residence in his gut. Any sound or sight that he couldn't immediately identify caused him to falter. The three Ardeigryph, despite what he was sure were their best efforts, were equally jumpy. A couple of times, he heard stifled cries of alarm from the hen called Lue. He cast a quick glance over his shoulder after the second time, and she mouthed a silent apology.

Brint and Tybrake had managed to keep a handle on themselves thus far, but Arias found himself wondering yet again why he'd allowed Bala to prevail in sending these three along with him. Especially Lue. She was small-bodied and flighty. It was hard to believe that she'd ever seen battle at all. The thought had hardly left his mind when he saw her stretch bolt upright and freeze. Arias and the keythongs responded similarly and watched, rapt, as she slowly used a wingtip to point. All eyes followed in the direction she was pointing, coming to rest on a single, shadowy figure perched among the highest branches of a dead tree in the not-so-far distance.

The Strigigryph was eerily still, a blur against the rest of the landscape. It appeared to be alone.

The party stood quietly and watched their new target, but the Strigigryph didn't change direction or move. Either it was watching something, unaware of their presence… or it was asleep. Perhaps Shadowbane's followers had become so confident that they didn't mind sleeping out in the open during the day. It was strange to see one at any time other than night.

Arias lowered his voice until it was barely a whisper before saying, "It's possible we haven't been seen yet. We could try to sneak on."

"But if it has seen us," Tybrake responded, casting a worried glance back toward the creature, "then we could be in more danger than we think."

He was right. No one knew exactly how long the Strigigryph had been there… it was possible it had been stalking them for some time now, staying at a distance so as to play the ruse of sleeping if detected. Arias shuddered a little, thinking of what would happen if that were true. They couldn't have the Strigigryph alerting anyone at Arborochre before they could reach the eyrie. If anything happened, it would mean the immediate end to first themselves, then Oceanside... then every other flock.

"Only one way to see if it's asleep," Arias said. "It'll be safer if we go as a group."

"Noisier as well," Brint whispered, eyes wide. It was the first time he'd spoken up since he'd joined in on the mission. Arias didn't disagree with him.

"We can't fly silently like they do. It'll hear us before we're even within striking range," Arias said. "But we can't chance it getting back to Arborochre. We have to take care of it." He couldn't believe the words that were coming out of his mouth as he added, "We can probably overwhelm it."

"What does that even mean?" Tybrakc asked, wincing as his voice rose a notch. Everyone watched the Strigigryph for signs of movement before swinging their heads back to converse.

"I see what he's saying," Lue said hopefully. "If we come at it from all directions…"

"Exactly," Arias said. "It'll only work if it's actually asleep, though. If it's pretending, it'll wake up the moment we take wing and move toward it. I'll go first… I'll fly over it, and then loop back around. I'm smaller than you all, so I'll hopefully make less sound, not to mention be less noticeable against the clouds in the sky. Meanwhile, you three should come at it from all sides. If it wakes up… give chase. We can't let it go, or we're all dead with certainty. Understand?"

"You've only just learned to fly, Arias," Tybrake said, "are you sure you're up to the task? The three of us are probably enough to take it out."

"I'll be fine," Arias said. "We can't take any chances on having it escape."

Arias pointed toward a decently sized opening in the skeletal canopy and spread his wings. With a final glance at the Strigigryph, he jumped skyward and pumped hard to clear the canopy in a few short bursts. The pain in his flank and chest were only a dull ache. As he rose, he kept an eye on his quarry. The brown smudge didn't move. Arias sailed over, making sure that there was plenty of space between it and him. The moment he looked down and back, he could see the Ardeigryph rising into the air, spacing themselves out so that they could come at the Strigigryph from a different angle. He almost felt smug that his plan had even worked this far. The feeling didn't last long.

Arias was still dozens of wing lengths away from the Arborochre Gryph when it started, opened its eyes, and turned its head toward him. With a combative hoot, it immediately threw itself toward him, broad wings churning as it propelled itself with a speed that closed the distance between them in mere murms. Arias's heart hammered in his chest. The Ardeigryph were too far off to offer any aid. The Strigigryph opened its talons to grab onto him, and his immediate instinct was to dodge and run. But maybe, just maybe, he could trick his adversary into thinking he was up to the challenge.

Against common sense, Arias opened his own talons and screeched as threateningly as he could. The Strigigryph seemed thirsty to meet his challenge. As they nearly met, Arias managed to close his wings to drop just out of reach. He heard the Strigigryph let out a cry of surprise, and then an even louder cry of shock as it turned and realized that it was surrounded. It zipped toward the forest, but Tybrake reached it before it could make it to the cover of the trees. Grabbing it with his thin talons, he drove it down toward the earth.

***

In the scuffle, it was hard to keep track as both Ardeigryph and Strigigryph fell. In some moments, Tybrake seemed to be totally in control, but at others he was reeling back to try to protect his face from the sharp claws directed his way. He was gradually losing his hold, however, ended up suffering an awkward landing. To Tybrake's credit, he gained his feet swiftly and set upon his downed adversary again, adrenaline fueling his fighting spirit as he crossed the distance, beak open. Arias, Lue, and Brint all looked for openings in the oncoming battle, but the Strigigryph was fully on the defensive now, and a force to be reckoned with.

Any attack Tybrake threw at the Strigigryph was easily dodged and reciprocated with a barrage of razor-sharp gouges and scratches. Tybrake hesitated with each injury he suffered, and finally backed away completely when the Strigigryph feinted forward and opened a cut above his eyes sending bright blood into his eyes. Vision blurred, he struggled to fend off the renewed strength in his opponent's attacks.

The Strigigyph forced Tybrake to the ground, and Lue launched herself into the battle to disrupt the deadly hold it was trying to place on him. What happened next was so unbelievable that Arias skidded and froze, shocked.

Hearing Lue's approach, the Strigigryph turned its head to address her, and the Ardeigryph hen reflexively positioned her beak between she and it to protect herself. It was a move which drove the sharp point of her bill directly through the Strigigryph's eye.

Time seemed to suddenly come to a halt. The victim of Lue's assault convulsed before falling to the ground, shuddering. Lue seemed equally as horrified as she was thrilled that she'd killed the creature, hurrying to wipe the blood off her beak.

Tybrake was thoroughly astonished. Finally, he managed to say, "I... didn't know you could kill things that way."

"Me neither," Arias said, reaching them. "But most of us don't have beaks as long as yours, either."

"I didn't really think about it," Lue said, using her talons to clean away the last of the blood. "But now we know. And chances are that if we haven't thought about it, they haven't either."

"Not altogether that helpful for us Gryphons, but I'll take it," Arias said. He rescinded his earlier thoughts toward Lue, feeling dumb. After seeing her in action, it was no wonder that she'd been chosen for this mission.

Tybrake pawed at his face, trying to see through the blood. "To be such a tiny cut, it certainly has no plans to stop bleeding," he said.

Arias thought to look for some mud, but one step reminded him that the ground was frozen solid. The barren winter surrounding them ensured there wouldn't be much else of use around. "Maybe if I can place some down over it, it'll stop," he suggested. The idea of taking any down at all in this cold weather sent a hearty shiver down his back, but he was still willing to try it. Tybrake shook his head.

"We can't waste time. If we engage anyone else and this cut opens back up, that's the end of me. I'm just a liability at this point. I'll head back to Oceanside on claw. We didn't see any danger until we got to this point, so I should be fine. And if I come across any predators that want to give me trouble, I'll give them something to think about."

"I don't like the idea of you going alone," Brint said, casting a sideways glance at Arias. "What do you think, Arias?"

Tybrake was obviously decided on heading back alone, but Arias had to admit that he didn't like the idea of it, either. He'd grown fond of the gangly wriggler-eater. "If you don't mind coming on along with me, Lue, I'll send Brint back to Oceanside with Tybrake to make sure he gets there safely."

"I'd be honored to go on with you," Lue said, and Tybrake's jaw dropped a little.

"Now look here, we aren't about to go wasting extra help!" he said.

"Time is more important than anything else, and we're wasting it now. Travel fast, and safe."

Arias turned and started into the forest, and Lue fell lightly into line behind him. Just before he got out of range, he heard Tybrake snort and say, "The nerve of that Gryph."

CHAPTER TWELVE

Arias immediately recognized the tall, dark trees that signified Arborochre's territory. Their thick needles provided welcome cover from roving eyes, although it was equally true that those same trees could be concealing hidden Strigigryph scouts. He and Lue utilized the vegetation well as they moved with caution. They had practically reached the eyrie itself, but the land around them was still hauntingly empty. Not a single Gryph was in sight. Where had everyone gone?

Arias glanced over his shoulder to make sure that Lue was staying close, and she responded with a grim tilt of her head. Even she sensed that something was wrong. Instead of going to the heart of Arborochre, Arias skirted his way west, looking for the telltale signs of Alissi's den complex. When he finally came upon the ravine and its snow-covered wood pile, he had second thoughts about continuing so brazenly. It felt too vulnerable. He couldn't even be totally sure that

Alissi would accept him here. But he needed someone who would hear him out.

Loud paw falls sounded behind Arias, and he whipped around at the same time as Lue. Approaching very deliberately and with no signs of aggression at all was Plithi.

"You definitely shouldn't be here," she said.

"Not exactly safe out there, either," Arias said.

Plithi didn't move. Her gaze was hard. "You took the chance to escape, and you've squandered it. Such a fool deserves to die."

Arias returned an equally hard gaze. "Why did you keep Shadowbane from killing Larin?"

"Even Gryphs with their deaths upon them deserve some measure of mercy," Plithi said. "The time for that has passed, however. Now it's time to atone for your failures." She dove forward, completely ignoring Lue's attempt to intercept her. She was just rearing up to strike at Arias when she instead darted sideways, eyes wary. Her tail lashed as she hissed.

Arias scrambled in his haste to regain his balance, having nearly fallen when Plithi stopped her assault. He was expecting her to rush him again, but she kept her distance now, circling slowly, keeping Lue in her periphery. Finally, she shouted, "Come out, you tongueless coward! I already saw you once. You can't hide forever."

There was silence, then a small movement from the thicket behind Arias. From its dark depths, Larin materialized.

Plithi gave a mirthless laugh. "I knew you were out here somewhere, Convert. You certainly are lucky, aren't you?"

Plithi took a step back. Larin took a step forward. Shadowbane's favorite hen had clearly shifted from being on the offense to focusing on self-preservation. Arias kept waiting for her to sound an alarm. Then he remembered how empty the forests were, and it made sense. Everyone must be somewhere else, far enough away to not be able to hear her.

"Why are you out here all alone?" Arias asked, matching Larin and Lue's pace as they cautiously closed in. "Seems a bit dangerous, doesn't it?"

"Hunting a Convert radical, of course. The moment you disappeared, it was time for her to pay. But she was smart enough to give me the slip. No matter. Plenty of other Converts paid the price for her. I've come to enjoy tracking her. She's the only escapee so far that I haven't been able to catch and kill."

Larin moved in. In the first few moments of their clashing, she surprised Arias by having the upper hand. Through sheer tenacity, she beat the experienced Strigigryph warrior back, and the look of surprise that crossed the Matriarch's face was nothing short of satisfying to see.

As Arias watched the two hens face off, it dawned on him that since most Converts had the ability to speak taken from them, most probably never told anyone what their pasts consisted of. Clearly, Larin had the background of a seasoned warrior. But she wouldn't hold the advantage for long.

Plithi was shouldering her way in, years of hard-won scuffles allowing her to exploit each small mistake. She kept trying to bait Larin into exposing her neck, but Larin was too leery to draw in. Arias took a step toward the fight and, without taking his eyes from the battle, told Lue, "This battle is between them, but we can't let Plithi escape. Fair or not, we can't let her warn Shadowbane."

He felt Lue ready herself beside him. The moment the two began to move in, Plithi broke away and fled. The three of them chased her, but it was only for a short distance. She didn't get far. Her end was merciful.

***

Arias marveled at the jet-black, shiny primary feathers that had grown in on Larin's wings with her last partial molt, and the two crossed necks joyfully, if only for an instant. She initially cocked her head when Lue kept referring to him as Arias instead of Quarnar, but she was excited to learn that it was his actual name. Their reunion was bittersweet at best; they both understood that their work was far from finished.

"Where are the others?" he asked, aware that if Alissi's den complex had been occupied, surely someone would've materialized by now to investigate the commotion. "I came to speak to Alissi. We have the numbers to try to end what's been happening here."

Larin pinned her ears and looked away, and he felt a sense of dread seep into his bones. "Larin?"

The black hen wouldn't acknowledge him for a few long murms, but she finally clicked twice and gestured for them to follow her. Arias hardly registered Lue's shock at realizing Larin had no tongue. He stooped into a low crouch and followed as silently as he could after his old friend. He kept forcing down spikes of paranoia as they moved a little more quickly and brazenly than he'd have liked, but he trusted Larin despite himself. After all, the forest had seemed empty… there must not be anything to worry about in the immediate area.

It was only at the heart of the eyrie itself that Larin slowed to a crawl and stopped to address her followers. She touched Arias with a wing and made a creeping motion, then pointed to Lue and touched her claw to the ground. Lue's confusion was expected, so Arias explained, "She wants you to stay here. Keep watch."

Lue opened her beak to ask a question, but closed it again without asking it. She made herself as small as possible against the boulder, sharp eyes scanning the surrounding area as instructed.

Larin and Arias picked their way toward the cavern where he and so many others had undergone initiation. It already seemed like an eternity ago. He heard the scuttle of many claws working feverishly against the grainy stone inside, and peered within.

Dozens of Converts were milling back and forth from the caverns connected to the cave, each holding beakfuls of blackroot. Working just as fast next to them were Strigigryph, bringing up the biggest prey items he'd ever seen. Each was carefully arranged in front of the pool, their bodies stiff with the cold. Converts hurried behind them to stuff as much blackroot as they could down the throats of the carcasses. Arias couldn't make sense of the sight, but then Larin directed his eyes to another part of the cavern. A mess of Gryph remains had been tossed carelessly into a corner. Arias couldn't tear his eyes away from the awkward angles of the legs and wings, and Larin had to tug him away. They rallied back to the point where Lue was nervously waiting for them.

"So?" she asked quietly the moment they reached her. "What do we need to do?"

Arias couldn't find his voice after what he'd seen. He looked at Larin. "Plithi said others paid because you ran away. Is that what she meant? Where's Alissi? Surely she wouldn't…"

Larin gave a shake of her head, and Arias breathed out in relief. Alissi, as far as she knew, hadn't been in that pile. But the fact that Shadowbane had slain so many Converts in reaction to his and Larin's disappearance further ignited his resolve to put an end to this place.

"They're all busy and in one location right now, which would be ideal for a surprise attack, but who knows how long they'll keep doing… whatever it is they're doing," he said.

Larin had never looked more frustrated by her inability to speak than after he said that statement. She bristled in annoyance and hissed at him, spreading her wings and doing her best imitation of a roar. The performance was so fearsome that Lue took a few steps back, her confusion tinged with fear.

The realization finally struck Arias. Naugi was coming soon. And it was possible that there was just enough blackroot in that cavern to poison a Hydra.

Larin's eyes widened. She fled away in a blink of time, and adrenaline fired through Arias's body as he flexed every muscle into a similar action. He saw the fear in his eyes reflected in Lue's as she dashed away, but a heavy weight on his back prevented him from doing the same. He was forced down onto the snow-covered ground, and he knew that there was only one creature that attacked like this. Unlike during his first capture, the claws holding him weren't attempting to be gentle. There was a flurry of activity a small distance away, the sound of Lue and Larin escaping. At least they'd made it away.

"I can't believe my luck," Shadowbane breathed into his ear. "You came back. And I'm guessing by the way you were just now sneaking around with those two that you aren't here to beg for my forgiveness."

The claws holding Arias tightened to twist at delicate wings. He grunted and clamped his beak shut so as not to scream, eliciting a laugh from Shadowbane.

"I liked you, you know. You're smarter than any of the others have ever been. Pity." He spread his wings with a silent sweep, and the air brushed against Arias's face. "There's a reason that we are the alpha species. The rest of you will soon learn your place in my new hierarchy… Naugi included." A deep hoot issued from the keythong, and a small group of Strigigryph hurried to surround them, awaiting orders. Shadowbane scanned over those gathered and frowned.

"Where's Plithi?" he demanded, and those in attendance shifted amongst themselves.

"She went out to patrol early last night," one of the Strigigryph said. "I expected she would've been back by now, but I haven't seen her."

"Me neither," another added.

Arias let a dark chuckle slip off his tongue despite himself. Every head whipped to stare at him. He could almost feel Shadowbane's eyes narrowing into the back of his head.

"You insolent buzzard!" he spat, shifting his

weight so that his claws pierced deeply. Arias winced and finally cried out as the delicate bones strained under the force, threatening to break.

"Where is she?" Shadowbane growled. "Answer, or you'll see just how slow I can make this."

"West from here, further past your territory than I thought I'd find anyone," Arias lied. "We left her alive, just didn't want her coming back here and outing us."

Shadowbane nodded to two of the Strigigryph, and they took off in search of his mate. Arias didn't bother to move when Shadowbane stepped away from him. He knew that his life was forfeit the moment he was caught; it was just a matter of how long. At least Lue and Larin had escaped. Maybe the flocks at Oceanside could prepare well enough to fight a worthy battle before dying. He was shoved to his feet and guided back toward the cavern.

"I want you to see the fruits of your labor before you die," Shadowbane said. "After all, none of this could've happened without you. It's a shame I didn't pick your brain more for your knowledge of plant life before you turned on me. I can't very well trust anything you may say now, can I? Take him somewhere dark and bind him well," he instructed his waiting guards. "I don't want any movement or a peep out of him during the ceremony. However," he said, eyeing Arias with distaste, "I want him to be able to see everything."

***

In the pitch black of the tunnel Arias had been led into, he lost track of time. Tough sinew bound his legs, wings, and even his beak, and his captors had taken no issue with dragging him unforgivingly across the gritty ground and into this little-used tunnel. The noise of activity above ground never ceased. They only changed as the Strigigryph and Converts worked in shifts to hurriedly poison the preymeat.

The only major sound Arias could concentrate on was the breathing of the Strigigryph guards on either side of him. The pain in his wings was almost comforting, a rhythmic pulsing of shooting discomfort that reminded him that he was still alive. So long as he was alive, he had a chance to find a way out.

The activities in the cavern went on, and the indefinite amount of time felt like eons. Eventually, however, the entire area reverberated with the sound of hooting, and Arias was jostled into high alert as his guards hauled him back into the main space. Cries of, "Naugi is coming! Everyone into position!" echoed over and over as each and every Strigigryph arranged themselves in a large circle around the meat, crowding the Converts into a corner.

A few Strigigryph, probably some of Shadowbane's more trusted servants, paraded to and fro, instructing others to straighten their backs or to preen plumage into shape. Converts who weren't packed tightly enough into the corner were beaten back until they were.

Everything evidently had to be just so. It all only took a matter of murms, and then Shadowbane was front and center, casting a discerning gaze over his flock.

His dark eyes came to rest on Arias, and he gestured to the guards beside him, saying, "Place him next to the prey meat. Perhaps Naugi will have a taste for Gryphon on this lovely visit!"

Arias stiffened at Shadowbane's words. He remembered the terrifying presence of Naugi all at once, and his flank throbbed at the thought. He struggled to move as he was rolled next to a very-dead ursos, but he'd been bound so tightly that he could hardly feel his extremities anymore. The cold, sunken eyes of the ursos stared at him, and he averted his eyes as a shiver ran up his spine. He was practically the same way as the beast, only he was tied up and still breathing. For now.

A massive roaring shook through the cavern, sending a shower of stalactites and bits of rock down onto those gathered. Gryphons and Strigigryph alike cried out in alarm, shielding themselves with their wings and looking up cautiously as the ancient Hydra made his grand appearance. He sent a torrent of wind through the enclosed space with the flapping of his wings, and his landing sent a wave of vibration through the earth, causing some of the lower tunnels beneath the cavern to collapse. Arias tensed as he waited for the ground itself to give up under the weight of the behemoth, but the shaking presently stopped. Shadowbane hadn't flinched from his defiant stance, and at a single glance, his flock straightened up, too. The serpentine neck of one of Naugi's heads snaked into the space, and he took in the scene before him. His eyes came to rest on Arias, but he quickly moved on. He considered the meat stacked before him instead.

Arias struggled against the sinew tying his mouth shut, but it wouldn't give even a fraction. His inner panic intensified as one of Naugi's heads went about spitting fire over the meat, and another began busily eating behind it. A third found and addressed Shadowbane.

"Your offering is acceptable. You may reside in my territory for another passing of the seasons, and my scale-kin will not prey on your kind. But by no means is this permanent. I shall return again anon. You must pay homage again in spring, when the frost melts."

"I wouldn't dream of missing it," Shadowbane said, quick to perform the lowest bow Arias had ever seen him make. His flock hurried to mirror the movement, and Arias squirmed harder as the fire spitting head started in his direction. Before he could fully feel the heat of the flame, Naugi abruptly stopped. The walls of the cavern groaned again as he stumbled backwards, and an expression of confusion spilled over him.

A look of suppressed glee crept into Shadowbane's eyes, but he was careful to replace it with faux concern. The serpent writhed, his necks tying and untying themselves as if they were struggling to escape from his body. He retched a stripe of flame and acid across the cavern, cutting through a quarter of the gathered Strigigryph, and sending the Converts running and flying in all directions. Howls of pain and anguish lanced through the air. Even Shadowbane ducked for cover behind a high stalagmite, fear suddenly etched into his eyes.

Heedless of the pain that accompanied his tight bindings, Arias inched forward at an agonizingly slow rate, breath rasping as fetid smoke rose from the victims of Naugi's direct blast. Nearby him, the still-flaming remains of a Strigigryph lay. He watched as the fire slowly started to extinguish itself, having eaten away most of the feathers and fur of its victim, and desperation crept into his frenzied wriggling. When he was close enough to feel the warmth of the dying flame radiating from the body, he didn't think twice about thrusting his forelegs into the weak flicker, flinching away only after the sinew bindings had weakened enough to snap. His eyes darted to find a path to escape. The only way to get there was past Naugi's flailing body.

In the pandemonium, Arias made his way toward the exit of the cavern. He dragged his hind end, having no time to undo the rest of his binds. Most of the other Gryphs were cowering in corners or flying about erratically, too afraid to go anywhere near Naugi, even to save their own lives. Arias feared being caught again more than being crushed, roasted, or dissolved to death by the Hydra. He kept close to the walls of the cave, breathing hard through his nostrils.

Naugi blew smoke into the sky, tilting backwards and snarling as he began to foam in his mouths. He snapped at the air, finally tripping over his own feet and toppling sideways, sending a huge plume of snow up into the sky. Arias squeezed his eyes shut as the icy cloud washed over him, concentrating on crawling past the stricken Hydra so he could position his body behind the same large boulder he, Lue, and Larin had hidden behind earlier.

Arias reached up and hooked his talons around the sinew holding his beak shut, pulling and digging until he was able to slip free. His lungs welcomed the chill as he gulped air down hungrily, his breath rising in steaming puffs as he lay limp, struggling to regain himself. He eventually worked himself up enough to pluck the sinew free from his hind legs, and just in time as well. The Strigigryph were beginning to reorganize, cautiously exiting the cave with Shadowbane in the lead. For the time being, Arias was forgotten. He dashed off for the forest, stumbling after having been tied for so long. He didn't choose a direction. He just ran.

***

The pain didn't catch up to Arias until he was well away from Arborochre. He'd been unable to reach the sinew that was tied mercilessly around his wings, and the appendages were beginning to ache terribly for lack of circulation. Worse than that, his talons burned with every step despite the coolness of the snow. He'd burned them well enough trying to free himself, and the protective scaling had completely sloughed off the bottom of his right foot, exposing the tender flesh beneath. It wouldn't have been a problem if he could fly, but...

Arias's ears flashed up as he heard the sound of something huge crashing through the trees. He caught a brief glimpse of a mass of grey before he pressed himself against the nearest trunk, and he couldn't believe his eyes as not one, but three basilisks zipped past him. The first was in the lead, but only as long as it took for one of the two flanking it to wrestle it into the snow.

Arias panicked as the reptilian creatures brought their fight closer to him, and he limped as silently as he could away from the tussle. It was a relief that the basilisks were too busy fighting one another to watch him creeping away. He felt no better when he realized that night was preparing to fall. Was this the night of the same day he and the Ardeigryph had gone stalking into Arborochre to try to contact the Converts? His extreme thirst suggested otherwise. He didn't even know how long he had been kept below ground in the tunnels of the cavern. He shuddered, thinking of those horribly dark spaces that had crumbled and been sealed off forever the moment Naugi had appeared.

Naugi. The gravity of the situation struck him as he slowed to rest. He couldn't believe that Shadowbane had used his own knowledge against him in such a terrible way. He was the only Gryph in the region who had such an understanding of herbs… Naugi probably automatically assumed he was the one who had devised all this.

Arias struggled to move on again. He needed
to let the others know what was happening so
they could do something, anything. He studied
the barest outline of the stars through the shifting
clouds, and charted his course more directly for
Glendale. The Alicorns would know what to do.
Blackroot had to have a cure. Maybe he could
send one of the Alicorns to Oceanside, and the
Gryphs could storm Arborochre, clear a way for
the Alicorns to reach Naugi... he nodded to
himself, grasping desperately at any semblance of
a plan. It was all he had.

Arias stopped on a small outcropping to rest,
his eyes searching the obstacle for ways to skirt
around. He frowned as he peered more closely at
the rocks before him. The huge boulders seemed
to be winding and unwinding, climbing up on
themselves. With dread, he realized he couldn't
stop staring. He couldn't move at all, even. And
when he picked out two serpentine eyes, he
quaked with the knowledge that he'd seen this
creature before, at the base of Naugi's roost. It
was Simik! The great basilisk could've nearly
rivaled Naugi himself in size. His long, forked
tongue flicked across the distance between them.

"Simik recognizes this morsel," Simik growled
in a voice so low, it may as well have come from
the earth itself. He hefted himself onto the
outcropping next to Arias, and it wasn't until he
blinked that Arias found himself in control of his
faculties again.

"Surely he wonders why he hasn't been eaten

yet," Simik purred, sending the tasseled end of his tongue against Arias's face. "Simik is preoccupied."

Arias gazed at the basilisk in wonder. There was no use in trying to run or hide.

Simik leaned his long neck down, and Arias swallowed as he stared into an eye that was nearly as large as he was. "Has this Gryphon glimpsed the final hours of Simik's better, Naugi?"

Arias wasn't sure how to react. He braced as the basilisk brought his head even closer to his. His rank, hot breath steamed in the air all around him as he growled, "Today is your day, Gryphon. Naugi has met an untimely fate. This one can feel it. When he dies, Simik will be there. All will accept Simik as leader. All leaders die, Gryphon, but they live on in their successors."

With a final snort that made Arias shoot straight up into the air, Simik continued along his way with his strange rolling gait, and Arias let out the breath he'd been holding in. Leaving a meeting with the fearsome creature alive felt surreal, but it seemed that any scale-kin he came across today had other goals that didn't involve eating him.

***

Dawn was nigh on the horizon by the time Arias sank uselessly to his hocks and stayed there. He was nowhere near Glendale. Each time he forced himself to take a few more agonizing steps, the distance seemed no less. Shadowbane and the Strigigryph would live. Naugi would die.

The Ardeigryph would suffer, and likely be killed. Then every other Gryph Shadowbane could get his claws on. Who knew what would become of the Alicorn herd. All because Arias hadn't just stayed put in Glendale when he'd had the chance. Even if he'd never left, however, Shadowbane and his flock still would've arrived in the region and started torturing and killing. Would things really have been different? Arias had tried, but nothing had been enough. He recoiled at the futility of the situation, closing his eyes. Maybe it would've been better had he never existed at all. At least then he never would've been able to witness the horrible injustices of the world.

***

Xio lay next to Hlaena in the warm meadow, its green a stark contrast to the rest of the forest in deep winter around it. He had his head resting on her shoulder, watching the herd as they nibbled at the tender grass, their tails swishing. Hlaena was napping, her eyelids fluttering as she navigated whatever dream world she was part of.

Xio frowned. He'd felt the beginning of something terrible, but he couldn't place what it was. It had started a while ago, and was growing more… tangible, whatever it was. The rest of the herd could feel it, too. It spread through them like a ripple, and they all paused in their eating and turned to face him with worried expressions. Hlaena stirred and opened her eyes.

Xio stood and pointed his horn toward the north, calling arcane magick to concentrate at its tip. If he focused, he could sense a strong presence in that direction, but this wasn't a presence that bothered him particularly. It had moved there quite some time ago… yes, the Aquila. Xio nodded to himself. *That's right,* he thought. *The thunderbird.* He turned eastward, where another ancient beast, older than Naugi even, was barely detectable somewhere in the ocean. He'd never discovered what that force belonged to, but he knew that it wasn't the cause, either. He wondered if Naugi would know; he'd never asked him. He froze. Naugi. How could he have missed the Hydra's presence so easily? He was usually the most prominent of any creature in the territory.

Xio walked into the woods, until it was hard to discern even Hlaena's familiar presence, and then closed his eyes and focused yet again. *Naugi,* he called into the ether, *Friend, what has happened?* Long murms passed.

There was no answer.

Xio ran back to the meadow, where the other Alicorns were waiting.

"Naugi needs our help," Xio said. "I don't know why, but we have to go to him."

"What about the forest?" one of the herd mares asked. "The winter will set in if we leave."

"Let it," Hlaena answered. "This is more important. We can reestablish the plants if the frost kills them after our return."

Xio led the way out of the forest, and his herd

filed behind him like ghosts, leaving behind their lush paradise. Behind them, the first flakes of snow in eons fell in Glendale, spreading an even coating on a land that had forgotten the touch of the cold.

***

Arias lay in the snow, unmoving. The light of the morning sun slanted weakly across him, offering no heat. He heard what he thought was just his fatigued imagination, and he shook it off as a figment of such. But then it came again, louder this time, accompanied by the unmistakable sounds of whinnying. He opened his eyes, wincing at the lance of pain that the sun's glow sent through them. With difficulty, he picked out figures the color of frost heading toward him. It was Xio, stallion leader of the Alicorns. And his whole herd was traveling with him.

CHAPTER THIRTEEN

Xio's group was traveling so fast, and Arias's coat blended in so perfectly with the snow, that he was almost trampled, unseen. He gave a sharp cry as the thundering hooves neared him, however, and Xio skidded to the perfect stop. It seemed to be the only thing capable of stopping the stallion, and he stared down with familiarity at the Gryphon that lay at his feet, puffs of steam rising from his snout.

"You're alive!" he said, and then more gravely, "What have you escaped from, little one? I've sensed something is very wrong, and I must see if there is anything I can do about it."

"You've seen the Strigigryph?" Arias croaked, meeting the stallion's concerned gaze.

"The newcomers that razed Skyhaven? Yes, we have. I thought perhaps you were among the slain, and I feared for you."

"They've done more than that. It's my fault, Xio. I gave them the knowledge to poison Naugi with."

Xio was aghast. "Why?"

"I didn't know. I thought I was helping… Their leader is the most evil creature I've ever met. I spent most of my time trying to stay alive. The only reason I was allowed to live without being tortured is because of the color of my coat. They believe I'm a Gryph they used to know, brought back to life, but they're crazy, Xio! They enslave other Gryphs and do horrible things to them. They're cannibals." He winced and forced himself to his feet. "It's all my fault, but I can't fix this. I need your help."

"What was it?" Xio demanded, using his teeth to clip Arias's wings free from their bindings.

"Blackroot. More of it than I've ever seen in my life. They hid it inside offerings of preymeat. Xio, I had no idea they would use it for anything other than healing those injured in battle!"

"Calm, Arias," Xio said soothingly. "I believe you. Hlaena, I must reserve my strength for whatever lies ahead. Can you please heal him? I wish to go on ahead."

The mare nodded, her muzzle wrinkled with concern. The rest of the Alicorns took off at a full gallop, and she nuzzled Arias in the silence after they'd departed.

"I've been worried about you ever since you left," she murmured into the feathers at his neck. "I hate to see that my fears were legitimate."

"I'm sorry," Arias said. The somberness in her voice threatened to rip what was left of him apart. "I should've never left."

"Hush, now. Everything will be fine soon enough." She gently pushed him over so that he fell on his side in the soft snow, and the very tip of her horn glowed with an iridescent maroon. Arias had seen this before, and he closed his eyes so he didn't have to watch. And then the pain of a thousand sharp claws dug into him as she thrust her horn directly into his chest.

The pain only lasted for a murm, perhaps even less than that, and Arias had hardly gasped before it was over. A warmth trickled through his veins, and when he stood to his feet again, it was with a vitality he hadn't felt for days. Hlaena swayed on her hooves for a moment, then steadied herself. A fraction of her forelock started to grey, and continued to do so until it was without any of its original color. Arias had an inkling as to what had happened, but he didn't understand the process itself.

"Thank you," he breathed, although the simple words of gratitude weren't enough.

"The Ardeigryph are suspicious in nature, and it's possible they won't listen to even an Alicorn," Hlaena said with undeniable fatigue in her voice. "We can use all the help we can get if what you say has happened has truly transpired. If the Strigigryph are as capable as we've seen them to be, then we've got a fight ahead of us to try to make things right. You can fly, correct?"

Arias nodded, eager to have a direct order to contend with. "I'll be there and back. Don't get hurt while I'm gone. Please."

Hlaena nodded and headed off in the direction Xio had led the herd, directly for Arborochre. Arias took a deep breath and leapt skyward with renewed strength. He forced himself to stretch to full speed, flying over the trees with a swiftness he didn't know he was capable of.

***

Arias reached Oceanside some time before sunrise. The Ardeigryph sent out an alarm upon seeing him, expecting hostilities, but settled down when they recognized him. Arias felt a huge relief when he saw a black figure outlined against the cliff side of the eyrie, significantly smaller than the others surrounding her. Seeing Larin safe was a small weight lifted from his soul. Bala was the first to meet him, along with three other warriors. It was all he could do to glide to a landing on the beach and try to catch his breath.

"No need to speak, the mute one and Lue filled us in about the ambush. How did you escape? Please don't take this personally, but we assumed you dead and fortified for what we assumed was the oncoming assault," Bala said.

"We… have to go… back," Arias puffed. It felt like no amount of panting could replenish him.

"What? Have you gone simple? We can't go back!"

"They've… poisoned Naugi," Arias finally said, struggling to regain his composure. "The Alicorns are going to try to save him… but if they can't get to him, they can't do anything."

Bala seemed to deliberate. "What exactly happens if the Hydra dies?"

Arias shook his head. "I don't know," he said honestly. "But I'm sure it's nothing good. Have you seen the basilisks? They've been fighting for his place in case he dies, and if that happens… Without Naugi's authority, there's nothing to keep them from hunting and killing us."

Bala's reservations were apparent. His flock looked to him with reluctant gazes. Finally, a high voice chirped up from the crowd that had gathered around, and Lue's lithe form pressed forward.

"If we don't take the initiative, they will come here for us. It won't matter whether they have the advantage on their own territory or not. But they likely won't be expecting us to rush them, and the Alicorns may be able to help us to fight. Won't they, Arias?" she asked.

Arias had never really seen the Alicorns fight before, but he found his head bobbing up and down anyway. He'd say anything to get them to head off immediately. Larin stood next to him and stamped decidedly. She locked eyes with him and nodded, and Brynne pushed her way to the front of her flock.

"The Gryphons have their heads screwed on right," Brynne yelled. "We fight or we die. The Pale will fight!"

A cry of genuine, excited bloodlust rose up from Brynne's flock. Arias hated it, but the gusto of the sound steeled him. He was so hungry for courage, he almost joined in the cry himself.

"Whether you come or not, we're going to battle. It's our best chance to get rid of these monsters once and for all. If they succeed, we're doomed anyway. Stop being so afraid and fight for your lives, for Halada's sake," Brynne growled.

Bala gave Arias another uneasy glance, least of all after what he'd told him in private in the cliff side den just a little while ago. Arias hissed in frustration and turned away from him.

"Let's go," he said.

At first it was just Lue, Larin, Brynne, and the Pale following alongside him, but as they cleared the beach, the sound of more and more pawfalls joined in. When Arias glanced over his shoulder, he saw the vast majority of Oceanside following behind, solidarity etched into their features as they flowed through the woods like a wave of fur and feathers. The Pale flew overhead with vigor, and their cries filled the wood with the sound of war. Arias's spine tingled as he moved forward. It was finally time.

***

Sunset bathed the cloud-streaked sky red as something the land had never seen before advanced forward. A combined flock of Ardeigryph and their fierce Gryphon neighbors neared Arborochre, spurred on by the singular purpose of survival. Arias caught sight of Bala not too far back, and admired the leader for joining despite himself. As they flew, here and there, Gryphons wordlessly rustled up from hidden spots in the forest to join them. The eerie homage of their clicking filled the forest below. Evidently, the escaped Converts knew exactly what the group's target was.

Arborochre was once relatively hidden among the dark conifers that surrounded it, but it was now easy to pick out from the sky. Naugi had leveled nearly everything in a quarter-mile radius, with parts of the forest illuminated by flames that still licked upward despite the frost. The cavern was just a pile of rubble, strewn through with the limp and occasionally charred bodies of its previous inhabitants. The Hydra lay dying at the center of the devastation, protected from outside interference by a wide circle of Strigigryph. A collective warble of apprehension rose up from many of the Ardeigryph at the sight of the scene, but Arias didn't balk as the Strigigryph noticed and divided into three ragged lines to face them.

Arias landed and picked out a single Strigigryph from the crowd to take on. Lue and

Larin seemed to have read his mind, because they both pressed hard to catch up to him. This fight wasn't about being fair.

The three of them converged on the single hen, and within murms they'd subdued the struggling figure long enough for Lue to execute her using her long bill. Many Strigigryph died swiftly as they paid no special care to the wriggler-spearing beaks that directed themselves toward the center of their wide eyes, indicating that Lue had wasted no time in telling the others how to utilize the technique. The Strigigryph were fast learners, however, and went to using the Ardeigryph's long necks against them. It was a horrifyingly effective tactic. One solid snap of that thin, elegant feature was all it took to drop an Ardeigryph just as fast as a pithed Strigigryph.

Out of the corner of his eye, Arias glimpsed a big Strigigryph hen overpowering Bala. She'd just begun to hook the tip of her beak into his neck, but Arias ran over and chomped into the tendon that ran up the back of her hind leg, eliciting a shriek of pain. Bala drove his beak into her skull, but there were already others lined up to challenge him. The bodies of fallen comrades were a constant reminder to both parties to not lose focus for even a moment.

Arias was so consumed with battle that the thought of the Alicorns had fled his mind, right up until the moment he heard a pearlescent cry rise up from the tree line. He glimpsed Xio and his herd fending off a swath of Shadowbane's flock, the Sire himself among them. It was all

Arias, Larin, and the other Converts needed to see, and they collectively abandoned their current fight to engage the new group. Arias almost stopped short when he saw the way the Alicorns moved among the Strigigryph, however. They bucked and plunged, colorful banners of magick snapping through the air in a blinding array as they manipulated the bodies of their enemies to form a path through. If it weren't so violent, it might've been beautiful.

The Strigigryph, skilled in killing less intelligent beasts, were at a loss as to how to handle the magick-wielding Alicorns. They managed to open bright wounds on the pale hides of the Alicorns, but scarcely could accomplish more than that. Arias leapt in to take on the Strigigryph's defense, and he set his jaw when he found himself standing before Shadowbane. The Sire hissed and ran full speed toward him, eyes dark with rage. If not nearly as impressive in stature, Arias easily matched his ferocity as he faced him down. Everything else dimmed in contrast to the finality of the oncoming conflict.

***

Xio saw a path to Naugi open as Arias's group made way, and he immediately darted toward the Hydra, his herd repelling any straggler Strigigryph that directed their attentions toward them. Naugi was unresponsive but alive, his armored chest rising and falling ever so slightly, his throats flaring as acidic saliva dripped down his maws. Xio could feel the eyes of dozens, perhaps even hundreds of the Hydra's less-ancient brethren watching somewhere out of view. Waiting for the moment their leader ceased to draw another breath.

Xio had known Naugi for so long that he wasn't sure what would happen if the Hydra died. He was nowhere near the end of his natural lifespan, just as Xio wasn't, and the thought was unnatural to even entertain. His herd squealed and sidestepped as they sensed the sheer number of scale-kin surrounding them. The Gryphs couldn't see or detect them… but they were there.

"I must try to save him," Xio announced, turning to face his mate. "You have to take care of the rest if I don't make it."

"No," Hlaena said, rushing up to block his path. "You cannot offer what is not yours to freely give. Don't forget the sacred vows."

The stallion's eyes softened as he gently pushed her aside. "If I don't try, the world as too many know it will surely be shattered. You'll do well in my absence, Hlaena. The herd will be lucky to have you."

He brushed past her, snaking forward until he was right next to the Hydra. The tip of his horn flowed with a blue iridescence, and his herd screamed fearfully as he thrust his horn into the mighty creature's body.

So small was Xio compared to Naugi that the fur over his entire body immediately greyed, dimming until there was no semblance of the original color. The Gryphs' battle was a distant lull to the stallion, almost unnoticeable among the grand scale of the act he was undertaking. Xio dropped to his knees, shuddering, eyes closing as the contamination he sought to cleanse instead overtook his body.

Hlaena rushed forward, intent to stop the event that was taking place. Xio didn't move from where he kneeled. He couldn't acknowledge her presence, but she knew that he could sense her there beside him. She joined him, and one by one, the rest of the herd united in the effort to bring the ancient protector back from the brink of death with their own sacrificial lives. Their manes gradually darkened with the weight of their task, until they were all the same as Xio's. Time seemed to stand still as Naugi's life hovered between the present and the afterlife.

***

Arias knew he couldn't defeat Shadowbane one on one. But he didn't feel fear anymore. He was almost… well, excited was the wrong word to use. But he was ready for this, even if it meant his own death. The two met in a snarling mass of snapping beaks and clawing talons, and feathers ripped into the air as they dragged against one another. Shadowbane's experience with fighting took no time to shine through. He opened a series of painful cuts that weren't meant to mortally wound, but instead were a testament to his superior abilities as a warrior. He was clearly playing with him, but Arias didn't care. Anytime he managed to connect his claws with flesh, he felt a rush of exhilaration that he was at least damaging his opponent.

"I should've killed you when I had the chance," Shadowbane growled, beginning to force him back. Arias initially resisted, but then, like a dawning, reason eked into his mind. It had been absent since the battle began, but now it cut through his instinct like a confusing new entity. He understood that he couldn't win like this. Brute strength and experience taken into account, Shadowbane could best him one thousand times over.

Arias put all his effort into breaking loose from Shadowbane's reach, diving backwards to safety the moment he felt the Sire let up. Shadowbane eyed him, sensing the shift in his demeanor, but not comprehending why. Arias slowly advanced on him, and when he was close enough, he kicked a mixture of snow, rubble, and char up from the ground and into the Sire's eyes. The powder flew up into a million glittering shards, and Shadowbane instinctively shielded himself from the spray.

The cheap shot sent Shadowbane rushing in with a flurry of attacks, the worst of which Arias managed to avoid. The keythong had flown into a frustrated rage, which was just what Arias had hoped for. Anytime something happened that Shadowbane felt was outside of his control, he acted to wrestle it back into a position where he was in charge. This was no different.

Arias ducked, countering the keythong's heavy blows, and danced sideways on the extraordinary energy Hlaena had granted him earlier. Shadowbane came at him again and again, but only rarely managed to land a glancing blow that caused him to just barely stagger. Arias knew that if he had the misfortune to encounter the attacks outright, they could easily knock him into a stupor. He flinched to the right in anticipation of an oncoming swipe, leapt when Shadowbane thought he'd duck, moved in for an attack whenever it looked like he should be retreating, and did his best to appear unsuspecting as he calculated Shadowbane's next move.

It wasn't long before a cry of frustration rose to Shadowbane's throat. The Sire had slowed considerably, tired after using so much effort to try to subdue Arias. Most Strigigryph who'd been fighting were all either injured, beginning to escape, or dead. The once-white snow they'd fought upon was stained with the blood of the fallen. A few isolated cries of victory rose up, and Arias tasted success as his companions surrounded him and his foe. Shadowbane glowered at them with disgust.

"Winning with numbers," he hissed. "Such a low-brained tactic. Different species have no business conversing together, working together, unless one is in servitude. You may think you've won, but you'll see that I was right. Eventually." He spat into the snow. "True peace comes with the guidance of a single leader. At least I achieved that."

Arias's eyes trailed over to where the Alicorns were next to Naugi, and only then did he note the spectacular act that was taking place. He had to do something to help. He stepped out of the way as the crowd around him moved forward, their intent clear. The Converts were the first to reach their old Sire. His end was swift, perhaps even swifter than he deserved.

Shadowbane would've never stopped doing what he thought Tsarine demanded of him, and so long as he believed that, his death was unavoidable. Arias turned away from the scene, heading instead to assist Xio's herd.

***

Xio and his herd were frozen in a mortal struggle from which they couldn't escape. It was quiet aside from the ambient sounds of the dying and the escaping. Arias and the other Gryphs stood, not sure what to do. When Arias reached out and touched Xio's shoulder, he felt an unimaginable force drain him like nothing he'd ever felt before. He tore away, gasping, and the other Gryphs backed away warily.

Xio's right eye barely opened, the eyelid trembling as though it were with great effort. He found Arias and held his gaze, just briefly, and then he tensed, a horrid shriek unlike anything Arias had ever heard before tearing from his throat. With a sound like the splintering of a branch, his horn fractured and broke, fragmenting into a thousand pieces. Xio slumped over and moved no more. Arias backed away slowly. He didn't have to approach him to know that he was dead. But then his panic and horror intensified as, one by one, the other Alicorns began to suffer the same fate.

Arias's mind raced for a way to help, unable to

312

tear his eyes from the terrible sight before him. His mentor, the kindest and wisest creature he'd ever known, and the only figure he'd ever known as a father was gone. The rest of his Alicorn family were quickly reaching the same fate, and he yelled out without thinking, "Save them!"

No one really moved as Arias rushed forward and grabbed ahold of Hlaena by her neck. He struggled to pull her away from Naugi's body despite the soul-sapping force that encompassed him the moment he touched her. Spots dotted the periphery of his vision. Some brave soul grabbed onto him and pulled backward as well, and they inched away as one unit before tumbling to the ground.

Arias wasted no time in looking the mare over anxiously, feeling a trickle of relief when he confirmed that she was unconscious, but still alive. A few other Gryphs had formed together to try to rescue the other Alicorns in the same manner. It seemed to help to have more than just one creature moving them. A rustle of fear pierced the group as a younger hen didn't have the strength to move a stallion by herself, and wordlessly collapsed. By the time the others pulled her away, she was as cold and dead as the snow upon which she lay. All told, perhaps half a dozen of Xio's normally robust herd had been salvaged. The rest had all met the same terrifying death as their leader.

Arias tried his best to rouse Hlaena. Her coat had lightened a few shades from the sickly grey it had become, but a worrying hair-thin crack now ran all the way from the tip of her horn down to its base. When he reached out and touched her, he still felt the disturbing draw of energy, but it was no longer quite as hungering as it had been. He flinched back a few times, and then carefully placed a talon against her side. It was hard to resist the urge to withdraw, but he felt hope as a few strands of her forelock achieved a wispy pallor in color. He grimaced as all the energy she'd given him when she'd healed him was taken away all at once. The mare heaved and choked as though breathing for the first time, and Arias sighed in relief. The other Gryphs, not fully understanding but reassured they could help in the same way, carefully mirrored what he'd done in groups to help revive the remaining Alicorns. And then they all froze as a gargantuan gurgle rose from the throat of the great Hydra that lay before them.

Naugi, the territory's ancient guardian, had breathed his last breath.

***

No word or feeling could describe the great trembling that shook the firmament as a tremendous screaming filled the air. Basilisks of all sizes materialized from the surrounding forest to rush toward their fallen brethren, serpentine bodies tangling amongst one another as they fought, venomous fangs flashing in the light. Arias grabbed Hlaena's limp body and struggled to make lift with her. Other unnamed faces crammed around him and took hold of various limbs to offer their wing power, flying upward. Most simply ran for their lives, too scared to think of anyone else. With nowhere to go and adrenaline fueling their actions, they headed for Oceanside. The basilisks seemed too consumed with killing and fighting their own battle to notice the flocks milling overhead. Those too injured to fly followed on foot or ran to hide as well as they could. Those too weak to escape were forgotten. There was nothing more that could be done.

The sound of the basilisks haunted the greater portion of the night. It kept the wing beats of the Gryphs steady if they tired and felt like slowing. Down below, hidden in the trees, who knew what horrors awaited a weary warrior?

Hlaena's body grew heavy in Arias's talons, and he was grateful when a familiar voice asked him to take over. He didn't expect to see the face of a Strigigryph when he looked over. It was Alissi. None of the other Gryphs seemed to bat an eye at the presence of the score of Strigigryph that had escaped along with them. There seemed to be a mutual understanding that the fight had been left behind in Arborochre. Questioning and accusations could be saved for later.

"Congratulations on learning to fly. I swear you must have some kind of blessing upon you. And I understand the look." Alissi's voice was tired. "I stayed out of the fighting, as best I could. As I said, I followed Shadowbane, but not because I was still loyal to him or to his cause. As soon as he died, I was more than happy to take your side." Murmurs of agreement rose from the other Strigigryph.

"He went too far," one said. "You can't follow

a leader who won't see reason… but you also don't want to die as a deserter."

Arias released his hold on Hlaena, and Alissi rushed to take his spot before the other two Gryphons carrying her succumbed to the extra weight. Carefully, most of the original Gryphs bearing Alicorns switched out similarly. Arias gave Alissi an appreciative nod as he angled his wings to capture the lift of an air thermal. He felt more tired than he'd ever been in his life. With the horrible cries of the basilisks seemingly rooted to the spot where Naugi had died, his eyelids now entertained the idea of shutting, leaving his wings to churn the air without direction. Whenever he drifted too far off course, a helpful comrade of some shape or form gave him a gentle nudge to encourage him to stay awake. He couldn't believe how many times he'd made the journey to and from Arborochre in the past days. He wanted this to be over, once and for all. What he'd hoped would end with Shadowbane's death seemed to be just the beginning of something new and even more frightening.

The air thermal Arias had been riding on gradually petered out, and he heard an audible groan ripple through the Gryphs around him that had been utilizing it. Everyone strained to stay aloft and, hoping to raise spirits a little, Arias called, "There will be others to exploit later. We aren't too far away from the eyrie, now. We can make it." A few heads bobbed in acknowledgement of what he'd said, but one Gryph in particular caught his eye.

It wouldn't have been odd had the Gryph looking at Arias spoken, but the stranger didn't. He felt their gaze boring into him for a few murms too long, and when he finally stared back, he found himself observing an Ardeigryph. They were darker in color, but somehow familiar. Before Arias could think any more on it, they banked hard to the right and disappeared amid a larger group. He followed where they'd gone with his eyes, but he couldn't entertain the thought of following them. To waste energy on anything other than heading to Oceanside was a ludicrous concept at this point. Still, the sighting bothered him.

The sky was paling with the light of morning by the time the Gryphs all collapsed at the Ardeigryph's eyrie. Only a few made it to the cliffs, and even fewer to the dens at the side of it. The Alicorns didn't stir from where they'd been lain on the beach, seemingly comatose. Arias couldn't think anymore. He dropped his head into his wing and slept without remembering closing his eyes.

***

It was nigh unto night again when Arias finally woke. Those who had stirred sooner had made themselves busy by hunting and casting for wrigglers, enough to feed at least a fraction of the burgeoning population Oceanside now hosted. He stretched, and regretted the action. He felt like a million tiny cuts had rooted themselves into his muscles, and he groaned as a wave of pain sank over him.·

"It's a pretty common feeling these days."

Brynne was sitting next to him, her amber eyes sweeping over the mass of sleeping bodies on the beach. "I never thought I'd say this—ever—but you were an absolute beast back there. I would've been afraid to face you, the way you were against Shadowbane. You were like a whirlwind; I had no idea you could be that fast. How'd you know what he'd try to do before he even did it?"

Arias shook his head. "I didn't. I just kept my eyes on him. I honestly feel like I probably couldn't do it again if you came at me right now."

She laughed and rolled her shoulder with a grimace. "What a battle, though!" She closed her eyes and yawned, her tongue curling in the air. "Pretty satisfying to finally give it back to those flat-faced freaks, right?"

"I don't think that's the word I'd use to describe any of what we did in Arborochre, but okay," Arias said.

Brynne's eyes sparkled nonetheless. "Where are those herbs when you need them, right?"

Arias didn't reply. Naugi was dead because of him. He didn't think he'd ever harvest herbs again.

Tybrake descended from the sky as soon as he saw Arias up and talking, and he clapped him triumphantly across the side, eliciting a hiss of pain.

"Tell me I wasn't great out there," he said, star struck. "Nowhere near to what you did, but I never thought I'd be able to take them head on like that! I've hardly been in any real fights in my life, and I'm alive! I held my own!"

"You were commanding the battle at one point!" Brynne praised. "I feel lucky that I was close enough to watch you take them down like that. You were amazing! We should spar sometime…"

Arias was happy for Tybrake, but he stepped a few paces away from them to nurse his sore ribs. He hadn't noticed how crisscrossed his pelt was with wounds. Considering how much Brynne had praised him, he must be quite a sight.

"Hey, Arias! I'll bring you a nice, fat wriggler to eat!" Tybrake said, noticing he'd stalked off from the conversation. He took off without waiting for an answer.

Brynne smirked as she watched him launch out over the sea. "They sure look up to you, Arias."

Arias let that statement sink in. Out of sheer desperation, he had stepped into a role he'd never wanted. How did he go from a scared cub, afraid to even visit an eyrie, to this? He wasn't a born leader by any means, and yet other Gryphs were impressed with him. It was still hard to think that any of this was real.

The Alicorns were scattered along the beach in

a line, where they had been unceremoniously dropped by the Gryphs that had enduringly carried them to Oceanside. Arias walked over to them and glanced over what was left of the herd. He knew all them by their faces and manes, but he admittedly cared the most for Hlaena. To think that this was all that was left... And poor Xio! His heart wrenched. He blocked it out. He couldn't think about it now. All that mattered was surviving whatever came next. He walked until he was near to Hlaena and placed his face against her muzzle. Her warm breath rose and fell, tickling his tattered ears. Still alive. Would she ever wake up? Could she? He nudged her softly, and her eyelids flickered, as if in a dream. He no longer felt the horrifying draining sensation that he'd felt when he'd originally tried to pry her away from Naugi.

"They're like your family, huh?"

It was Lue, who was now sitting a few respectful paces away. He nodded, and she edged a little closer. "Some of the other Gryphons who know you and your tale filled me in," she said. "I'm glad you came here, outsider. And I'm sorry we were originally going to toss you into the sea to drown! You made the difference for us. I hope they recover soon. We wouldn't be alive if not for you, or them. No way we could've taken on all those Strigigryph without help."

Arias didn't know how to reply. He still felt like he'd failed everyone. Why couldn't they see that? He looked out over the sleeping mass of Gryphs, all different in shape, size, and age, at peace for the moment. What would've happened had he stayed in Glendale the way he should have? Shadowbane, for one, would never have gotten his talons on the knowledge of what blackroot was. Naugi would still be alive. And perhaps the Strigigryph never would have been able to enter into the Alicorn's sacred paradise to cause violence… he could have lived a blissful life, ignorant of the suffering of the rest of his kind just beyond the enchanted forest.

Was that a better outcome?

In a rustle of wings, Larin landed next to him, and he still had to still stifle his surprise at seeing her fly. It felt nice to know that at least one thing that had been forcefully taken from her had been restored. She settled in close to drape a protective wing over him, and he crossed necks with her and closed his eyes. He'd been through so much with the hen that he felt best when she was near him. He wished he could make sure that nothing ever happened to her again. But after what had transpired, he knew he'd never make that promise to anyone as long as he lived.

Arias drifted off into a waking sleep, feeling like it would take a lifetime to ever be fully rested again. Something landed with a *thwap* nearby him. He opened his eyes to look at the huge wriggler that now lay in front of him, and a Tybrake that was obviously proud of the catch. He flew off to cast for more, and when Larin roused, Arias asked if she wanted the wriggler. He wasn't hungry.

While Larin ate, Arias took a survey of the
eyrie. Pretty much anyone who wasn't off casting
was deep in slumber or nursing wounds.
Something was bothering him. A sound filled his
ears, and one look at Larin told him that she
heard it, too.

It was subtle at first, and hard to place. A
crinkling sound, like the sound of dry leaves
when they were crushed under paw. And it must
have been some distance off, as it slowly grew
louder and louder with a frightening pace. Arias
listened for what felt like eons, heart pulsing
loudly in his body, wondering what could
possibly create such a ruckus. And then he made
out the screaming of basilisks: of many, many
basilisks.

"Up," Arias said immediately, not bothering to
think. He pecked and shoved a nearby Gryphon
to his feet. "Up!" he roared, eyes peeled up the
beach, toward the forest. The sound was
emanating from there. Every Gryph that had
been slumbering on the beach jumped up, crests
raised in alarm. The ground was quaking now,
and with cries of shock, clouds of Gryphs
erupted upward and to the safety of the sky.

The terrified masses soared higher as the
sound intensified. There was a rumbling like a
massive landslide, and a huge plume of flame
spread over the tree line. Its heat was so intense
that entire drifts of snow immediately vaporized,
leaving only a blackened graveyard of charred
trunks behind.

Simik, the great basilisk who once stood watch at the base of Naugi's roost, blew another swath of flame before returning to a brawl that consisted of what seemed to be an uncountable number of scale-kin, some rivaling him in size and strength, others smaller but unwilling to give in. They moved forward like a tsunami, their flames shooting unpredictably across the land, claws leaving gouge marks deep enough to scar the earth for years. The energy behind their attacks on one another stood testament to how much vitality they all still had left. With every significant movement, they left a trail of the deceased in their wake.

"Clear the beach!" Bala yelled, as throngs of Gryphs zipped toward the safety of the sea. As Larin fluttered away from his side, Arias started to follow, but his eyes ripped back to the Alicorns that still lay wantonly across the beach. His breath caught in his throat.

"The Alicorns!" he cried, but his voice may well have been a whisper in the din of terrified screaming. The other Gryphs were all too busy running for their lives. He struggled against Hlaena in desperation, trying to dismiss the fact that she easily weighed twice as much as he did. He strained his wings, failing to rise even a few feet. He could feel every pinion as they combed the air uselessly. The basilisks bore down upon him, roaring as they sent snow, blood, and sand up from the ground in fantastic explosions punctuated by bursts of flesh-melting flame.

Arias closed his eyes and channeled all his

energy into moving the mare, and miraculously—
he felt movement! Larin had returned to grab the
Alicorn alongside him, her newly feathered wings
pumping hard to rise under the heavy load. The
tussling basilisks passed beneath them, and only
from the sky did Arias see the sheer devastation
that stretched out across the region, accented by
the bodies of exceptionally large basilisks that had
lost the battle for leadership. The thickest smoke
rose in a dark blur, indicating the remains of
Arborochre, the center of where the conflict had
begun. Arias concentrated on the task at hand.
He knew better than to look back at the beach
where the other Alicorns had lain. He couldn't
bear to.

CHAPTER FOURTEEN

The Gryphs had flown far enough that the basilisk's flame couldn't reach them, and they now circled nervously in the air, unsure of what to do next. The entire region looked like it was on fire from their vantage point, a million orange flickers against the winter sky.

Brynne and Bala exchanged withering looks as they tried unsuccessfully to quiet their ranks. They banked to hover next to Arias.

"Maybe we can take them down one at a time…" Brynne started, before being silenced by incredulous looks from all around.

"We'll never know until we try," she continued. "The Strigigryph I've talked to say they've hunted some creatures called drakes in their homeland, and they don't sound that different from these."

"Absolutely not," Arias said, looking down hopefully as Hlaena stirred in his claws. The mare opened her eyes, squinting, and after a few murms she struggled to escape. Larin and Arias released her, starting a bit as she dropped a few feet before regaining herself under her own wing power. She snorted and shook her head, disoriented, but it only took one glance toward the beach for her to understand what had happened.

"We've failed…" she said so quietly that Arias figured it must have been meant for only her own ears.

"What lies across the ocean?" Alissi flew up to join in the conversation, and the acting Sire of Oceanside seemed taken aback by the question.

"No idea."

"What do you mean, no idea? You live on the ocean, don't you? You've never tried to travel across it?"

Bala continued to hover silently for a moment before saying, "Our ancestors did. That was ages ago; for all I know it could've just been a tale. Consider that we don't even know which direction to try to travel. Even Ardeigryph fear a death by drowning. How well do you think you'll be able to convince your land-based friends that their best chance of living is across an immeasurable amount of water? The waves out there aren't like these ones below us now. They're huge swells; hardly anything survives a fall into them."

Brynne seemed disgusted that the possibility of leaving was even being considered. "This is our homeland, and has been for as long as Gryphon-kind can remember. I'm not going to have fought this hard just to move over for some oversized scale-kin. The Pale will not be leaving this region, we aren't cowards. We've invested too much. You can all speak for yourselves."

"Brynne, see reason," Arias said. "That's a death sentence down there. Even if you do manage to kill the basilisks, and that's a huge *if*, what is there left to return to? There's no good forest, the prey animals will have either moved on or perished, and we don't even know how long the basilisks will fight. It's possible whoever the new successor is won't honor any of Naugi's old treaties, and you and your flock will be hunted day and night like prey."

"He's right," Hlaena said with a fatigued voice. "It took Naugi eons to develop the level of temperance he had. Even then, he still had his moments, as we all do. His were just on a grand scale that left entire populations wiped from existence. I can't even remember the last time I saw another Hydra; he may well have been the last we'll see in our lifetimes. A basilisk won't rule over their territory in the same way he did— they'll use sheer strength to foster submission from others. They see no need for bribery, and possibly aren't advanced enough to even understand the concept of it. The best possible scenario for whatever life remains here now would be if Simik were to emerge as victor. He is probably the only one of them old enough to possess his level of reasoning, although empathy will never be a part of his decision making."

Brynne scowled. "I say we let the basilisks tussle it out, and then take the victor head on. They'll be tired, and we have the advantage in numbers!"

"I would not advise that," Hlaena snapped. "One sweep of that flame, and you and your entire flock cease to exist. Don't be foolish. If you must lead anyone to death, lead yourself, and leave your followers to survive." She looked over the open sea. "We've failed. I've failed. This place doesn't belong to anyone anymore, least of all to our kinds. Let us go."

The lone Alicorn mare started out over the ocean, and slowly, without questioning, a throng of Gryphs followed after her. The Pale was the last to follow, splitting into indecisive groups that hovered between the land and the sea. But eventually, they relented and joined the massive processional heading slowly toward open water.

***

The sea had almost become a friendly force to Arias since his time spent in Oceanside, but he saw that Bala had been right in that the further out they flew, the scarier it became. The swells bulged into monstrous white caps that broiled like humongous fangs, snapping for a meal. The only good thing was that there were many air thermals present, and the Ardeigryph readily found and rose high on them, their long, thin wings hardly stirring as they soared. The Gryphons and Strigigryph followed, their short, broad wings providing a massive disservice to them as they attempted to capture the same elegant efficiency that their Oceanside counterparts exhibited.

The sound of the basilisks and the sight of the burning mainland were long gone, swallowed up by the distance of the journey. Bala flew toward the back of the flock, encouraging the old, young, and injured to continue to stay aloft. Tybrake kept an eye on the swells below. More than once he swooped down to pluck a tired Gryph from water so they could regain flight. Brynne warned him that wasting his energy was a bad idea when they had no idea how close land was. He argued, but he also stopped searching the surf.

Nanchu was kept firmly in the middle of the group, so she could feel secure in whichever direction she was headed. She'd never left the eyrie before or been so far out to sea. The sounds—or lack thereof—were unsettling to her, and Arias had flown next to her for the greater part of the day, reassuring her as best he could. Larin stayed at her other side, giving her a constant presence to focus on so she could stay calm. It seemed to help.

Brynne, meanwhile, had traded her anger for despondency. She lagged behind the group in general, carrying a quiet, smoldering kind of rage. Arias left her alone.

Hlaena remained at the front of the group. She

ignored Arias when he settled into flying next to her, and the action made him feel worse than anything, but he decided that he deserved it.

"I'm sorry," he said, though the words felt emptier out loud than they had in his head. "Nothing I can do can make up for what's happened. If there's anything I can do at all, I'll gladly do it."

The mare looked over at him. Hlaena had always been the one he'd gone to for comfort when he was younger. But her eyes lacked their familiar compassion, and the alienation was stifling.

"It's not your fault, little one. But… for now, I wish to be alone." She pulled ahead with a finality that ended the conversation, and Arias couldn't stop the small whimper that clawed its way from his throat. What had he expected? Ratina had been right in everything she'd told him. It seemed so long ago already. The only thing left to do was to survive. The rest would have to be sorted out later.

He slowed until he was nearby Larin again, and she glanced at him sympathetically, but he looked away and instead focused on the line that was the horizon. It was the only way to try to ignore his own thoughts and the tightness that had crept up and taken residence in his heart. A single thought kept eking into his mind, however.

Xio… everyone. I'm sorry. I know that's not enough. Please, let me have survived for a reason. Let there be a reason for everything that's happened.

As darkness engulfed the sea, he poured his entire being into hoping the last bit was true.

Thank you for reading! If you enjoyed this book, please consider leaving an honest review for it. Also, consider joining the mailing list:

https://www.kathrynobrown.com/

Read them all!

The Quill and Claw Series

Book One: A Gryphon's Journey

Book Two: A Gryphon's Trial

Book Three: A Gryphon's Mercy

"We're running out of food," Brynne said, lying on her back with her paws in the air.

Arias turned, frowning. "What?"

"We've been hauling in less and less by the day. There's been a sharp decrease in prey over the last three."

"The wrigglers, too?"

Brynne shook her head. "No, but not all of us eat those things."

Arias thought in silence. It made sense. This island had probably been thriving without major predators for a long time before they'd arrived. And they'd brought huge numbers.

"Well," he said. "There's only one thing to do. Eating less isn't feasible; we'll still run out with how many we have. We have to leave."

Neither of them liked the prospect. But if the choice was between either a slow death of starvation or a swift end with whatever that thing out there was, Arias knew which one he'd pick.

"The idea won't be a popular one," Arias said, "but if we can get the leaders and influential Gryphs on our side…"

"The stragglers will fall into line," Brynne finished. She stood up, shaking the sand from her coat. "Right, then. I'm on it. Let's have a meeting.

www.ingramcontent.com/pod-product-compliance
Lightning Source LLC
Chambersburg PA
CBHW051604100726
47898CB00001B/226